OTTO PENZLER PRESENTS
AMERICAN MYSTERY CLASSICS

DEAD MAN INSIDE

VINCENT STARRETT (1886–1974) was a Chicago journalist who became one of the world's foremost experts on Sherlock Holmes. A books columnist for the *Chicago Tribune*, he also wrote biographies of authors such as Robert Louis Stevenson and Ambrose Bierce, various books on books and book collecting, plus Sherlockian pastiches and numerous short stories and novels. A founding member of the Baker Street Irregulars, he is perhaps known best today for *The Private Life of Sherlock Holmes*, an imaginative biography of the great detective.

OTTO PENZLER, the creator of American Mystery Classics, is also the founder of the Mysterious Press (1975), a literary crime imprint; MysteriousPress.com (2011), an electronic-book publishing company; Penzler Publishers (2018); and New York City's Mysterious Bookshop (1979). He has won a Raven, the Ellery Queen Award, two Edgars (for the *Encyclopedia of Mystery and Detection*, 1977, and *The Lineup*, 2010), and lifetime achievement awards from NoirCon and *The Strand Magazine*. He has edited more than 70 anthologies and written extensively about mystery fiction.

DEAD MAN INSIDE

VINCENT STARRETT

Introduction by
OTTO PENZLER

AMERICAN MYSTERY CLASSICS

Penzler Publishers
New York

This is a work of fiction. Names, characters, places, and incidents either are the product of the author's imagination or are used fictitiously. Any resemblance to actual persons, living or dead, businesses, companies, events, or locales is entirely coincidental.

Published in 2023 by Penzler Publishers
58 Warren Street, New York, NY 10007
penzlerpublishers.com

Distributed by W. W. Norton

Cover image: Andy Ross
Cover design: Mauricio Diaz

Paperback ISBN 978-1-61316-394-8
Hardcover ISBN 978-1-61316-391-7

Library of Congress Control Number: 2022917400

Printed in the United States of America

9 8 7 6 5 4 3 2 1

DEAD MAN INSIDE

INTRODUCTION

One of the first things they teach in writing courses (I hear; it is obvious that I've never taken one) is to grab the attention of the reader immediately. An opening line is good, and so is an opening scene.

Vincent Starrett's *Dead Man Inside* opens with people at an expensive clothing store staring at a corpse, unable to enter because of the sign on a square of white paper attached to the front door:

DEAD MAN INSIDE!

I AM DEAD. THIS STORE WILL NOT OPEN TO-DAY

It is a complicated case and the detective who will solve it doesn't really want to be involved and doesn't really want to be roped into being a detective at all.

He's Walter Ghost, the laconic amateur sleuth who first appeared in *Murder on "B" Deck.* He has no interest in detecting and is quick to tell that to anyone who will listen. "I won't be seen crawling around on my hands and knees," he says early in his appearance, a definite allusion to Sherlock Holmes and his methods. Further, he adds, "I would positively refuse to disguise myself, even if it were possible," also referring to one of Holmes' great skills.

Ghost does not appear to have a job but there are no restrictions on his checkbook. He is a dilletante, with expertise in William Shakespeare and a number of arcane subjects, but he is not to be confused with two other famous detectives of his time, S.S. Van Dine's Philo Vance and Ellery Queen's Ellery Queen, both of whom would stop an investigation to offer a lecture on a subject so esoteric that everyone involved in the case sat mute and bored while the sleuth rattled on about a particularly fascinating insect or an artist unknown to mere mortals.

Unlike Queen and Vance, Ghost has a sense of humor and is always willing to modestly downplay his curious bits of knowledge, a trait he shared with his creator.

In addition to being a novelist of crime fiction, Vincent Starrett (1886-1974) was a journalist, essayist, poet, bibliophile, and scholar, best known today for his profound knowledge of and affection for Sherlock Holmes.

Born in Toronto, Starrett was taken to Chicago as a child and lived there for most of his life, though his extensive travels took him to virtually every major city in the world. Although his goal was to be an illustrator, he first worked as a journalist for several Chicago newspapers, producing countless essays, biographical and bibliographical works, and critical studies of a wide range of authors. For a half-century, he was regarded as one of the twentieth century's most distinguished writers about books and bookmen. He presided over the famous "Books Alive" column in the *Chicago Tribune* for many years.

Starrett's finest work is undoubtedly the charming and erudite study *The Private Life of Sherlock Holmes* (1933), the first full-length book to treat Holmes as a real historical figure. In addition to his notable non-fiction, Starrett wrote many first-rate Golden Age mystery novels and short stories.

With *The Unique Hamlet* (1920), he wrote what is often regarded as the finest Holmes pastiche ever written--one in tune with his bibliophilia—as the great detective is faced with recovering the missing inscribed first printing of *Hamlet*, the most prized Shakespearian rarity in the world.

Many of Starrett's mystery and detective short stories were collected in *Coffins for Two* (1924); *The Blue Door* (1930), which contains tales of theft, murder, and blackmail, featuring such characters as Jimmie Lavender and G. Washington Troxell, an antiquarian bookdealer and amateur detective; *The Case Book of Jimmie Lavender* (1944), the whimsical amateur detective who looks "like an actor or an army officer" and investigates crime set mainly in the Chicago of the gangster era; and *The Quick and the Dead* (1965), ten macabre tales of grim crime and horror.

In addition to the three detective novels featuring Walter Ghost—*Murder on "B" Deck* (1929), *Dead Man Inside* (1931), and *The End of Mr. Garment* (1932), Starrett also wrote two mysteries in which Riley Blackwood serves as the sleuth. It is clear that Blackwood was based on no less fascinating a character than Starrett himself, as both men were bibliophiles, both admired Sherlock Holmes, and both had a bit of a sharp tongue and of similar physique—tall and gangly. Blackwood's adventures are *The Great Hotel Murder* (1935) and *Midnight and Percy Jones* (1938).

Not worth mentioning is Starrett's only stand-alone mystery novel, *The Laughing Buddha* (1937), a paperback original released by a small house whose editor felt comfortable scattering his own additions to the text throughout. It was restored to its original form and published as *Murder in Peking* (1946).

This is not Starrett's only brush with publishing misadventure. When *The Case Book of Jimmie Lavender* was issued, the publisher misspelled the name of the protagonist on the dust jacket!

American Mystery Classics has also published the first Walter Ghost mystery, *Murder on "B" Deck*, as well as the first Riley Blackwood novel, *The Great Hotel Murder.*

DEAD MAN INSIDE

TO
SCOTT CUNNINGHAM
WHO WATCHED IT GROW

The incidents
and characters of this tale
are entirely fictitious

CHAPTER ONE

To Rufus Ker, slowly approaching from the north, the phenomenon was as surprising as would have been an unpremeditated "To Let" sign upon his own front window. There was a placard on the glass-paned door of Bluefield, Incorporated!

He snorted with indignation. In all the years as man and boy that he had opened that door to trade, no such vulgarity had been permitted. Had Bluefield, slightly mad, overthrown all the sacred traditions? Or was this the prank of some miserable clerk, newly hired, to make the house ridiculous?

There it was, underneath the chaste gold letters of the firm's remarkable name: a hasty square of paper pasted to the inside glass.

He shuffled forward in fussy anger. With the proper key between his fingers he paused and bent his near-sighted gaze upon the outrage. Then the bunch of keys fell jingling to the frosty morning sidewalk. It was perhaps a miracle that Rufus Ker did not drop beside them.

DEAD MAN INSIDE!

said the square of white paper. And Rufus Ker would have sworn that the letters were a foot in height and vocal as the record of a phonograph. The words were blocked in office ink. Beneath them, in somewhat smaller lettering, he read another dreadful message:

I AM DEAD.

THIS STORE WILL NOT OPEN TO-DAY.

For a moment, stunned, he stood before the once familiar door, screening the placard with his body. Then he stooped quickly, snatched the fallen keys from the sidewalk, and let himself in with fumbling hands. In an instant he had torn the square of paper from the glass. He stood trembling and triumphant, while the door closed smoothly on its automatic mechanism.

It would be twenty minutes or half an hour before another clerk arrived. . . .

He looked about him fearfully. The shop, its curtains drawn, its lights extinguished, was melancholy as an empty church. Yet all was apparently as he had left it the evening before.

He shuddered and pushed a button in the wall, flooding the place with light. Then relief came to him swiftly, and he laughed aloud.

All was as it should be, as it always had been. At the back, the door of Bluefield's office stood open. He could see within. The desk was neatly ordered, as usual, and the chair before it was vacant. The square of paper was some ghastly joke whose perpetrator would be discovered and discharged. Some disgruntled employee, leaving among the last, had contrived to stick the thing upon the glass and escape unnoticed. There it had remained throughout the night—a malicious wafer calculated to hurt the reputation of the firm.

Great God, what a thing to have had happen! What a libel! How many persons already had read the screaming sign upon the door? It was a marvel that it had not been reported to the police.

"And how glad I am," said Rufus Ker aloud, "that I came down a little early this morning."

His mind began a canvass of the members of the staff. Regan—Jacobs—Humphries—Phildripp—Thain. These were the newer and younger men about the shop. Was it possible that any of them . . . ?

His blood began to boil. For a few moments he hated them all.

They would be coming to work soon. Or would one of them fail to appear? Would the scoundrel guilty of such an outrage dare to show his face again upon the premises? Was not this horrible jest the last insult of a man already sure of a position some place else? Of course the fellow would deny authorship. Young clerks were always dissatisfied, and they were usually liars.

Rufus Ker glanced at the big clock ticking on the side wall and began his duties of the morning. The racks of overcoats and suits looked singularly gloomy in their enveloping shrouds; the long tables revealed almost sinister outlines under their coverings. Terrible doubts again assailed the ancient clerk. He moved from rack to table and from table to rack with tremendous courage, snatching the coverings away with dramatic gestures. He was a little late now, and he would have to hurry.

All was as it should have been—as it always had been. His doubts left him. Again he was filled with fury at the unknown trickster who had wrought this agitation.

He swung back the inner curtain and stepped into the shop window, still darkened by the closedrawn hangings and the shade beyond. The wax dummy of a man, correctly attired in evening wear—he had been nicknamed "The Ambassador" by the younger clerks—sat immovable, as always, in his gilded chair, with hats and sticks around him. Crossed gloves and a silver cigarette case were on the low stand beside him. On miniature standards, like a row of footlights across the window front, were the latest in cravats and handkerchiefs.

The house of Bluefield was famous throughout the fashionable world.

Rufus Ker swung back the heavy silk hangings and anchored them at the sides. He let the shade up to the window top. It was like the rising of a curtain upon a section of the world. "Act One: A Street in Chicago" might have been the title of the episode, supposing an auditorium to lie behind the window of the shop.

But there was no longer any drama in the incident for Rufus Ker. He had looked out too often upon that section of the world. At the moment he noted only that a light rain had begun to fall and that passers-by had buried their heads in their collars. One citizen, attracted perhaps by a movement in the window, glanced in as he went past, and for a moment his startled eyes rested upon the gangling figure of Rufus Ker, the lanyard of the window shade still clutched in his hand.

"Umbrellas to-day," murmured Rufus Ker, peering out into the mist. "I must get that line of black silks ready."

He backed gently out of the window and reentered the shop, dropping the curtains behind him.

For a few happy moments he had forgotten the hideous message, now crushed inside his pocket. Umbrellas only were upon his musty mind. . . . They were in a stock closet at the rear of the shop. . . .

He turned the handle of the door and put his head inside.

Then Rufus Ker bleated weakly, once, like a frightened sheep, and reeled backward against the nearest support. With eyes that bulged with horror he stared into the closet gloom and into the face of the waxen dummy, sometimes humorously called "The Ambassador."

Hanging quietly by his coat collar, from a hook, the human semblance was impersonating a hanged man with singular fidelity.

On a gilded throne, in his own shop window, Amos Bluefield, a modest enough executive, who was ordinarily somewhat difficult to see, sat quite still, looking out with blind eyes at the mounting congestion of the boulevard.

CHAPTER TWO

ALL THAT was on a Friday morning.

It was quite late, however, Friday night, before Miss Holly Moment, glancing idly at the evening paper—which had been tossed aside by her father a little time before—came upon the column destined to upset her slumber. She uttered a little squeal in which were blended somewhat of discovery and somewhat of dismay.

Then in shocked tones she observed, "Good heavens!"

Her father laid aside his book. "What is it now, dear?" he asked mildly. Then he waited, confidently expecting to hear of a staggering reduction in feminine wearing apparel somewhere in the Loop.

"Mr. Bluefield has been murdered!"

Chandler W. Moment returned to his book. "Yes," he said, "I noticed it. Quite a fantastic affair. I used to buy my hats there. Probably it will turn out to be suicide, after all. Why do you read that sort of thing when you sleep so badly?"

But he put aside his book again at her next remark.

"He was murdered, Father—and I am probably the only person in Chicago who can prove it."

"What!" cried her father, like a character in a book. "What are you talking about, Golly?"

That was a name he sometimes called her—a campus corruption of her actual name as written in the family Bible.

"I didn't tell you before because I had forgotten about it; but last night Stephen Robey and I passed Bluefield's—quite late. We went to Sperry's, as I told you, after the show, and had something to eat. It was after midnight when we left, and we walked to the corner to pick up a cab. Naturally, we passed Bluefield's."

"And saw the proprietor murdered," observed her father; "after which you forgot about it!"

Miss Moment frowned.

"Don't be silly, Father," she said, annoyed. "I didn't say I saw him murdered. What I saw was the murderer. It must have been he. As we were passing, I happened to look up. At that minute the window curtains were drawn aside and a man looked out into the street!"

"Probably Bluefield himself," said her father. "Did Stephen see him, too?"

"No, he didn't; but I told him about it. Of course, as soon as he saw us, the man inside disappeared. Stephen thought he was probably a caretaker or a night watchman."

"Probably was," agreed Chandler W. Moment. "After all, nobody can say at what time Bluefield entered the shop. My advice to you is to forget all about it."

It was excellent advice from a parent, but Miss Moment—luckily or unluckily—was a young woman of conscience. She was also small, dark, and the possessor of her mother's jaw. Professor Moment noted the resemblance and sighed.

"I wish you would keep out of things that don't concern you, Holly," he complained. "And don't set your jaw at me that way! It makes you look like General Andrew Jackson."

"I shall call up the police the first thing in the morning," asserted Miss Moment. "It is my duty, Father."

"Duty," retorted her father evenly, "be damned!" He entertained a pleasant passion for minding his own business: a circumstance which he often mentioned.

"That is all very well," said his daughter, "but the reason Chicago is as bad as it is, is that its citizens don't coöperate with government."

This was a line he had himself read to her from a morning newspaper editorial.

For a few moments her parent studied her through a thin fog of tobacco smoke.

"Very well," he said, at length, "if you are determined, I'll call up the chief of police myself in the morning. I happen to know him slightly. But I doubt that you have anything to contribute."

In point of fact, it occurred to him, the chief of police would probably listen politely, make a note or two, and then forget the matter. It was what he wanted to do himself.

Nevertheless, he was vaguely uneasy. Holly, he recalled, had always been a problem.

"You can, of course, describe the man who looked out of the window," he continued suavely, after a few minutes of silence. "You noticed his hair, his necktie, the color of his eyes?"

Miss Moment was startled. "Why, no—I can't," she confessed. "It was just a glimpse, you see; really only a part of his face. Then the curtains dropped, and he was gone. It was dark, too, and—" she hesitated—"I'm afraid I really *couldn't* describe him."

"Splendid!" cried her father, relieved.

He greatly disliked publicity—of the wrong sort—and was now certain that there was no danger of it in the immediate future. It was possible, indeed, that by morning his daughter would be in another frame of mind. It was even possible that he would, himself, forget to call up the chief of police.

He did not forget, however. The morning papers were rather full of the sensational affair. Bluefield, after all, had been a citizen of distinction, and the spectacle of him seated, dead, in his front window, was well calculated to enrich the public imagination. There is no telling how many lives were uplifted and ennobled by the double column photographs on the back pages of the morning journals—for the enterprising camera men had been on hand before the body could be removed.

Over the breakfast coffee Chandler W. Moment and his daughter digested the reports. . . .

The possibility of suicide had not been ruled out; but the notice on the shop door was not being taken very seriously. The thing was not in keeping with Bluefield's known habits of restraint. The books of the murdered man were said to be in order, and it was agreed that if the haberdasher had contemplated suicide he would have selected a less public place to die. It was announced that an inquest would be held that afternoon at two-thirty o'clock.

Rufus Ker, it appeared, had been taken into custody. The rest of the clerks and clericals of the establishment were under surveillance.

"An excellent word, too," commented Chandler W. Moment. "Nobody can pronounce it, so it has an appearance of significance. It suggests at once great police activity and intelligence. Sand in the eyes of the public. Can't the jackasses see that no clerk employed by Bluefield would have imagination enough to commit such a crime?"

"Why not sand in the eyes of the murderer?" asked his daughter. "If he thought suspicion centered on the staff of the shop, wouldn't he feel safer? Wouldn't he take greater chances? Besides, what can you know about Bluefield's clerks, Father? Why shouldn't a clerk have imagination? It was that dummy in the window that suggested it all, of course!"

"Theatrical!" said her father contemptuously. "Do you know who I'd look for, Holly, if I were handling this affair? I'd look for the author of the latest three-act thriller. Nobody else would have thought of such a thing. But, no! The police must line up all the clerks and errand boys and give 'em the third degree. 'Did you murder Amos Bluefield and stick him in his window?' 'Certainly not!' 'Where were you on Thursday night when this affair must have occurred?' And how many of them will care to answer that question, in this day and age? Half of them were probably out with chorus girls. A nice thing for their wives to find out!"

He chuckled sardonically and returned to his reading.

"But apparently they have two strings to their bow. Listen to this: 'Detectives hurried at once to the dead man's hotel—an outlying hostelry of fashionable reputation, where the wealthy haberdasher kept sumptuous bachelor quarters.' No mention of the hotel by name, of course: it probably advertises in the papers. Note the subtle suggestions in that single line of type! 'Fashionable reputation—wealthy haberdasher—sumptuous bachelor quarters.' Instantly we have a picture of disorderly parties, young women in négligé, and three rings for ginger ale and ice. *Cherchez la femme*, eh? The second canon of police dogma. As if a woman could have committed such a crime!"

"Not enough imagination?" queried his daughter, faintly ironical.

"Rubber-stamp detective methods," said Chandler W. Moment. "No wonder murderers escape. In ancient Italy they used to employ the toughest criminals they could find to keep the cities free of the rest of the tribe. Paid 'em well, too. It's an idea we might take over to-day, with modifications. Call in another murderer on a case like this, and we'd quickly know who did it."

Miss Moment laughed. "He'd have to be at least as clever as the first one. Your idea would be splendid in the case of gangsters and gunmen, perhaps; but suppose this murderer to have been a clergyman or a professor of history?"

"Did he look like either?" asked Professor Chandler W. Moment swiftly. "If he was a professor of history, he did it because he couldn't afford a new hat. Probably he had a daughter who afforded too many."

They agreed upon one thing: that the real mystery was the manner of Bluefield's death. There had been no wound upon the body, no sign of terror upon the face. It had been, apparently, a rather benevolent face that had looked out of that dreary morning window—fat, placid, and with the high cheekbones of Bluefield's Dutch ancestors of New Amsterdam and, perhaps, the Dry Tortugas.

"For Blauvelt, you must know, my dear," said Chandler W. Moment to his daughter, "was in his day an eminent pirate. There is still a seaport carrying his name, somewhere in Central America—in Honduras, I believe. And what an end for the descendant of a famous pirate! Not this murder—which, after all, is rather fitting—but to make his fortune as a haberdasher. I remember I used to think that something persisted in the Bluefield strain. I have paid him as much as twenty dollars for a hat."

His daughter sighed. "What a passion you have for hats," she said. "Yet I never see you wear one."

"Because one is never to be found," said Chandler W. Moment. "They hide themselves at my approach. It's a case of the perversity of inanimate objects. One notices it also in the matter of pipes and blotters."

"Where is the one you bought last week?" asked his daughter—"the one that was too large? I could cheerfully murder the haberdasher who sold you *that.* You look like a reservation Indian in it. On the day the Great White Father issues hats to his children. Pirates indeed!"

"The truth is, my dear," asserted Chandler W. Moment, "all business is just piracy, operating under the law. Legalized scoundrelism! I can't say that I feel particularly sorry for Bluefield; but it must be admitted that his murder is a very neat problem for the dabbler in detection."

Thus Professor Moment discussed the death of Amos Bluefield with his daughter Holly, who had seen the murderer in a window. He rose from the discussion immensely edified and kept his promise at the telephone.

"Great Jonathan!" exclaimed the chief of police, when he had listened to the report. "Can you put your daughter in a taxicab, Professor, and send her down here to me? And that young man who was with her—where can I get hold of him? I want to see them both."

Reluctantly the professor revealed the name and address of his daughter's midnight companion.

"I'll bring Holly down to you myself," he said; "but, as I've already told you, she didn't really *see* the man at all."

"In about half an hour, then," said the police chief jubilantly. "Make it snappy, Professor."

Then the chief of police hung his receiver back on its hook with unaccustomed gentleness and sat back in his chair. He rubbed his hands together with soft impatience. Not that he expected anything sensational to develop from the testimony of Holly Moment, but it helped to fix the hour of the murder, for one thing; and for another it gave him something to tell the newspaper gang. They had been hounding him for twenty-four hours.

A swell picture of a swell girl who had seen the murderer was *something* for the damned highbinders, anyway.

CHAPTER THREE

ALL THAT was on a Saturday—Saturday morning, along toward noon.

A statue was to be unveiled in Lincoln Park at two o'clock: an equestrian statue to the memory of General Thaddeus Burke. Thaddeus Burke who had stemmed the tide at Antietam. It was a regular rocking horse, according to the art critics of the town—morose gentlemen who contributed columns of jargon to the Saturday journals. The great bronze animal reared gloriously upward from its granite base as if about to leap a barrier, and high upon its back sat the almost forgotten warrior, flourishing a bronze sword.

This remarkable effigy had been presented to the city by a wealthy manufacturer of sewing machines whose mother had been a Burke.

The ceremonies planned for the event by the park commissioners were elaborate, but the rain practically ruined them. Only a huddle of officials and an unhappy scattering of citizens turned out.

There were, however, half a dozen newspaper reporters on hand, and it was one of these who first saw the little square of paper affixed to the shrouding canvas.

"What's that?" he asked aloud, and pointed upward at a spot that approximated the height of three tall men.

He was addressing no one in particular, but the principal orator, who was mounted somewhat higher than any of the group around him, took it upon himself to answer.

"It's—why, it appears to be a piece of paper," said the orator, with just a touch of irony in his voice. He craned upward again, for an instant, and added: "Yes, it is a piece of paper."

An official bustled forward, annoyed. "Well, what the dickens is it doing there?" he asked. "Funny we didn't notice it before. There's something written on it, isn't there?"

He was in a mood to be incensed by little things.

A shocking idea entered the mind of the newspaper man. He looked at his confrères with startled significance.

"Holy smoke!" he exclaimed. "Do you suppose it could be another of those . . . ?"

His associates looked back at him as if he had suddenly gone lunatic. Dawson was a funny skate, anyway. Always suspecting mystery where there wasn't any mystery. Now every square of paper he would see, for six months, would inflame his imagination.

Nevertheless, they drew together at the edge of the platform and stood looking up at the square of wet paper. The light rain fell upon their upturned faces.

What held the piece of paper to the canvas? Could it be the rain?

Their spokesman, the imaginative Dawson, drew the head of the official delegation to one side and whispered fiercely in his ear.

"This may be serious, Mr. Wallingford," he said. "I advise you to have a look at that square of paper before you go ahead."

"Nonsense!" asserted the man called Wallingford.

"Will you give me permission to climb up and have a look at it?"

"Certainly not! My dear boy, we have an audience out there in the rain waiting for us to proceed."

"But, look here—" began Dawson.

"Oh, forget it, Larry," interrupted his accomplices. "Let's get this damn thing over and go home."

"H'm," said young Mr. Dawson, and subsided. He returned to his post under the temporary shelter.

But his mind raced. What a story, he thought, if it should turn out that . . . !

Lord, what a story!

His friends watched him narrowly. They cast occasional nervous upward glances at the square of paper. The trouble with Dawson was that sometimes his hunches worked out. There had been that case of the prisoner in the old church, for instance!

The ceremonies went damply forward. The address of the principal orator was not a success. To the reporters it sounded like long streams of gibberish, punctuated at intervals by names calculated to elicit applause. The names were uttered in dramatic capitals. They popped out like the balls of fire in roman candles. . . .

Washington . . . Hamilton . . . Jackson . . . Lincoln . . . Grant . . .

It was an apathetic audience.

At length the name was mentioned for which they all were waiting.

"Burke!"

The unhappy citizens cheered and clapped their hands. The orator stepped down with a satisfied smile. He shook hands with the sewing-machine manufacturer and the president of the Lincoln Park Board. His place was taken by a little girl attired in white. Three men hurried forward to show her what to do.

"Burke!" she echoed, with a happy smile, and fumbled with the cords, only slightly assisted by the three men who stood beside her.

"I warn you, Mr. Wallingford," said the reporter again. "You ought to have a look at that paper. It's not a price ticket. If it says 'Dead Man Inside'—well, there'll probably *be* one." He was squirming with eagerness and something that resembled apprehension.

The man called Wallingford stared. "Are you crazy, Dawson?" he asked.

"I'll think *you* are if you don't take my tip," flashed the reporter. "You read the papers, don't you?"

"Good Lord!" whispered the official, suddenly understanding. "You don't mean to say that you think—that you think . . . ?"

Young Mr. Dawson laughed a trifle madly. "Oh, hell!" he said. "Go ahead and pull the cord."

"Wait!" cried the man called Wallingford.

He moved toward the group gathered around the little girl, but he was just too late.

A signal already had been given. The shrouding canvas parted slowly and began to fall away. A plumed hat appeared, and the tip of a bronze sabre. For an instant the canvas stuck, caught perhaps by an epaulette or sword guard, then it fell swiftly, crashing to the earth with a miniature roar.

"My God!" said the president of the Lincoln Park Board.

In the dreadful pause that followed, six reporters took to their heels and fled wildly toward the nearest telephones.

CHAPTER FOUR

The murder of Hubert Gaunt shocked the city principally because of its grotesquerie.

Amos Bluefield had been a citizen of note, an item that had enhanced the theatricality of his demise; but Hubert Gaunt, as far as anyone could discover, was not a citizen at all. He was simply a man dead in extraordinary circumstances. A man tagged with a tiny placard similar to that which had announced the murder of Bluefield. Every amateur detective in the metropolis shook his head sagely when he read about that placard, and observed that there must be a connection somewhere between the two.

The name of the second victim had been found where names are usually found when men are done to death by other men. It was written on a label sewed to the lining of his inside pocket. The pocket contained nothing else of interest. The garment of which it was a part, however, proved to be of some importance in itself. Outfitted with strange pockets, in sleeves and tails, it was almost certainly, the police pointed out, the coat of a professional gambler.

But how had a professional gambler come to die mounted upon the bronze horse of Burke of Antietam?

As in the case of Amos Bluefield, no single clue was found upon the man's body to indicate the nature or method of his death. A small, fair man of possibly forty years, he lay—when found—stiffly twisted across the bronze horse, in the valley made by the rearing neck of the animal and the upright form of the bronze rider.

The trade mark of the murderer, the newspapers reported, had been recovered from the heap of canvas. It was unlike that found by Rufus Ker on the door of Bluefield, Incorporated, in that there was no second message. It was a simple statement of fact: "Dead Man Inside!" The words had been lettered, not written, and there was no other clue to the author of the crime.

The late editions of the evening papers, which carried the full account of the sensational event, carried also the report of the coroner's jury in the case of Amos Bluefield. As might have been predicted, an open verdict had been returned. The suspicious nature of the case was stressed and action recommended to the police.

"Person or persons unknown."

The police, distracted by the new horror, responded with their only trump card. The murderer of Amos Bluefield had been seen, they said, and by a woman—by the daughter, in fact, of Professor Chandler W. Moment of the University of Chicago.

"Perhaps," said the chief of police to the reporters, "that will hold you for a 'moment'!" And he smiled happily at his own little joke.

Thereafter, for a time, the life of Holly Moment became a bit of a burden. Only her sense of duty saw her through the ordeal with tailored stride. It was true that she had little to contribute—but she was charming. The camera men photographed her from every possible angle and in all parts of the house.

They even endeavored to persuade her that it was her duty to be photographed outside the premises of Bluefield, Incorporated, pointing to the spot upon the window behind which she had seen the murderer's eyes. Miss Moment, however, knew the extent of her responsibility to the public.

This most engaging feature of the case "broke," in the vernacular of the press, for the Sunday papers, and Holly Moment viewed her features on the second page with more attention than ever she had given them in her glass. She was more than a little shocked by the excitement her simple tale had created. Her father, when the press men clamored at the door, thoughtfully retired to his library and would not emerge. He had, as he had so often asserted, a grand passion for minding his own business.

The murder of Hubert Gaunt had its effect also in other quarters. Rufus Ker—the elderly dotard who had opened the chapter of crime by his unfortunate discovery of the wax model of "The Ambassador" in a closet, seven-and-a-half minutes after he had seen it in the window—was released by the police and went immediately to bed.

There was no earthly reason to suppose that he had murdered Gaunt and, in point of fact, it was admitted, he could not have done so. He had been taken into custody on Friday morning. The body of Gaunt had been unveiled, with ceremonies, on Saturday afternoon. But as late as six o'clock Friday evening there had been no corpse across the bronze horse of Thaddeus Burke, in Lincoln Park. Workmen had testified to this: workmen who had finally adjusted the shrouds around horse and rider.

Thus Rufus Ker, since by the police theory he could not have committed the first murder without having also committed the second, was automatically out of the picture.

The relief to Rufus Ker was considerable.

In a sense, the same line of reasoning should have applied to the other clerks in the Bluefield establishment; but for some reason—possibly because they were younger men—it did not. None of them, however, had been taken into custody. Their homes merely had been shadowed by plainclothes detectives and their wives terrorized by telephone calls from the newspapers. Those who had no wives had, naturally enough, gone to call upon their sweethearts; and these had been trailed by cumbersome dicks, to and from the trysts.

One clerk, greatly daring, had ventured to celebrate his vacation by going to a theater—that was Phildripp—and his particular tracker enjoyed a very good comic opera at the expense of the production.

The murder of Hubert Gaunt, indeed, was a sort of mixed blessing. It at once simplified the case and made it harder.

What the hell, as the chief of police earnestly asked, could Gaunt have had to do with Bluefield?

The county of Cook—that is to say, in effect, Chicago—being of a pious and Sabbatarian impulse, does not call its inquests on Sunday. The bulky newspapers of that day, in consequence, announced that the inquest upon the body of Hubert Gaunt would be held on Monday afternoon. The autopsy performed upon the body of Amos Bluefield had revealed nothing of a suspicious nature, it was pointed out, but in view of this second death mystery, so obviously akin to the first, a more thorough post mortem might be expected in both cases.

All the Sunday papers printed reproductions of the two death notes and indicated the similarities in the lettering. With reference to fingerprints, it was asserted that too much confusion existed for anything like a satisfactory clue. The square of paper taken from the shroud of General Burke had been soaked by rain and torn by the falling canvas. That removed by Rufus Ker from the door of Bluefield, Incorporated, had been crushed by Rufus Ker, in his zealous frenzy, and was covered with the finger prints of Rufus Ker.

So much for summary.

There remained a safety pin. Curiously, the notice pinned to the shroud of Thaddeus Burke had been affixed to its background by a safety pin.

The almost immoral similarity of safety pins, however, was also explained by the press.

Professor Chandler W. Moment and his daughter read the accounts in the newspapers with the careful attention of participants in epochal events. They were both deeply interested in the new development and both heartily sick of their own part in the case. It had been a wearying day when at length the hour came to retire.

"Why, after all," asked the professor thoughtfully, "should any sane murderer, having committed his crime, take it into his head to look out of the window?"

He still harped occasionally on that original incident. From it had dated all other nuisances.

"Whatever his reason may have been, he did it," said the professor's daughter. "Probably he *wasn't* a sane murderer. He may have been insane. And what makes you think he had already committed his crime? He may even then have been waiting for Mr. Bluefield to come in. Anyway, I think it's just what he would have done. He was there in the darkness, behind that window. He heard footsteps outside—Stephen's and mine—and he peeked out to see what was going on. Probably he'd have looked out even if he *hadn't* heard us. Possibly he was just getting ready to leave the place or to stick up his notice. Naturally, he'd want to be certain he wasn't observed. When you're a murderer, I imagine looking before you leap becomes a sort of subconscious action."

Miss Moment was getting a little tired of having her word doubted. The chief of police had seemed a bit skeptical. Young women seeking notoriety were not a novelty in his life, he had hinted.

"Well," observed the professor, at length, "it is, to say the least, an extraordinary case." He repeated: "An extraordinary case!"

As he was preparing to ascend the stairs he used the adjective again. "What an extraordinary thing it would be, my dear, if the whole mystery were to be resolved by a safety pin!"

It was at that instant that the telephone bell rang for the eleventh time that day. Reporters who for years have been calling men up at three in the morning to inquire into the state of their health or the amount of their embezzlement get to be hardened animals.

Professor Moment answered.

"Yes?" he said. And a moment later: "Good God, no! Certainly not!"

"What is it, Father?" asked his daughter.

"The *Courier & Examiner* wants to know if you will look at the body of Mr. Gaunt and try to say whether his face resembles the one you saw looking out of that window."

"Absurd!" said his daughter. "Tell them I shall do nothing of the sort. I am through with the whole case."

Professor Moment merely hung up the receiver.

"I almost wish I had not gone to the police at all—now," continued his daughter spitefully.

"I almost wish neither of them had been murdered," said Professor Chandler W. Moment.

CHAPTER FIVE

On Monday a stranger reached the city whose arrival was a blow to the investigation. He came from Portland, Maine, he asserted, and within half an hour of his arrival the hotel reporters were reading his neat signature on the Marlborough register: "Adrian Bluefield"; with a fine Dickensian flourish under both names.

Mr. Bluefield was fat and a bit pompous. His jowls, white and heavy, overlay the edges of his soft collar and lent him a pleasantly Falstaffian appearance, dispelled by the hardness of his little eyes, which were lost in rolls of surrounding tissue. It was as if another and larger face lay behind the one immediately visible. The features, however, seemed to be those of an ancient medal, struck to commemorate his triumphal progress through time. He was immensely affable.

Yes, he admitted, he was the only brother of the murdered Amos. A sad, a very sad affair!

Mr. Bluefield smoked cigars in an amber holder. His finger nails glistened as he raised the toy to his lips. He had no doubt, he declared, that his brother had died of a heart seizure and that the notice posted upon his door had been his own grim jest. Realizing his condition, Amos Bluefield had paid a last visit to his famous establishment, made his preparations for death, hung the waxen dummy upon a hook in the closet, and calmly seated himself in the window.

"A last grim jest," he repeated, shaking his great head thoughtfully.

Amos, he asserted, had been a fellow of considerable humor. He had always resented the almost sacrosanct atmosphere of the shop. He had carried on the tradition of his father, however, until there seemed no longer any reason for so doing.

"I knew, of course," he added, "that Amos's heart was bad. He knew it himself."

Realizing that he, Adrian Bluefield, the brother and only heir, would at once dispose of the famous business—as he fully intended to do—Amos had determined to advertise his retirement in a fashion that would at the same time advertise his disgust. It was a fashion that he, Adrian, although profoundly shocked by the event, understood and, in a way, appreciated. A last grim jest.

"Amos, I happen to know," said Adrian Bluefield, "was heartily sick of Bluefield, Incorporated. He often told me so."

It was not a particularly plausible story. It suggested principally that Adrian Bluefield would be glad to come into his inheritance, get rid of it for cash, and return to Portland as rapidly as possible.

A reporter, greatly wondering, ventured a question.

"Gaunt!"

The sudden cry was almost a scream. With an effort Mr. Bluefield recovered himself.

"Why, no," he said, "I must confess I have not heard of what you call the Gaunt episode. I have seen no newspaper since I left Portland. I have the morning papers here—" he indicated a heap upon a chair beside the door—"but I have not yet had a minute to glance at them. Gaunt? Gaunt? I know that name."

With portentous calm he listened to the story of the second death. He began to walk about the room, at first slowly, then with increasing speed. It was obvious that this new development had shaken him; obvious too that it was really new. Incredible as it had at first seemed, the man had really had no word of the murder of Hubert Gaunt. The tidings had struck him suddenly with a force that could only be conjectured.

He paused in his march around the room.

"Then it *was* murder," he said. "Poor Amos! It was from him that I heard the name you have just mentioned. I have had several letters, only recently, I recall, in which this Gaunt is spoken of. Amos had lent him money—a considerable sum, I believe. It was for old times' sake. They were at school together, I think. A gambler, was he? But he needn't have murdered Amos. I am sure my brother was not pressing him. Amos didn't need the money. And now Gaunt is dead, too! Suicide, of course. The same fantastic turn of mind is evident in both cases."

Again he was thoughtful.

"Well, gentlemen, I am sorry, in a way, that he killed himself afterward. I should have liked to send him to the Chair. As it is, I suppose there is nothing for it but to accept the unhappy facts. My poor brother!"

A reporter ventured a suggestion.

"No, no," said Adrian Bluefield. "I see no reason for reopening the inquest. What does it matter, after all, what means was employed? Gaunt is dead. My brother is dead. Nothing can bring them back for explanation or for punishment. No doubt the inquest upon this fellow Gaunt will disclose the means. Some subtle poison, no doubt. Dreadful! And my poor brother, there in his own window! You know, of course, how he hated publicity, how he shunned it in his lifetime."

He bowed his head and shook it slowly from side to side.

"Naturally, I shall be here for several days," he continued more briskly. "I shall await the report of the inquest upon Gaunt. We shall probably hold my brother's funeral to-morrow. At some quiet chapel, I think, and quite privately. I shall retain a lawyer to look after the property until it can be disposed of. My own interests, in the East, of course, make it impossible for me to carry on a business here; and, anyway—" he smiled a trifle deprecatingly—"I am afraid I am not cut out for a shopkeeper."

He had not seen his brother for some years, he explained, but a warm bond always had existed between them.

"Thank you very much, gentlemen," he said. "I shall visit the police, of course, sometime during the day. Perhaps they will come to see *me.* Not that there is anything I can tell them. But I must see an attorney first. I can't have this inquest reopened, as you tell me there is some talk of doing. It would serve no useful purpose, and I must return shortly to Portland."

He passed around a box of excellent cigars and watched his visitors depart. "Certainly a grand guy," observed one of the reporters, entering the elevator.

"He doesn't care a thing about the money he's going to get. Just thinking of his poor brother!"

Whereupon two other newspaper hounds laughed raucously and vulgarly.

They smoked their cigars, nevertheless, and found them none the worse for their contact with a Bluefield.

The police, however, welcomed Adrian Bluefield with open arms. Nothing is more annoying than an unsolved mystery in which the public and the press happen to be interested. When it is a fantastic affair, and the clues are slim, a matter-of-fact brother from the East is little less than a godsend. Adrian Bluefield's statement that he could furnish letters from his brother in which Gaunt was actually mentioned as being in the haberdasher's debt was almost too good to be true.

In justice to the police it must be said that the idea that Gaunt had murdered Bluefield and then killed himself had already been given consideration. On the face of things it was not a bad theory. Adrian Bluefield's acceptance of it was all that was necessary to make it the only possible theory.

By the same token, it was no longer imperative that the Gaunt mystery should be unduly pushed. Gaunt—obviously a ne'er-do-well—had owed Bluefield money which he had been unable to repay; there had been a meeting between the two, and a scene, as a result of which Bluefield had been—very cleverly—abolished. But Gaunt was too dead for punishment, and there was no one else to punish. *Quod erat demonstrandum,* as Euclid remarked.

To be sure, the inquest on Gaunt would have to go ahead, and it might develop something significant. If it did, the mystery of the manner of death would be solved, and the newspapers would have a story. That was all. If it did not, what did it particularly matter? Nobody had come forward to worry about Gaunt.

Nevertheless, the autopsy on the corpse of Hubert Gaunt was as careful as a clever young coroner's physician could make it—hurried by the very nature of his profession, in a city like Chicago. It resulted precisely as had the autopsy on the body of Amos Bluefield. It had no result whatever.

"Yes," said Adrian Bluefield, when he had heard the verdict. "Yes, yes! A very dangerous man, I should imagine, this Gaunt."

He shook his head slowly from side to side. "Perhaps it is as well that he is out of the way. With his curious knowledge of God-knows-what, he might have been a tremendous menace even to the police. I regret that my brother should have had to be his victim, but at least the murderer is dead."

He announced that his brother's funeral would be held the following afternoon—Tuesday—in the stained-glass chapel at Hillcrest, and that only friends would be present.

On the same day, at approximately the same hour, the body of Hubert Gaunt was buried in the potters' field.

The same leaden sky looked down upon both spectacles. Slate gray and slate blue.

It had been raining, off and on, for a number of days.

CHAPTER SIX

In Chicago, as no doubt elsewhere, the theater curtains rise at two-thirty for the Wednesday matinées. It is not an immutable law, but the practice is followed with commendable unanimity.

In anticipation of the event, a sardonic Director of Mundane Activities (Chicago Division) contrives, upon alternate Wednesdays, to tie up traffic in the streets in such fashion that hundreds of customers reach their destinations late.

"Only in the third city in the world," as John Rainfall disgustedly observed to his taxi driver, "is it possible for a bridge to rise politely at two twenty-three and allow thirty cents worth of mud to pass up the river while a million dollars' worth of business waits at the bridgehead."

Catching the ironic purport of the communication, the taxi man nodded his head. "You said something that time, brother."

The democracy of the fellow had been notable throughout the drive.

After a moment he contributed a secret thought of his own. "Look at that big sunflower in the middle, will you! He stands there like he don't know what it's all about."

The traffic policeman, damp and desperate, was some feet beyond the reach of the speaker's voice. He could not have heard the insult, however, had it been shouted at him, so great was the din.

A block behind, new motor cars were adding themselves to the collection in the street and adding their raucous bellowings to the symphony. It was apparently the belief of all concerned that a traffic tangle is best straightened out by a continuous staccato shrieking of motor horns. In the intervals of the uproar, the warning bell at the bridgehead could be faintly heard, either in competition or collusion.

The light mist continued to fall drearily.

Rainfall—John Rainfall—Dr. John Rainfall of the Gatacre Memorial Hospital—leaned back cynically in his seat and lighted his third cynical cigarette. If he was going to be late, he was going to be late; that was all. Saxon, he hoped, would have sense enough to go to his seat without waiting.

But the noise at length was subsiding. Rainfall glanced at his wrist watch, then at the clock in the Wrigley Building doorway. The bridge was on its way down. The tall tug, dragging after it its train of barges, was slowly leaving the neighborhood with a last derisive hoot. The big sunflower was endeavoring, godlike, to bring order out of chaos.

He caught the doctor's eye and waved a blue arm in cheery greeting. "Grand weather for ducks, Doctor," he roared, coming alongside. "And for sunflowers," smiled Rainfall, handing him the habitual cigar.

In a moment now, he noted, the stream would be in motion and the bridge would be choked, Rainfall dug quickly into his pocket. "I'm getting out here," he said. "I can do it better on foot."

In spite of his limp, which was aggravated in damp weather, he was one of the first to pass the barrier. Cutting across

Wacker Drive, he reached the thoroughfare called Wabash, where he flagged another taxi, headed west, and in five minutes was at his destination. The sidewalk in front of the theater was deserted, save for a seven-foot doorman. He was exactly twelve-and-a-half minutes late.

The curtain was already up, and with a feeling of guilt he trod softly in the wake of an attractive usher, who looked like a boy and was a girl. The shifting impact of her torchlight on the carpeted aisle conjured queer figures in the pattern underfoot; then it remained stationary upon a pair of gray spats under a seat that was beside his own. He smiled down into the face of Howard Saxon.

His own seat was on the aisle. With a murmured apology for his tardiness, he seated himself, pinched his companion's knee, and gave himself over to contemplation of the play. His overcoat he had hurled at a check boy as he entered the theater.

On the stage a reedy made was saying: "Quite true, Mrs. Caldwell. By all means let us bring the offender to justice. Yet if we all got justice, which of us, I wonder, would escape!"

It was the stage detective, Halleck, vouchsafing his epigrammatic philosophy of life.

"At fifty-two," replied the woman addressed as Mrs. Caldwell, "one's ambitions are modest. I no longer yearn even for justice. Like charity, it is only a word—in the dictionary."

Terrible!

Her voice, too, was thick and annoying. "Adenoying," it occurred to the cynical physician. He screwed his head around and stole a glance at Saxon, wondering what his friend was thinking of the stage detective. Saxon, he recalled, loathed detective stories and read them for the enjoyment of laughing at them. That, at any rate, was Saxon's story.

The outline of the play was already known to Rainfall. Patrick Lear had told him all about it. Saxon, the doctor assumed, was unacquainted with its ramifications.

The sporting editor of the *Telegram* was studying the stage detective with amused attention. The idea, apparently, had been to create something intellectual as a contrast to the roughneck police captain who, no doubt, would shortly appear. The fellow's real name was Ridinghood, as betrayed by the program, which also struck the newspaper man as humorous.

Saxon was glad that Rainfall had arrived before anything of interest had occurred. Rainfall and Lear, he knew, were old friends. How far out into the audience, he wondered, could an actor see? It was a point that had never come up in his reading. Would Pat Lear be able to pick out his friends ten rows back? Probably not.

A tall, clean-shaven woman, striding like a man, walked onto the stage from the right. Or was it the left? Was the right hand of an audience the left hand of the actors, so to speak? She asserted loudly that she didn't know what was coming over the Master, these days, that she didn't, what with his goings-on with that outlandish foreign gentleman and his looking under the bed the way he did every night before he retired. Oh, she had seen him, she said, even though perhaps she shouldn't have been looking; but now that Miss Miriam was at home, bless her dear heart, she looked at a lot of things she never had thought of looking at before; and what was more she would go on looking, too, rather than that any harm should come to that dear lamb. Family curse indeed! she said. She could tell a story about that, too, if she had a mind to; and it was a good thing for some folks that she wasn't one to talk much [*laughter*], for if she ever got started the Lord only knew where she'd end or who would be hit.

She looked very hard at Mrs. Caldwell as she said this, and Saxon grinned happily. Fifty per cent of the morons in the audience, he knew, would at once begin to suspect Mrs. Caldwell of whatever misdemeanor was to follow. The other fifty per cent, slightly more cunning, would suspect the loose-tongued housekeeper.

Mrs. Caldwell's name was Beulah, it appeared, and when there were harder eyes and faces, thought Saxon, Beulah would have them.

Lear was about due for an appearance. A grand fellow, and certainly a very popular actor. The house would roar its applause as he came on, and Lear would pause in his entrance and bow, ever so slightly, to his massed admirers.

"I come on at the second 'Sh-h!'" he had said, the afternoon before. The first was just leaving the lips of Mrs. Caldwell. "I think Mr. Carraway is coming now," she continued warningly.

Then a curious silence fell upon the stage. It was as if a signal from the wings had frozen the second "Sh-h!" upon her tongue.

Was it conceivable that the woman had forgotten her lines? That Lear had forgotten his cue?

The silence continued. After a moment, and quite suddenly, it was unbearable. Saxon leaned forward in his seat. There was an odd menace in the situation that he felt but could not name. A sense of impending revelation. Something had happened—something not upon the boards.

The sporting editor of the *Telegram* half rose from his seat, so sure was he of his intuitions. The silence, brief as it had been, was now almost intolerable. The stage detective and Mrs. Caldwell were faking a voiceless conversation. They were stalling for time.

A puzzled murmur became apparent in the audience. Then slowly the curtain began to come down.

Rainfall sprang to his feet. His hand was on Saxon's shoulder. "What do you make of it, Howard?" he asked in a whisper. "If Lear has had another heart attack . . . !"

"Wait!" said his friend.

A man had stepped from the wings and now stood before the curtain in silence. The long vista of a painted street was immediately behind him. He raised a hand to hush the rising murmur of the house. His voice was low but clear, and every ear was bending to catch his announcement.

"I regret to have to tell you that Mr. Lear has been suddenly taken ill. He is unable to go on, and, unfortunately, no understudy is available. Obviously the performance cannot proceed. If you will turn in your seat checks at the box office . . . "

"Come on!" cried Rainfall.

He almost dragged his companion to his feet. As they hurried to the rear of the auditorium and around to a side aisle the voice of the announcer on the stage continued to issue instructions. The public, at any rate, was to get its money back.

Passing through a door behind the lower tier of boxes, Saxon and the doctor traversed a short corridor and climbed a narrow flight of steps. They passed another door and found themselves, with some suddenness, behind the scenes. A number of men and women, some of them in costume, were whispering together, with occasional glances toward a room whose door opened a few feet beyond. At close quarters their greased faces looked strangely inhuman.

"Where is Mr. Lear?" asked the physician.

They pointed silently to the door of the room beyond. The

thin youth who had played the part of the stage detective added dryly: "In his dressing room."

Rainfall pushed into the dressing room, with Saxon at his heels. Then both stopped motionless.

Patrick Lear, surrounded by managers, assistant managers, stage managers, and house detectives, sat quietly in a chair before his dressing table. He did not turn as they entered. His eyes, widely open, stared with mild surprise at his own face looking out at him from the mirror. He seemed to be pondering, whimsically, the unaccustomed experience of being dead.

In another chair, some distance removed from the futile group, a white-faced woman was sobbing quietly, unobtrusively. In her Saxon recognized with surprise the actress known in the play as Mrs. Caldwell.

Rainfall stepped forward and seized the wrist of the dead man. He tore open the actor's shirt at a spot above the heart and placed a hand inside. He bent down and for an instant stared fixedly into the blank eyes. Useless gestures, all of them. The doctor knew a corpse when he saw one.

Then again, quickly, the group about the dead man turned. The elderly stage housekeeper, who had garrulously prattled about the Master, had just stepped into the room. As she did so, she stooped suddenly and came up with a square of white paper. It had been lying in the corridor, just across the doorsill—ignored.

"Let me see that," snapped Sultan, the house manager. He snatched the paper from the woman's hand.

Again he cried out, and they crowded toward him in a body. Over his shoulder they read the words blocked upon the paper.

DEAD MAN INSIDE!

CHAPTER SEVEN

NEWSBOYS SHRIEKED the tidings in the streets.

With an enterprise they had not equaled since the world's series baseball games—when final box scores were on sale at the park before the crowd had left the grounds—the newspapers flung forth their extra editions. Somewhere in the audience there had been journalists other than Howard Saxon. A line of customers still struggled to reach the box office as the shouts began outside. Those who had received their money back, but who still hung about the theater, were able to purchase swift, inaccurate reports of what had occurred almost before their eyes. There was something mysterious and fascinating in the phenomenon.

Meanwhile, a bulky patrolman had replaced the seven-foot doorman on the sidewalk, and in the dressing room of Patrick Lear a minute investigation was going forward.

Captain Michael Frogg, head of the Detective Bureau, was present in person, with a staff of technical experts. Finger-print men with cameras and flashlights were in everybody's road. There were detectives enough to populate a village. Among these latter were two men of considerable note—John Kelly and William Sheets. Both were thief catchers of reputation, and more than one murder mystery had been solved by their combined perseverance. It was a pleasure, thought Saxon, watching them, to see them at work.

"Nothing Holmesy about those dicks," he observed, *sotto voce,* to Rainfall. "They wouldn't know a steamfitter from a country parson by his coat lapel; but if one of these actorettes has anything on her conscience you can bet these birds will pry it loose."

With Rainfall, the newspaper man had remained to see it through.

"A couple of rat terriers in a roomful of mice," said the physician. "They know their business, though."

A sheet had been draped around the body of Patrick Lear, and Saxon and the doctor were feeling somewhat better in consequence.

The more important members of the company were now isolated in their dressing rooms, attended by inquisitive detectives. The rest of the cast had been herded into a corner of the wide stage. Swift questions were fired at these, from time to time, as the burly sleuths prowled about in search of clues. In all parts of the house a scene of vast activity was apparent. The theater seemed to be bursting with policemen. Over the several disturbances, at intervals, sounded the hoarse roar of Captain Frogg, urging his men to greater effort.

But there was little enough that could be learned. It was obvious, after an hour of search and inquiry, that the murderer, if he were not among the members of the company, had made his entrance and his exit by way of the fire escape that led directly from the star's dressing room to the alley below. There were even marks upon the window ledge.

"Only," observed Captain Frogg, in his rhinocerine bellow, "we just don't know yet who made the marks and when he made them. Maybe they were there last week. Maybe this Lear made 'em himself. Maybe that's the way he used to leave the theayter, to escape his admirers. Maybe *I* made them, last night, walking in my sleep. Just the same," he concluded with hoarse satisfaction, "I'm betting that the man who made them was going away from here—in quite a hurry." His voice dropped suddenly to a dulcet purr, strangely incongruous, as he repeated: "In quite a hurry!"

He thrust his head out of the door, smiling with a sort of ferocious humor at the huddled group of actors and actresses. The idea in his mind became suddenly apparent. "There ain't any of you people who come into this show late, I suppose? Second or third act, maybe? Lots of time for somebody to do a little job of murder, hop out of the window, and hustle over to the stage door again, eh?"

"I asked about that, Captain," said the detective Kelly. "The man at the stage door says nobody came in twice. He says if anybody had climbed the fire escape from outside he'd have seen him. He doesn't stay inside all the time. He moves around a bit. Takes a smoke in the alley every once in a while."

"Anyway," contributed Sheets, "to climb that thing from the alley you have to pull it down first. It goes down when you step on it, but it's a good twenty feet above you when you're under it."

The captain shrugged his massive shoulders.

"Anything you say, boys," he retorted. "But it could have been done. I could do it myself. What about a parked car, right underneath the escape, eh? There's parked cars up and down every alley in the Loop. Wouldn't have had to be his own, either. Where's that doorman?"

"That's right," agreed Kelly, without embarrassment. "It

could have happened that way." He started for the door. "I'll get after that fellow again."

Sheets followed more slowly, and Rainfall, Saxon, and the police captain were left alone with the corpse of Patrick Lear.

"Could have happened, anyway," continued Frogg. His obstinate, good-natured growl seemed to fill the little room. "Moves around and takes a smoke in the alley, does he? Not when it's raining, he don't! When it's raining he sneaks his little smoke indoors, just like we all do. Of course he didn't see anything. Nobody *ever* sees anything. The man that did this job wasn't aiming to be seen. Ask a watchman whether he saw a murderer climb a fire escape twenty feet away, and of course he'll say no. Because he knows damn well it's his job to see things, and he knows damn well he wasn't on the job. That's human nature, ain't it, Doctor?"

"Absolutely," said Rainfall, smiling faintly.

Captain Frogg lowered his voice. He became almost confidential.

"I know you, Dr. Rainfall," he said. "You're one of the big guns in medicine. I've heard of you before. Well—what about it?"

The physician stared. "What about what? This case?"

"This death," said the police captain. "What killed him? That's what I want to know. And those other birds, too. What killed *them?* Could it have been poison?"

"Yes," answered Rainfall, "I think it could have been; but I don't believe it. The coroner's pathologist is a competent fellow. I know him. If it had been poison he'd have spotted it."

Frogg nodded acquiescence. "Then what the hell was it?"

"Any reputable physician, looking at Lear, would probably say heart failure," answered Rainfall. "I'd say it myself if it were not for those other cases. But it ought to be settled, this time."

"You're darned tooting it ought to be settled this time," growled the captain. "If it ain't, I'll have every newspaper in town on my neck. This fellow ain't Bluefield and he ain't Gaunt. He's a public character. We've got to find out what killed him, and we've got to get the man that did it. Did he have heart trouble?"

"He had had one attack that I know of."

"Shock, maybe," mused the captain. "Murder by shock, eh? Scared to death!

How's that?"

"I doubt it," said Rainfall. "It's possible, of course."

"Look here," said Frogg. "What's your idea? I suppose you have one."

"Well, I have and I haven't," confessed the physician. "What I *do* want to see, though, is a first-class autopsy, this time. I'm not knocking the coroner's staff. They have to work quickly, and in an ordinary case they're all right. This isn't an ordinary case, as I see it. It's a queer business, don't you think?—three men dead and no reasonable explanation of their deaths!"

"Yes, I do. Look here! Why not do the job, yourself?"

Rainfall's glance wandered to the body of Patrick Lear, monstrously outlined under a white sheet. He shook his head.

"Lear was my friend, Captain. I don't quite fancy it. But, by the Lord Harry, I *will* do it rather than have it go undone. The other autopsies were pretty casual, from all reports. Examination of the vital organs isn't enough." He hesitated. "I suppose the coroner would object, anyway."

"Why should he?"

"He'd think I was butting in on something that was none of my business, wouldn't he?"

"To hell with the coroner," observed Frogg, without malice.

"Tell him you're working for me. I'll tell him myself. He'll be here at any minute."

"Very well," said Rainfall. "I'll do it. That is, I'll stand by and oversee the job. He can hardly object to that."

Frogg, however, had just had another idea. "No," he decided, "there's no use giving Powell all the credit. We'll let him go ahead his own way, and when he flops again—as he probably will—we'll call you in. That way the department gets the credit, and Captain Michael Frogg gets his name in the papers."

He chuckled raucously.

"All right," agreed Rainfall. "I don't care how it's done as long as we get at the truth. As a matter of fact, the coroner may find it out for himself."

"No fear of that!" Frogg was confident the coroner's office was hopeless. "Tell you what we'll do: we'll—"

The detective Kelly came hurrying back. He interrupted the gruesome conversation without apology.

"Well," he announced briskly, "you were right, Captain. There *was* a car parked near that fire escape. The doorman saw it. He thought it had been there all morning."

"Oh, he did!"

"Yeh, thought it belonged to somebody in the next building."

"Well, maybe it did," grunted Frogg. "But the murderer used it, whoever it belonged to. If he came at Lear from outside, he did. He wouldn't have to be a monkey to do it, either. Anybody can climb on top of a car and swing onto a fire escape. I could do *that,* myself. Naturally he watched his chance."

"It couldn't have been there all morning," mused the detective. "It'd have got a ticket."

"Maybe it would and maybe it wouldn't," said Frogg. "It would depend on whose car it was. If it was the mayor's car, or the fire marshal's car, or *my* car—then it wouldn't! Likewise, if it happened to be the car of some friend of a certain mounted policeman, it wouldn't get a ticket, either. Well, look up the mountie on this street, Kelly, and see what he knows about it. How about all these play actors?"

"Some of 'em walked, some of 'em came in taxis. Even this Lear didn't have his own car."

"And none of 'em know a thing about what happened, eh?"

"So they say."

"What about the girl who was doing all the crying in here?"

"Miss Carvel? She was on the stage when it happened."

"What does she say?"

"That's what she says. Oh, about her crying! Well, she says she was nervous and upset."

"Nervous and upset, was she?" inquired Frogg ironically. "Well, she was the only one of them that was, then. Nobody else was doing any weeping. How do *we* know she was on the stage when it happened? She was there when Lear failed to show up—sure! And a swell alibi, too, Johnny, me boy. No, it all depends on when it happened. And nobody knows when it happened. Lear came in at two o'clock, so it must have happened after two. He wasn't dead when he walked in, that's certain. By God, we'll need a time chart of this play before we're through!"

The sporting editor of the *Telegram* had been silent quite long enough, it occurred to Howard Saxon.

"How about that piece of paper, Captain?" he asked.

"*What* about it?" retorted the captain suspiciously.

"Well," explained Saxon, "I've an idea that it has nothing whatever to do with this case."

"The deuce you have! Now where did you get *that* idea?"

Rainfall, too, looked amazed at his companion's contribution to the discussion. He had almost forgotten Saxon.

"Here's the way I figure it," said Saxon. "Lear had a bad heart, as Dr. Rainfall has told you. Well, he had another attack, and it carried him off. Somebody in the company, who had been reading about these other cases, fixed up a ticket of his own. Maybe somebody who didn't like Lear. Bingo! A new murder mystery and a free advertisement for the show."

Captain Frogg frowned thoughtfully for a moment. Then he sighed.

"The worst of it is," he observed, looking at Rainfall, "he *could* be right! Not about advertising the show. A fellow'd have to think quick to pull that, after discovering a man dead. But maybe it *doesn't* have anything to do with those other cases at all! Maybe somebody just wants us to think so."

Saxon nodded. "Well," he replied, shifting his ground expertly, "in that case, you'd probably have the murderer of Patrick Lear, at least."

"So we would, so we would," agreed Frogg, without enthusiasm. "Ain't it grand, Doctor, to have a newspaper imagination! Well, I've changed my mind again. I want to know something about this case. You'll act for me at the autopsy, will you, Doctor?"

"Yes," said Rainfall. "I'll perform it, if necessary."

"Swell!" observed Captain Michael Frogg. "Now we'll get somewhere. That'll be Powell now. He always makes a lot of noise." They turned abruptly to greet the coroner of Cook County.

CHAPTER EIGHT

THE INQUEST developed a number of matters of interest.

Deputy Coroner Kipp was in charge—a small man with a walrus mustache and a habit of stroking it gently. Once he had been a Sunday-school superintendent. His passion for publicity was still enormous. The reporters loved him. His adjectives and his asides made admirable press copy. It was always a pleasure for Deputy Coroner Kipp to discover them in print.

However, he knew his business, and he got about it promptly.

A coroner's physician took the stand and revealed his profession. He confessed that, in pursuance of his duty, he had conducted an autopsy upon the body of Patrick Lear, at the County Morgue, on the preceding afternoon. In that autopsy he had been assisted by the well known surgeon, Dr. John Rainfall, acting for the police.

Deputy Kipp leaned backward in his chair. "Just tell us, Doctor, in your own words," he suggested, "the nature and the results of your examination."

"As to its nature," answered the physician, "it was an autopsy such as is usually conducted in a case of this sort. Perhaps a little more careful, in view of the importance of the case. As to its results, they were at first disappointing. The man apparently had died because his heart had stopped beating."

The deputy brought the legs of his chair back to position. He placed his finger tips together and half closed his eyes.

"You mean," he asked, "that you found nothing suggestive or significant?"

"At first, nothing. Nothing whatever."

"Remarkable!" observed the deputy, glancing at the press table.

The exclamation, however, was intended only for the reporters. To Deputy Kipp the information was not even surprising. He had received a complete report of the autopsy some time before, and it was even then before him on the table. His inquests, filled with deliberate suspense, were merely good theater for the public and the newspapers.

"Now, Doctor, I will ask you to be a little more explicit. If you had been signing a death certificate for this man, what cause would you have assigned for his decease?"

"Heart disease—probably *angina pectoris.*"

"Coronary sclerosis," translated the coroner's assistant, complacently. "I need not ask you whether you looked carefully at the eyes and mouth of the deceased."

"The autopsy was complete, up to a point. The eyes betrayed no trace of drugs or opiates. The tongue and lips had not been bitten as a result of spasm. The body showed no external bruises. The organs were taken out and sent to the laboratory. There were no traces of poison in the viscera."

"Extraordinary!" said Deputy Kipp. "And as to the heart?"

"The heart was markedly dilated. Blood in one chamber.

Marked evidence of sclerosis of the coronary vessels. Marked myocardial degeneration."

"Meaning exactly?"

"Nothing at all, sir. It is a condition that exists in all men of forty or over." The witness smiled genially. "I have no doubt that I have it, myself. I may add that the kidneys were posted for alcoholism, but without important results."

The raggle-taggle jury, which already had viewed the body in an adjoining room, was beginning to feel that it had known the dead man intimately. The several actresses who were to be called had not been required to listen to the details of dismemberment. They were not present in the room. But the press-gang methods of the coroner's office had, as usual, assembled a singularly polyglot crew to sit in judgment. A number of the jurors appeared to be slightly ill.

"Thank you," said Deputy Kipp, with a little bow. "I understand, however, that you were nevertheless successful in your examination."

"Dr. Rainfall, acting for the chief of police, assisted me in my investigation. We agreed that the head of the deceased also should be posted, and this was done. In ordinary cases we do not always post the head. It depends upon—well, circumstances! In two previous cases, recently before the public, it was not done, in consequence of which, Dr. Rainfall believes, valuable evidence was lost. I agree with him."

Deputy Kipp nodded his own agreement. "Precisely," he observed. "And the cause of death, Doctor?"

"A singularly ingenious wound within the brain. It is difficult to suggest what the weapon used may have been. Hatpins are out of date, I believe; and a hatpin, if used, might have broken off inside the wound. Something long and hard and slender, I suggest—driven up under the skull cap, just to the right of the final vertebrae. Possibly three inches up. Death, of course, was instantaneous."

"Fiendish!" exclaimed Deputy Kipp. "And there was no mark whatever to indicate the entrance of this weapon?"

"A faint one—hidden under the line of the hair, at the base of the skull. Hardly more than a pin prick. The exterior wound is so negligible, indeed, that it might never have been discovered. The smallest possible puncture. Possibly only a single drop of blood resulted. With that wiped away, and the spot vigorously massaged, there would be practically nothing to indicate the entrance of the weapon. Inside the brain, of course, the evidences of hemorrhage were considerable."

"A long needle, perhaps?" asked the deputy.

"Conceivably, but unlikely, I think. That too might have broken off. But something as slender as a needle and of a finer temper. Something that wouldn't break. Something, I should imagine, with a solid handle. The upward thrust would have had to be reasonably vigorous."

"A hypodermic needle?"

"I know of none long enough or strong enough."

"Thank you," said Kipp benevolently. "It is probably a matter we can safely leave to the police. Dr. Rainfall, if you please!"

But Rainfall had little to add to the story already told. The coroner's physician had made a thorough job of his testimony, in keeping with the best Kipp traditions, and had covered himself and his office with glory. Rainfall added his authority to the statement and took his seat.

The second sensation followed immediately.

It was established that Patrick Lear had been a married

man and had, in consequence, left a widow. Astonishingly enough, the widow was none other than the hard-faced young woman who had played the part of Mrs. Caldwell—the young woman who had wept in the dressing room of the dead actor. The wedding, it appeared, had been secret, and the name Stacey had appeared upon the licence. It was Lear's proper name. The more Shakespearean pseudonym had been adopted for stage purposes.

This was a police triumph that had been kept away from the press. To the constabulary mind it was a significant discovery. It furnished, at any rate, a conceivable motive for murder. Lear had been a reasonably wealthy man, and no doubt there had been another woman in the case.

Kelly and Sheets, detective sergeants of reputation, were elated. One must begin some place to investigate a mystery, and often one clue is as good as another. The main thing is to keep busy and to keep the reporters satisfied. How Miss Carvel had managed the deed—if she *had*—was perhaps another matter, but they were not at the moment worrying about it.

To Howard Saxon, seated next to Rainfall at the rear of the inquest chamber, waiting his unimportant turn upon the stand, the revelation wore another and more puzzling aspect. He thought of the white-faced, sobbing woman in the actor's dressing room, then of that same woman as he had seen her, on the stage, only a few minutes before.

Had she been there upon the stage when the thing happened? Was there any reason to doubt it? And how long had Lear been sitting before his mirror awaiting the cue he could not answer?

The woman had been admirably at ease in her part, even when she must have known that Lear, in some fashion, had been stricken. She had carried on bravely while the audience waited. That, supposed Saxon, was her training. Yet tears, also, no doubt, were part of her training.

On the other hand, there were the murders of Bluefield and Gaunt. The connection between the three was shriekingly obvious. At any rate, it was obvious that there was a connection.

Young Mr. Saxon had discarded his idea that Lear's case was unrelated almost as rapidly as he had adopted it. It seemed clear to him now that when the bodies of Bluefield and Gaunt were exhumed they would reveal the same sinister brain hemorrhages.

Ergo, to imagine Mrs. Lear—Miss Carvel—as murdering her husband, required also a belief that she was at least cognizant of the other murders. Certainly, however, she had not herself murdered Amos Bluefield—and set him up on a throne in his own shop window! Nor could Saxon quite see Miss Carvel enticing Hubert Gaunt, that more mysterious victim, to a spot beneath the towering statue of Thaddeus Burke for purposes of slaughter.

Her testimony from the witness stand had been dignified and without emotional display. She concluded it by denying any knowledge of her husband's death up to and until the moment she had seen him dead.

Young Mr. Saxon was greatly puzzled. That the actor's widow was a legitimate enough suspect, for the time being, went without saying; but for that matter everybody behind the scenes was temporarily suspect. She had been cool upon the stage and tearful in her husband's dressing room, and in both cases she might have been justifying her excellent reputation as an actress. But what of Bluefield and what of Gaunt? If she had had any part in the other murders, she could not have been alone.

The thing ran somewhat in a circle in Saxon's mind. With

a mental shrug, he returned to his more immediate rôle of detached spectator and prospective witness.

The coroner's deputy was calling another name. Miss Carvel was walking slowly to her seat. The reporters were looking anxiously at their watches.

"Mr. Moore!"

There appeared in answer to the summons an actor named Moore. Mr. Moore, it appeared, had acted as stage manager for the production so suddenly closed by the death of Patrick Lear.

He told his story with simplicity and outward restraint.

For the first time the crowded inquest chamber began to get a picture of the Alhambra stage as it had been set for murder, just twenty-four hours before.

CHAPTER NINE

LEAR HAD been a likable fellow, it appeared.

An eccentric, of course! He held himself aloof from the rest of the company; but in this, it seemed, he was not unique among stage celebrities.

It was his habit to appear for a matinée promptly at two o'clock and shut himself away in his dressing room. It was Moore's habit, promptly at two-thirty o'clock, to knock gently upon the star's door as an indication that the curtain was rising.

Lear knew the moment of his own entrance to the tick of a clock. He had never before been known to miss his cue.

"Never before having been murdered," muttered Rainfall to Saxon, with grim humor.

Sometimes, at Moore's mnemonic tap, Lear would be heard to respond, but the tradition was not established. When, therefore, he had failed to respond upon the afternoon of his death, the stage manager had felt no anxiety. With the advent of the star's actual cue, however, and still no sign from the dressing room, Moore had become alarmed and had entered the room.

"Mr. Lear," he said simply, "was seated at his dressing table—dead!"

"You knew at once that he was dead?" Kipp's innocent query was suave as cream.

"I think I did. There was something about him—"

"You had seen the bodies of dead men before?"

"Only in their coffins," admitted Moore.

"At any rate, you were sure that Mr. Lear was dead?"

"I was afraid so. It was significant that he had not responded to his cue."

"You had seen him enter at two o'clock?"

"I saw him when he came in—yes, sir. He seemed to be in the best of health and spirits."

"And, as usual, he went at once to his dressing room? Quite so! Was he alone?"

"Quite alone."

"What of his wife? Was it not her custom to arrive with him?"

"We knew nothing about his wife," answered Moore simply. "I, at least, knew nothing about her until to-day. Miss Carvel—the young lady who appears to have been his wife—used to come to the theater by herself, usually in a taxicab."

"And you heard no one with him, at any time, after he entered his room?"

"I heard no one at any time."

"Very well, then. You found him, as you supposed, dead. What did you do then?"

"There was only one thing to do, and I had authority to do it. The curtain was up—the house was waiting. The actors on the stage were stopped in their tracks. Mr. Lear had no permanent understudy. I knew his lines myself but never actually had played the part. For one evening—or two—in case of an ordinary illness, I could have filled in. But if Mr. Lear were really dead—as I feared—you see? Anyway, the curtain had to come down. I ordered it down."

"Dramatic!" commented Deputy Kipp.

"Dramatic!" wrote each reporter at the press table. Then, having completed a certain number of pages, each handed his copy to a slant-eyed junior, who hurried with it to the nearest telephone.

The coroner's assistant stroked his curving mustache. His fingers played with a square of white paper on the table. After a moment he lifted the paper with a theatrical gesture and presented it before the actor's eyes.

"When you entered Mr. Lear's dressing room, Mr. Moore, immediately before you discovered that he was dead, were you aware of this piece of paper any place within view?"

The stage manager's reply was prompt. "I was not. It was discovered later—just outside the door."

"You are quite certain it was not pinned to the door? In your agitation, you might not have noticed it, perhaps. Is it not conceivable that it was dislodged when you opened the door? That it then fluttered to the floor where later it was found? It is not very large, you see. It would have been easy to overlook."

The stage manager was puzzled. "I suppose it is conceivable," he admitted. "I have no memory of it."

The deputy handed the square of paper to the members of the jury. It passed from hand to hand. The jurors gazed upon it owlishly, then owlishly upon the stage manager. In the mind of each was a conviction that Stanley Moore had pinned the paper on the door himself and was now denying it.

"Are you familiar with the handwriting of Mr. Lear?" asked the deputy coroner. "I realize, of course, that the words on this square of paper are printed in ink rather than written; but is there any suggestion of the handwriting of the deceased?"

"None that I can see—no, sir. I suppose he *could* have written it—printed it—but in that case—"

"Ah, yes! In that case?"

"It would surely have meant that he knew—that he was going to die!"

"Precisely! And suppose he *did* know he was going to die, or perhaps had some premonition of death, do you think he might then have written—printed—such a note and left it to be found upon the door?"

"No, sir, I do not."

"Why, Mr. Moore?"

"In the first place, why should he have printed it? He knew how to write. But he wouldn't have done it, anyway. If he had thought he was going to die, he would have called for somebody. If he had thought he was seriously ill, he would not have allowed the performance to begin. An actor owes something to his public, and he doesn't forget it: if he's any good, he doesn't. Mr. Lear was one of the best. He would never have let an audience down like that."

"I see! In your opinion, then, this square of paper was not left in Mr. Lear's dressing room, or outside Mr. Lear's dressing room, by Mr. Lear himself."

"Yes, sir."

"Have you any idea who else might have done such a thing?"

"I have not."

"There are, however, jealousies upon the stage, as elsewhere? It is at least conceivable that Mr. Lear had enemies?"

The stage manager shrugged. "I suppose so. But jealousy and enmity aren't the same thing, Mr. Coroner. A man may be jealous of another man without wanting to kill him. And the man who wrote that thing was advertising—murder!"

"Tut, tut, Mr. Moore! The word murder has not been used. It has not yet been established by this jury how Mr. Lear met his death."

"It has been pretty well established by the doctors."

"Still, it is for the jury to decide."

This was merely one of Kipp's engaging fictions, since he dictated all decisions himself.

"When two other men meet their death in the same way—" argued Moore, a bit obstinately; but again Deputy Kipp good-humoredly interrupted.

"We are investigating the death of one man only—Patrick Lear, otherwise Stacey. You have been reading the newspapers, Mr. Moore, and forming premature opinions. Let us admit, if you like, that jealousy and enmity are not synonymous. What can you tell us of any jealousies existing among the members of the company headed by the deceased? Did you, for example, feel any jealousy toward him yourself?"

"Certainly not!" The stage manager spoke with some heat. "We were the best of friends."

"Excellent! And what of the others?"

"They were fond enough of Mr. Lear, I believe. He was perhaps a bit of a martinet, at times. A little impatient with others less gifted than himself. Mr. Lear's effort always was to bring the entire production up to that high level of artistry reached by himself alone."

"And some of the company resented this attitude?"

"Not that—no! There may have been some private grumbling, but no more than that. There always is. Nothing was ever said, that I remember."

A reporter who had just scratched a hasty question upon a scrap of paper, got up suddenly and handed it across to the inquisitor. Deputy Kipp looked at it with bleak eyes. However, it was the next question that he asked.

"To return to the square of paper, for a moment, Mr. Moore: I want you to clarify your earlier inference. Do you believe it possible that it may—the paper, not your inference—have been dropped upon the floor, where it was found, *after* the discovery of Mr. Lear's body?"

"You mean by someone entering the room immediately after I had left it?"

"Yes—or still later by some member of the company gathered about the body when the excitement was at its highest."

The stage manager hesitated. "Well, yes," he replied, at length. "I don't know whether that is what I was actually suggesting, but it might have happened that way."

"You had no particular person in mind?"

"No, sir. Certainly not! I am merely certain that Mr. Lear didn't write it himself."

"Very well! In short, then, Mr. Moore, you know of no incident whatever, however slight, that might throw some light upon the death of Mr. Lear. You are as anxious as we, I am sure, to clear up this mystery. Think carefully, if you will. What can you suggest?"

"Nothing! I am as mystified as anybody could be."

"Thank you. You may stand aside. Mr. Sultan, please."

But neither Sultan, the house manager, nor any of those who followed him, could add to the testimony of Stanley Moore, the little man who—excepting always the tacitly assumed murderer—had been the last to see the star alive and the first to see him dead.

CHAPTER TEN

Murder, as a rule, is a secret profession. The idea of the average murderer is to abolish his victim and then escape with what speed he may be able to muster. It is his ardent wish to remain unknown. He hopes and perhaps prays that he has left no clues behind that will betray him to the police.

Sometimes a murderer more cunning than the average practitioner will leave a deliberate trail for the detectives to follow. This, obviously, is more than likely to be false—at any rate, misleading.

The case of the "Dead Man Murders," as it was quaintly called by the newspapers, was of another kind. There had been secrecy, to be sure—of a sort. Invitations had not been issued to the murders; but certainly the world had been invited to attend the investigation. The newspapers again were filled with it.

Of deliberate clues, so to call them, there were perhaps three: three squares of white paper, marked with ink. They had ticketed, in each of three instances, the unique tomb of the murdered victim. They were not, however, particularly helpful. Anybody can print letters with a pen, and nearly everybody's attempt will be more or less like the other fellow's.

One thing seemed certain, now—that the three murders

were the work of a single hand; at least, of a single brain. To the police, another thing seemed obvious—that that brain was diseased. It is always easy and distracting to cry "Lunatic!" when a piece of villainy is out of the usual groove.

The press recalled a series of sanguinary crimes in Vienna, in 1916, the work of a madman who had been subsequently discovered in an asylum. He had contrived his incarceration very cleverly on other grounds.

Saxon, however, was still dubious.

"Bunk!" he observed heartily. "All bunk, Rainfall! To the extent that any man who commits murder is crazy, I suppose this fellow is—but the whole thing looks to me like some sort of a come-on."

"Yes?" Rainfall was lazily interested. "How so?" They were in a taxicab, returning from the inquest.

"It's too evidently what he would like people to believe—what he *expects* the police to believe. In every case, except maybe that of Lear, he set up a background of sheer lunacy. Bodies in windows and on statues! Even Lear's case smacked of it. What's the word for that kind of a psychosis? Exhibitionism?"

"No," smiled the physician. "He certainly isn't exhibiting himself, whatever else he's doing." After a moment he asked: "Well, what do *you* think, Howard? I'm open to conviction, although it does look like insanity to me."

"How about egotism?" The sporting editor of the *Telegram* chuckled. "Of course, that's first cousin to insanity!" He sobered. "Well, I'll tell you what I think: I think the fellow who did those three crazy jobs was a smart fellow—a fellow with an imagination. Therefore it's going to require an imagination to catch him. Three men, apparently unassociated, fantastically murdered and their bodies exposed in public places! Lear's wasn't, perhaps, but I'll gamble the murderer would have preferred to kill Lear in the middle of the stage—in full view of the audience. Only, that way, he could hardly have hoped to escape. But he left his card—didn't he?—to indicate that the same man was at work. Every deed was labeled—and very whimsically labeled, if you ask *me*—to call attention to the singleness of purpose involved. There's a phrase for you—singleness of purpose! I'm getting rhetorical. Here's another: all three murders were the work of a single hand which, in effect, now boasts of what it has done, calls upon the world to witness, and defies detection."

He smiled a little at his own enthusiasm and asked: "How's that?"

The physician shrugged. "One man may have murdered Bluefield in his shop at night. One man may have murdered Lear in his dressing room yesterday—although how he managed it is a caution. But one man didn't murder Hubert Gaunt, then lift his body onto that iron horse. He couldn't! That required help."

Saxon was taken aback. "You may be right," he admitted. "One man *could* have done it, I think; but it would have been quite a chore. *Quite* a chore! By George, I can almost see him trying it!"

"He'd have needed a stepladder and a corps of assistants," said Rainfall.

"Gaunt wasn't such a big fellow, though," argued the newspaper man. "Rather small, wasn't he? Oh, I don't know! Who am I to play detective?"

He was silent for a moment, while the cab sped northward. Suddenly he began to speak again.

"Why do you suppose Lear sent us tickets for that particular performance, Rainfall?"

"Eh?" The physician was startled. "I was just thinking the same thing myself. Great minds! You think there was something more than coincidence in it, then?"

"Don't you? I can't help wondering. It seems such an extraordinary coincidence."

"It does," agreed Rainfall. "His physician and a famous newspaper man! It almost looks as if he had been *expecting* something to happen and was preparing for emergencies."

"Well, it's a valid thought," said Saxon.

"Another thing," said the doctor: "Is it your idea that Lear knew those other fellows—Bluefield and Gaunt?"

"He almost had to, didn't he?"

"Because the murderer planned to kill all three? It doesn't necessarily follow. But if Lear knew them, why didn't I?"

"I suppose Lear had friends or acquaintances unknown to you. Why not?"

"I've known Lear, as I told you, since he came to me—a patient—years ago. I've corresponded with him, off and on, for a long time. I've seen him whenever he was in town. I was his friend and—as far as Chicago is concerned—I was his physician. Surely I would have heard their names mentioned."

"I don't think so." Saxon shook his head. "Lear may have had reasons for not mentioning them. He needn't have told you everything about himself. If Bluefield and Gaunt were 'wrong,' as may have been the case, he wouldn't have mentioned them to you. Did you know his name was Stacey, not Lear?"

"Yes, he told me that, years ago."

"It wouldn't mean anything, of course." Saxon was thoughtful. "Lots of actors change their names. Patrick Lear! What a name, eh? Almost too perfect for his part in life. It simply couldn't have been his own."

Rainfall laughed. "The Lear, I believe, is from Aristophanes."

Saxon looked at his companion reproachfully. For a time they fell silent again, while the cab jolted on its way toward the Gatacre Memorial Hospital.

"Yes," said the newspaper man, at length, "the fellow who did all this had imagination, Rainfall. What an advertising man he would have made! What a novelist! Bluefield, a millionaire recluse and haberdasher, sitting dead in his own shop window! Gaunt, a gambler and a mystery, sprawled dead across a bronze horse in the city's principal park, waiting exhibition at the hands of a schoolgirl! Lear, the nation's most popular romantic actor, dead in his dressing room, before a mirror, while a thousand people wait for his appearance on the stage. What a beginning for a mystery story! I wonder what form his confession will take."

"His confession?" echoed Rainfall.

"His mind appears to be fantastic. On the heels of what he has already shown us, we are entitled to look for something unusual in the way of a denouement. Perhaps he will disguise himself as a sky writer and smoke his confession across the clouds—just before he disappears forever behind one of them. I believe that has not yet been done, even in fiction."

The physician smiled wryly. "Perhaps he will disguise himself as a ton of coal and be delivered at your door," he said. "You are gifted with a trifle of imagination yourself, Howard."

Howard Saxon laughed. "My employers," he admitted, "have often accused me of the same crime."

The open verdict returned by the coroner's jury, they agreed, was the only thing that could have been returned. Where the inquisitive Kipp had left off, it was the business of the police to begin.

"They'll get farther following up the Lear case than they will with the others," said Saxon.

"And you may depend on it," said Rainfall, "they will keep a none too friendly eye on everybody concerned: Mrs. Lear, Moore, Sultan, you, I, the housekeeper—what was her name?—Ballantyne!—and particularly, I should say, on that stage detective, Ridinghood. He will be almost notably suspect. Not that he is any more involved than anybody else, but because he played the part of the detective. Without being aware of it, the police mind inclines toward paradox."

He laughed shortly. "What a name that would be for a murderer, Howard! *Ridinghood!* Little Red Ridinghood! Can't you see the newspapers? It would be reversing the fairy tale with a vengeance."

Saxon laughed also. "A good enough name for a detective, too. They ought to have let him keep it for the play." After a time, he added soberly: "There's one thing I haven't told you, Rainfall. There was one really smart man at that inquest, today. Not you and not me. He was that reporter who asked the last question put to Moore. Kipp let on it was his own question, but it wasn't. The fact is, that square of paper *was* dropped on the floor of Lear's dressing room *after* the herd had entered."

"The deuce it was! What makes you so certain?"

"Because it wasn't on the door, and it wasn't on the floor, when you and I entered. I said nothing about it at the inquest. I'm no super-Hawkshaw or anything silly like that. Amateur detectives give me a pain. But if I've learned anything at all from experience I've learned to use my eyes. I used them when we entered that room."

"Well?"

"The paper wasn't anywhere around. In other words, it was dropped there, where it was found, after we all had entered—and why not by the murderer himself?"

CHAPTER ELEVEN

MEANWHILE, AT the Gatacre Memorial Hospital, a tall man, whose phenomenal ugliness had for a week been a jest among the dapper internes, shifted restlessly in his too short bed and awaited tidings of release. It was his first experience of a hospital as a patient, and he was heartily tired of it. He was too polite, however, to mention the circumstance. Cigarettes were his solace—a pipe being frowned upon—and Sister Hertha was sure he would burn the building down.

He lay now, as daylight waned, waiting the coming of Dr. Rainfall, chief surgeon of the institution. Outside the window of his private room—only a few feet from a black-lettered Zone of Quiet placard—a child, alone in a motor car, played ceaselessly with the squawking siren. In the corridors, rubber-tired service tables with metallic tops rattled past like adumbrations of battle. It was the hour for dinner—the evening meal—and the bored patient looked forward without appetite to the impersonal repast that shortly would be placed before him. His nerves, he realized, were beginning to get frayed.

Two days still lay between him and freedom. On the morrow his several stitches would be removed, and on the day following, God and John Rainfall willing, he would be permitted to pay his bill and depart. He touched his abdomen gently. A great deal of inconvenience might have been spared the world of men, he reflected, if its citizens had been divinely equipped with zipper fronts. What under the sun could have given *him* a diseased appendix? His inclination was to abuse the city. He had no love for Chicago—a gray, cold place in the late autumn, with few attractions for a citizen of the world. At this moment he should have been en route to dinner at his favorite club in New York. The whole episode indeed, reflected Walter Ghost, had been quite ridiculous.

He had been stricken the day of his arrival, at the very moment he had leaned over an ancient map in the Newberry Library.

Beyond his open door an elevator crashed open and then crashed shut. There was a sound of wheels, and a whiff of ether floated in to him as a long stretcher was rolled past. Some poor devil returning from the operating room. An emergency affair, no doubt, since it was late for such performances. He had come downstairs himself like that, only a week before—swathed in ether and bandages, like a modern mummy. What a week it had been! Only the conversation of Dr. Rainfall, the surgeon, had helped to correct his opinion of the windswept metropolis. John Rainfall, author of his humane wound and of all this delay, was a man of sense and humor. His daily visits were little oases in days of arid stupidity.

A small volume of Shakespeare lay face downward, ignored, upon the tumbled counterpane.

"There is no doubt about it," murmured the ugly man. "I am becoming exceedingly bored."

A buxom nurse thrust her cap in at the door and smiled seraphically. His private nurse had gone upstairs to dinner.

"Did you ring, sir?"

This, also, was forever happening. His voice and eyes, the uniformed young women admitted among themselves, were things to be romantic about. What a gentleman he was! And no more than forty, surely.

"I didn't," said Ghost, "but it is always pleasant to see you. One gets weary of looking at the ceiling."

He was lonely, however, by his own desire. There were friends in plenty who would have flocked to him if he had advised them of his predicament. The picture of himself, badly shaved and helpless upon his back, was not an attractive one, he felt. He had no wish to make it a public spectacle. Hospital conversation, too—tempered to the supposed seriousness of one's illness—was a bit of a nuisance. At funerals people frankly whispered, but in hospitals they were simply embarrassed.

"Your dinner will be along in just a minute, I think."

"They prepare it in very large basins, don't they?" he asked mildly. "You couldn't get me an evening paper, I suppose! I haven't seen one for days."

"I'll try, sir. I'll ask the head nurse, right away. There's a book of cross-word puzzles in the library."

"Thanks! But don't trouble about the book." He smiled whimsically at his ignored Shakespeare. "I have a book, you see! That isn't a joke—it's a serious matter. Your name is Tapscott, isn't it? An interesting name. I am a man of one book, Miss Tapscott, and as such, the Spaniards say, to be distrusted. I wonder what passage I quoted coming out of the ether! I must ask the doctor. Pay no attention to my levity, Miss Tapscott. I am also a word of three letters, in vulgar use, signifying a beast of burden. Has Dr. Rainfall come in yet?"

"I don't think so. I haven't seen him. I'll see about the paper for you right away, sir."

A trifle bewildered, as usual, and secretly convinced that the admired patient was more than a little mad, the young woman hurried from the room. She was back again quickly, however, with a lurid evening newspaper—a journal immensely popular among women recovering from operations. From one of these she had borrowed it. Ghost buried himself in its pages until the service table crashed across his sill and came to rest against his bed.

"Thank you," he said, and watched with relief the departure of the young woman in charge.

He had come across a murder mystery on the front page, of so frantic a complexion that he was certain at least half of it had been invented by the ingenious reporter. Three dead men—and a situation that would have made the fortune of a sensational dramatist.

It was all the more interesting in that his friend Dr. Rainfall, apparently, had known one of the victims. It was even more astonishing and interesting in that the daughter of his old friend Chandler Moment apparently had seen the murderer. What a small world it was, after all, he took no shame in thinking. He picked fastidiously at the dishes that had been set before him, and read the newspaper account of the murders, until the arrival of his physician.

Rainfall came in briskly, followed by Saxon.

"Well, Mr. Ghost, I imagine you are getting rather tired of our persistent hospitality. Let me introduce a friend of mine—Howard Saxon. He is dining with me, shortly—hence his reluctant presence in a hospital! Sorry you can't join us."

The two men shook hands, measuring each other with friendly eyes.

"I'm sorry, too," said Ghost. "As it happens, I have already dined." He indicated with some distaste the clutter of small dishes on the service table.

The physician laughed. "Hospital food *isn't* exactly what one would order in a restaurant," he admitted. "On a desert island, on the other hand, you would find it excellent." He laid a thumb and finger lightly upon his patient's wrist for a moment. "Well, you're in pretty good shape, and no doubt you'll be ruining your digestion again soon enough. I've had a look at your chart. No other complaints?"

"None! Everybody has been very good to me. In spite of which, I shall be glad to get away from you all."

"I've been telling Saxon about you," continued the doctor, in his best bedside manner. "He thinks it not particularly to Columbus's credit to have discovered America, and hopes you will succeed in proving that he didn't."

Saxon was only a little embarrassed. "That was only nonsense," he smiled. "I'm really very much interested in your research. Your idea is that not Watling's but some other island was the actual site of Columbus's first landing, is it not?"

"Yes," answered Ghost. "It is one of a number of subjects upon which I am a bit of a crank. Having nothing better in the world to do, I go around trying to disprove the conclusions of other men. I seem to have that kind of a mind." He smiled apologetically, and Saxon noted that when the man smiled his ugly face became singularly attractive.

"I wish my own line were half as important or interesting," said the sporting editor of the *Telegram*, quite sincerely.

"I've just been reading about you both," said Ghost. He indicated the scattered newspaper.

"The deuce you have!" exclaimed Rainfall. "Are we already in print?"

"You are casually mentioned as having been friends of the actor Lear, and present in the theater when he was murdered. I suppose he was murdered?"

"He was murdered, all right," said the doctor grimly.

"You can gamble on it," added Saxon. "So were the others. It's perfectly wild, Mr. Ghost. Nobody knows anything about it. We've just come from the inquest."

"That's usually the case, isn't it? By the way, was Lear his real name?"

"No, it wasn't," answered Saxon. He looked at the long patient with a certain new respect. "Why did you doubt it?"

Ghost laughed quietly. "Don't look at me as if I had asked something very clever," he begged. "It's a very natural question. I'm a student of the man who invented Lear. The name was bound to strike me as unusual. But an excellent choice for a stage pseudonym."

"His real name was Stacey," said Howard Saxon.

"What killed him?" asked Ghost, looking at Rainfall. "Was that revealed at the inquest?"

"I revealed it myself, after a fashion," confessed the physician. He explained the nature of the wound that had killed the actor, in words he thought his patient would understand.

"I see," said Ghost, nodding. "Very clever! An attempt apparently to create the appearance of a basal apoplexy. Discovery of a traumatism—"

"My dear sir!" cried Rainfall, surprised.

Ghost laughed silently. "I think I forgot to tell you that I am myself a physician," he said. "Well, perhaps I'm not! But I once graduated in medicine and surgery. I've never actually practised. I'm somewhat of a dilettante, I'm afraid. Too much money has spoiled me for work. I do only the things it interests me to do. Medicine and surgery attracted me earlier in life."

"What else do you do?" asked the physician, looking down at his astonishing patient.

"I read Shakespeare, I look for queer islands of the sea. A good cipher will keep me out of mischief for days."

"You ought to go in for detective work," said Saxon. There was just a suspicion of irony in his tone. "Did that ever occur to you?"

"Heaven forbid!" said Ghost piously. "I've played at detective two or three times in my career, and always with a certain distaste. Mysteries attract me, but not detection in the ordinary sense."

"You didn't solve the mysteries?"

"They were solved. I don't quite know how. Certainly by no brilliance of mine. I simply haven't the sublime egotism—or lack of selfconsciousness—necessary to a story-book detective, Mr. Saxon. I *won't* be seen crawling about on my hands and knees, and I would positively refuse to disguise myself, even if it were possible."

His smile was infectious, and Saxon laughed. "I'm with you there," he said. "The transcendent detective merely amuses me. Marvelous fellows on paper!"

"That's all very well," observed Rainfall, "but we could use one of those same fellows in a case like this one. I hardly see Messrs. Kelly and Sheets in the rôle, however. No doubt they have certain excellent positive faculties, but I fancy they are rather lacking in what might be termed retrospective penetration."

"Intuitive analysis," said Ghost. "It exists, though, in many men and in many women. Women are frequently quite astounding. They seem to be able, by some curious alchemy, to reconstruct an entire temperament from the smallest detail."

"I suspect you could do it yourself," accused Rainfall. "What opinion have you formed of this case, for instance?"

"I haven't collected my thoughts at all. I've only read this single newspaper account of the latest tragedy. The earlier cases are only touched on. However, I would venture to suggest that all three men were murdered by the same person or persons. Bluefield *might* have taken his own life, but it is most unlikely that he would have done so in his own window. Gaunt might also have committed suicide, but not on the statue of General Burke. Lear's case is the least sensational, and if there had been no others it is likely that there would have been no investigation. The three taken together, with the placards calling attention to their similarity, indicate, of course, a definite sequence of murders. They indicate, indeed, something more serious, I should say—that the sequence may not yet be complete."

"Eh?" cried Rainfall, startled. "You mean . . . ?"

"Nothing has occurred to suggest that the murderer has finished. There may be other dead men and other placards. Why not? Who can say what curious scheme of vengeance the murderer may be following? It is a little far-fetched, perhaps, but one might even go a step farther and suggest that each murder, with its attendant death notice, is in effect a warning to the next man marked for death."

"Sa-a-y!" The sporting editor of the *Telegram* also was startled. "You *are* a story-book detective, Mr. Ghost, whatever you may say to the contrary."

His respect for this curiously ugly and attractive man was growing. After a moment he chuckled.

"I'd like to hear about those other mysteries, some day, Mr. Ghost—the ones you *didn't* solve!"

CHAPTER TWELVE

HOWARD SAXON was that curious anomaly, a sporting editor who could wear evening clothes and get away with it. He was that even more curious anomaly, a sporting editor whose name was in the Blue Book. His father had been the notorious J. Andrew Saxon, at one time a mighty name in the city. His mother had been Sally Blankenship, the actress. The crash of the Saxon fortunes, some years before, had been a notable event in the financial world, but it had failed to dent the social standing of the J. Andrew Saxons.

The elder Saxon was now dead. He had saved enough out of his reverses to take care of his wife, and the sum—comfortable but not enormous—had passed to the younger Saxon upon the marriage of his mother to another man, almost as wealthy as had been J. Andrew.

Young Mr. Saxon was a newspaper man by choice. The union of finance and the stage had given him a curious heritage. His first impulse had been to run joyously through his money. This he had done, gracefully and without scandal. His second impulse had been to refuse the munificent offers of assistance made by his mother. When it had become apparent that he would have to seek employment, he had cast about him, leisurely, for something that would offer excitement along with the necessary remuneration. He had found it in newspaper work, greatly to the horror of his mother and her friends, and to the delight of the younger members of the dwindling phalanx known as Society.

He knew everybody, which was an advantage. It was at times a disadvantage that everybody knew *him.* Since he had become sporting editor of the *Telegram* it was particularly disadvantageous, for everybody asked him for tickets. Tickets to the fights, tickets to the football games, tickets for everything for which it was supposed he had received large quantities of free passes. He was more popular in season than the drama critic.

Young Mr. Saxon, in short, was a likable individual; and he was twenty-six years of age. He was supposed to be remarkably good-looking.

He had known Lear, the actor, for a number of years. They had met casually at teas and prize fights and other functions whenever the actor had come to town. They had met at some such gathering, in fact, only the day before the murder of Patrick Lear at his first Wednesday matinée—an affair at which the busy Rainfall also had managed to be present. It was after this meeting that Lear had sent the two of them tickets to the performance—a circumstance that, later, both of them had been inclined to regard as significant.

The police, when they got around to it, thought so too. They had noted the seemingly innocent fact, mentioned by both men in their testimony at the inquest, and it became one of their several lines of investigation. Rainfall's sardonic prediction that both he and Saxon would, in time, be looked upon with suspicion, bore fruit with a rapidity that surprised even the cynical physician. The interrogations were friendly, however.

Saxon, by good fortune, was able to prove at once that he had left his office in the *Telegram* building with just time to make the theater comfortably and take his seat. For some hours previous to his departure from the office, he had been more or less under somebody's eye in the sports room. It was impossible that he could have murdered Lear, even if his hands had been red with the blood of Bluefield and Gaunt.

For a time his subordinates had considered the colossal joke of denying this airtight alibi and sending Saxon to the Chair; but they had decided in the end that his successor as sporting editor might be less amiable and easy-going than the good-natured Howard. With a certain humorous reluctance, they cleared his name of the stain of homicide and were ironically thanked for their generosity.

Rainfall's explanation was made more difficult by the admitted fact that he had reached the theater late. He had not, he asserted frankly, the faintest idea who the taxi driver was who had driven him from the hospital. The police idea, rather obviously, was that he might have murdered Lear in the actor's dressing room while the latter was waiting for his cue; then in some manner have escaped unseen, strolled around the block a number of times, and returned to the theater tardily to join his waiting friend.

In the nick of time the doctor remembered the jam at the bridgehead and the episode of the noble sunflower, upon whom he had bestowed a cigar. The noble sunflower, interviewed by his confrères, recalled the incident, and the day was saved. The police graciously retired from both fields, and, since the sporting editor of the *Telegram* and the chief surgeon of the Gatacre Memorial Hospital were men of distinction, were careful not to broadcast their earlier suspicion.

Other minor suspects fared less well. They received publicity enough to last them for the rest of their lives. In the eyes of their landlords, they became definitely criminal characters.

Saxon, cleared of the suspicion of murder, felt himself more than ever a part of the strange case, and in Walter Ghost, it occurred to the newspaper man, he had found a fellow with whom he could discuss it. Ghost, he decided, was a man very much to his liking. A curious fellow, however, very curious indeed. A fellow who was genuinely different. But a man with a name like that would have to be.

Ghost also was sinfully ugly, except when he smiled, when, quite suddenly, he became almost beautiful. His voice and his eyes were magnificent. His personality was quiet yet overwhelming. All this was to young Mr. Saxon very attractive—and their common dislike of story-book detective methods was another bond between them. Yes, he liked this Walter Ghost. He liked him a great deal.

There was something, too, about Ghost that it was difficult to name—charm—personality—more than either, really—what was it?

When Ghost spoke of Columbus, dead four hundred years and more, and an island in the Caribbean all but unknown to any but ships' captains and cartographers, one's more immediate and timely interests somehow faded into insignificance. Chicago, not the remote island, was a mere speck upon the map. Newspapers became rather meaningless and unnecessary.

Decidedly, the fellow had a way with him. Yet he could think about immediate matters, too. His suggestion of a murder sequence as yet only begun had seemed at first a staggering piece of melodrama; yet, when one came to think it over, it was more than just plausible. By the Lord Harry, it had all the earmarks of an inspiration!

In a day or so this unusual man would be leaving the hospital—perhaps had already done so.

"H'm," mused the sporting editor of the *Telegram.*

He visualized the telephone at Ghost's bedside. Then he laid aside his cigarette and lifted the receiver at his own elbow. In a few seconds—miraculously enough—he was talking to Walter Ghost.

"I say," said young Mr. Saxon, "I want you to come to my rooms when you're discharged. Will you? I'm way out south, you know—away from the noise. It'd be a very decent place in which to convalesce. Hotels are pretty lonesome, really. I've a spare bed—and a spare table—and a spare typewriter, if you use the damn things—and—well, what do you say?"

A fine chuckle came to him over the wire.

"It's kind of you, Saxon. I'm afraid I'd be a nuisance. I'll have to move carefully for a time, I suppose. Well, I'll consider it. I have to go some place soon. I'll look in on you, anyway, sometime."

"Look in before you sign up," urged Saxon. "I'm immensely interested in your researches, you know. Also, I'm interested in your murder-sequence idea. Not professionally! I'm not a reporter."

Again he listened to the low rumble of Ghost's laughter. "Are you forswearing your aversion? Are you going to be one of the hounds?"

"By Jiminy!" said Saxon, into the rubber mouthpiece, "I may be one of the hares! Kelly and Sheets have already been after me for my alibi."

"Shelley and Keats?"

"Kelly and Sheets—the detectives, not the poets. They're on the theater end of the case. They seemed to think I might have committed the murder and have forgotten to mention it. Maybe they still think so—I *hope* they do."

"'There has been much throwing about of brains,'" chuckled Ghost. "Did you?"

"Not that I remember. It's an experience one would be likely to bear in mind, don't you think?"

"There is precedent for believing so. Though it have no tongue, we are told, murder will speak 'with most miraculous organ.' You see, I have been reading my book again."

Saxon laughed. "I'm a little rusty on the Bard, but I'll read him, too, if you'll accept my invitation."

"I'll think about it," said Ghost. "Thank you."

The sporting editor of the *Telegram* returned to his duties in a pleasant frame of mind. It had been a happy thought to ask Ghost to share his lodgings.

In his room at the hospital, however, Walter Ghost leaned back upon his pillow and decided that the arrangement would not do at all.

Not that there was anything wrong with Saxon. He liked Saxon well enough. But another idea had entered his leisurely mind. It was just possible, he thought, that he would find himself, shortly, at home with the Chandler W. Moments, as he mentally designated the professor and his daughter. The invitation, after all, had been standing now for several years; and what better time to accept it? Supposing, of course, they wanted him. But he rather fancied they would want him. It was just conceivable, it had occurred to Ghost, that Holly Moment was in considerable danger. An active search was going forward for a most ingenious murderer, and she was the only person known to have seen him.

Not that she could have seen much! But what did the murderer know of that? He read the papers, no doubt—but what might not the police be concealing from the press? In the mind of the unknown murderer, Holly Moment was definitely a puzzling problem, and it was possible that she was regarded as a menace.

A strange solution, thought Ghost, lay behind those three fantastic murders. Some curious passage in life—now hidden or obscure, like the meaning of a disputed stanza, yet capable of being resolved by a patient scholar. Was he not himself perhaps, that scholar?

The mystery fascinated him. He admitted it, smiling wryly. In some fashion—and as usual through no particular fault of his own—he had been brought into this odd affair, and he felt that he must see it through. Once more, in spite of his pretended aversion to the profession, he might be Walter Ghost, Detective—a sorry enough figure, doubtless, as measured beside the famous amateurs of fiction, but a fellow of some little talent, after all. It was not detection that he disliked, but theatrical detective methods. Mystery attracted him in every form, and it was at the heart of everything.

Just as in most persons there was a latent criminal, enabling them to flee in fancy with the hare, there was in most persons a latent detective, in whose person they hunted with the hounds. The criminal instinct, on the whole, was more than balanced by the instinct to support the rule of order. In his own case, Ghost realized, he had always been a detective, although his quarry only occasionally had been crime. Was not his quest of the Columbian landfall sheer detection? To a very considerable degree, in point of fact, it was not only detection but deduction.

Well, the Columbian investigation could wait, if necessary; it had waited a long time for solution, anyway. And the proof that the two historic Shakespeares—the poet-dramatist and the actor from Stratford—were one and the same?

What of that! He smiled. That, too, could wait a little longer. The problem in Chicago concerned a number of his friends, for one thing, and it was as immediate as it was alluring. The murderer was still alive and dangerous. At most, the solution could go back no farther than a decade or two in human history.

"Yes," murmured Ghost, "I shall pitch my tent with the professor and his daughter—if they will have me."

Later that evening, when his private nurse had left the room, he called the Moment home and revealed a part of his intention: to wit, that he would be happy to accept an invitation of long standing if it were still in force.

"Why, you old rascal!" shrilled Chandler W. Moment. "To think that you have been here for more than a week and didn't let us know. Two weeks? Terrible, Walter! And in a hospital, too! But I warn you that you are coming to a place that is marked for death and destruction!"

He laughed in a high, unnatural key.

"What do you mean?" asked Ghost sharply. "I've read about your daughter in the papers, but nothing of that sort. Are you joking, Chandler?"

"My daughter," said Chandler W. Moment, "is going to be packed off to Florida as rapidly as I can get her ready. We have received a letter threatening her life. It may be a joke, but I'm not taking any chances."

"Listen," said Ghost. "Listen to me, Chandler! Don't be an

elderly idiot! Do you understand? Don't send Holly to Florida or any place else. Why, good God, man, don't you realize—But of course you don't! She might be murdered before she ever reached her destination. On the train—on the way to the train—on her own doorstep as she was making ready to leave! The safest place for Holly Moment just now is in her own home, and it is your job to see that she stays there."

"Well," grumbled the professor, relieved, "that's what she thought, herself, I must confess. But it'll be quite a job to keep her in the house. Quite a job, Walter! You see, the little fool isn't a bit afraid."

"You tell her to stay indoors until I arrive," ordered Ghost crisply. "Do you hear? Until I arrive! I'll be along as soon as I can get away."

CHAPTER THIRTEEN

THE LETTER, of course, was anonymous.

"That will be about all from you," it began abruptly. "One more reminiscence, and we will change the ticket."

The words were in the familiar blocked letters that had been a feature of the earlier sensations. Ghost read them with a feeling of relief. Nothing, at any rate, seemed to threaten at once. The girl had revealed nothing of genuine importance. It was what she might later reveal that was bothering the author of the letter. Obviously, he feared she had seen more than she had reported—or might later remember something she had forgotten.

Chandler W. Moment was in a high state of nervousness.

"You see what it means, Walter?" he shrilled. "Of course, you see what it means?"

"'Change the ticket,' is the threat," agreed Ghost. "In other words, if Miss Holly continues to talk to the police and the reporters, a fourth ticket will appear, with the words 'Dead *Woman* Inside.'"

"And still you think I ought not to send her away!"

"I can't imagine anything that would be more foolish. The arm of murder is always a long one. She is safer here than she would be any place else, except perhaps in jail. At least we can keep an eye on her here. We can be on hand to protect her. But, really, I'm not as much alarmed as I was. I think the fellow is uncertain. His letter is a shot in the dark—just in case she knows more than she has told. And since she has told all she knows and can have nothing further to report, she should be safe enough. I don't mean that we ought to let her walk around the streets unaccompanied."

Miss Moment herself, the subject of the discussion, looked hopelessly from one man to the other. "I can't remain in the house forever," she said.

"It won't be necessary," said Ghost. "For one thing, the case won't last forever." He smiled. "Since I am somewhat of a prisoner myself, being convalescent, you will at least have company."

"Very good company," agreed Miss Moment, "but I imagine you will want to take the air, occasionally. Couldn't we go to Florida together, Mr. Ghost?"

"It would hardly look respectable, would it?"

She made a face at him. "Of course, you know it isn't that I'm afraid to stay here. But I won't be shut up in the house. It's too silly. You've just admitted that there's no danger."

"Not exactly that," he demurred. "There's always danger. I shall probably be in some danger myself, if it becomes known that I am here and investigating the murders."

"Then you are going to investigate them?" Her question was swift and delighted. "That alters the case. I'll help you—and we'll protect each other!"

"Agreed!" said Ghost, and they both laughed. "I haven't been asked to do anything," he continued more seriously, "and probably nobody will thank me. And, of course, I'm not planning anything stagey or sensational. I merely meant that I intended to give the case some thought—principally because it interests me, and, being idle, I need something to interest me. I'm not strong enough to run around picking up clues, even if I were so minded."

"What can you do, Walter?" The professor was curious.

Ghost shrugged. "Possibly nothing. But heaven knows there are enough indications already to hang somebody."

"Those little papers?" asked the girl. "This letter?"

"Not only those. The nature of the crime is one clue, I think. I mean, the way the murders were committed. But the biggest clue of all—how I dislike that word, don't you?—would seem to be the past histories of the men who were murdered. I hope the police have sense enough to realize it."

"What have you discovered about them?" Again it was the professor who was curious.

"Not a thing, upon my word. But surely it is obvious that, somewhere, at some time, in some place, their paths must have crossed. Not only were they known to the man who killed them, but they were known to each other. So I believe, anyway. They had to be. The pattern is too perfect for its figures to be unrelated. Perhaps it was only last month the thing happened. Perhaps—"

"What thing?"

"The thing that made the murderer take three lives. I don't know what it was, of course. Perhaps it was twenty years ago. Something happened, however, that made necessary—or seemed to make necessary—the murder of three men. Possibly there are other murders yet to be committed. Possibly the fellow is planning to wipe out an entire circle of which he was once a part. I don't know. We do know that three murders have been committed. There are innumerable possible motives in most cases, I suppose. In this case I think the motives can be boiled down to three—all basic—fear, revenge, and greed."

"Fear?"

"Suppose these three men to have known something about the man who killed them—something that might, if told, send him to death or to prison. Do you think he would hesitate to take their lives? It would be, in effect, self-preservation. Or, if revenge were the motive, we may suppose that these three in some way had injured the man who ultimately killed them. Greed, of course, supposes a sum of money at stake—which, by the elimination of others with equal or prior claims, would accrue to the author of the murders."

Miss Moment applauded lightly.

"Bravo, Mr. Ghost! You talk like a detective in a magazine."

"Do I?" Ghost was comically dismayed. "I hope not! I'm really only applying a little logic and common sense to the problem. Any policeman, I'm sure, would think exactly what I have thought, although he might express himself differently. But a magazine detective! O Lord!" he sighed. "I thought they always spoke in paradoxes and solved their mysteries by intuition. Divine intuition! Don't they always have mismated eyes, too?—one brown and the other blue—or hair that is white only on one side?"

He was silent for a moment, then quite soberly he continued: "Exactly what did you tell the police, Holly? Were the newspaper accounts accurate? Just how much of this man in the window did you actually see?"

She looked helpless all at once. She had been over all that so often. "Practically nothing. I'm beginning to think all I really saw was a movement of the curtains. You know?"

"I know. And, naturally, since you were not thinking of the

man in connection with disclosures yet to be made, you paid little attention even to the movement. But you did think enough of it to call Mr. Robey's attention to it."

"That's true. It seemed odd, at that time of night, to see a man in a shop window. The shop was so obviously closed. That's what was in my mind, I guess."

"It was his eyes, of course, that you saw first. You must have seen his eyes. Probably that was *all* you saw."

"I don't even know that I saw his eyes. I think I did, but I may have visualized them because of the impression of movement. You know? I thought I saw a face—but just for an instant. Then—the movement again—as the curtains dropped."

"He would not have exposed much of himself," commented Ghost. He looked around him a little helplessly, and his eyes fell upon the heavy hangings between the room in which they sat and the room behind it. The eyes brightened.

"Suppose we try a small experiment," he said, rising to his feet and pulling down the window shades. The room was suddenly as dim as twilight. He crossed the floor to the entrance of the other room. "I step behind these curtains—so—and you no longer see me."

He vanished as he spoke, but his voice continued to speak from the room beyond.

"You are farther from me than you were from the window, that night, I imagine. Sidewalks are fairly wide, of course, on the boulevard, but you were walking close in, near the buildings, were you not?"

"About the middle of the sidewalk, Mr. Ghost."

"Well, you are near enough as it is, then. It's a pity there is no glass to complete the illusion. Was there a light near at hand, do you remember?"

Miss Moment puckered her forehead and tried to think. The room was curiously dim and eerie. "It's hopeless," she answered, at length. "I really don't know. I think there must have been, or I would not have seen *anything.*"

"Well," said Ghost, "you didn't see much. A lamp some distance away would have given sufficient light, I suspect, for all you really saw. Perhaps even a lamp across the street."

"There *was* a lamp across the street!" she cried quickly. "You know, Father, that little fountain with the stone wings? It is directly across the street, and there is a lamp beside it. I'm sure there is, for I remember the fountain very clearly."

"Probably there is," said Ghost, his voice still muffled by the intervening curtains. "You turned from looking at the fountain and felt the movement in the window. It was really feeling it as much as it was seeing it, I think, and it was all quite casual. Now, I part the curtains very gently and put one eye to the aperture. You are on the sidewalk outside of Bluefield's. . . . Turn quickly, now, and what do you see?"

She spun excitedly toward the hangings, which immediately dropped into place.

"I saw your eye and the fingers of one hand," she said, "and just a little of your coat, Mr. Ghost—the right side." After a strained instant she asked: "Are you wearing something on your coat, Mr. Ghost—on that side?"

"Nothing," said Ghost, stepping into the room. "What did you think I was wearing, Holly?"

"How exceedingly strange!" she exclaimed. "I thought I saw a little glint of something bright—as if you had pinned a little star there—or were wearing a button in your lapel. Do you suppose—"

"It's very interesting, at any rate," said Ghost cheerfully. He recrossed the room and let up the shades. “I haven’t the remotest idea what it means, or what you think you saw; but I’m going to do some worrying about it. Very odd, Chandler!”

“Very,” agreed Chandler W. Moment dryly. “You had me scared to death for a minute, Walter. Good heavens, what an atmosphere you created out of nothing! And in my own home! I had no idea how unfamiliar familiar things could look. I seemed to be in another house.”

What under the sun, Ghost asked himself that night, as he lay awake in bed, could the fellow have been wearing?

CHAPTER FOURTEEN

The show, meanwhile, had started again. A minor star, hastily imported from New York, had mastered Lear's part in an incredibly short time. Once more the doors of the Alhambra were flung open and the public rushed in. It was a master stroke. Lines of law-abiding citizens stood before the box office. The queues extended into the street, crossed the alley, and turned the corner. If ever there had been any doubt as to the success of the piece, there was doubt no longer. Lear's murder had advertised it to the ends of the country. Simple souls believed, perhaps, that a new star was to be murdered every night. After the first performance dramatic critics observed profanely, among themselves, that the wrong star had been assassinated. In the business office there was some talk of changing the name of the piece from *Green Terror* to *Dead Man Inside.*

An additional popular feature was the continuation in the part of Mrs. Caldwell of Doris Carvel, widow of the murdered Lear. The actress herself asserted, ruefully enough, that until matters had been adjusted, her husband's estate settled, and the mystery of his death solved, she would have to remain in Chicago anyway, and it was necessary to make a living. Widows do not enter hurriedly into their inheritances where a police activity has clouded the issue of death.

Wherefore Miss Carvel played nightly, for a time, in *Green Terror*, and the public waited patiently for her to crack.

She never cracked. She was a bit nervous, however, the first night of the new dispensation. It was thought that she swayed slightly at the second "Sh-h!"

Suddenly it became necessary to find a new stage detective and a new Mrs. Caldwell. With a bang, the morning newspapers "broke" the story. Clay Ridinghood, playing the part of the detective Halleck, had been seized at his hotel, late the night before.

The charge was not specifically the murder of Patrick Lear. It was freely hinted, however, that the dapper young man was supposed to have had advance knowledge of that event. Mrs. Lear—or Miss Carvel—was also an object of suspicion. While not technically under arrest, she was being carefully guarded at her hotel.

Kelly and Sheets were responsible. Trailing the actor and Miss Carvel, who had been seen together frequently, after the murder, the detectives had interrupted a passionate love scene, not upon the stage. The scene, in point of fact, was a private booth in a notorious night club. Kelly—or Sheets—or perhaps both of them—had heard enough to convince them that, whoever had killed Patrick Lear, Doris Carvel and Clay Ridinghood were very glad he had been killed.

Later, an interview was given by Miss Carvel to a silky youth from one of the smaller journals which caused the gloating public further to erect its pointed ears.

"Yes, I'm glad he's dead!" she had cried defiantly. "Why shouldn't I be? He was a beast. I hated him. I was his wife when it suited him—that was all. He had a public of girls—flappers. They adored him. Two generations of them adored him. Once I adored him myself. He said that knowledge of his marriage would kill him with his public. My God! He was forty-three and getting bald! He painted and powdered like a woman. Trying to stay young—for his public! To the public he was charming and romantic. To me he was a brute. We occupied different rooms at the hotel. Nobody knew we were married. He wouldn't permit it. I could tell you of his cruelties—I could send a message to the girls who keep his picture on their dressers . . . "

And a great deal more to the same effect.

"Ridinghood! Yes, Ridinghood did know we were married. I told him so myself. He pitied me. If he could, he would have married me. But he didn't kill Pat Lear. He *would* have killed him if I had asked him to. But he didn't do it. He couldn't have done it. He was on the stage when it happened. Everybody knows that. A whole theaterful of people know it. They saw us, talking together there—speaking our lines . . .

"But I'm glad he's dead. I'm free now!"

And so on. It was a vigorous piece of denunciation, and it carried a certain conviction. The trouble was, however, Ridinghood *could* have killed Lear, in spite of the theaterful of people. Nobody knew just when Lear died. He simply had not responded to his cue. For all anybody knew to the contrary he might have been sitting dead in his dressing room for half an hour before the performance began. With caution, Ridinghood might have entered the room a minute after two o'clock, killed his man, and left the room, all without being seen. Nobody was bothering much about either of them. Everybody had his own work to do, his own preparations to make. Lear was a solitary and eccentric person, and Stanley Moore could not be everywhere at once.

What Ridinghood could have had to do with the murders of Bluefield and Gaunt could only be conjectured. He was free, of course, after the evening performances. Bluefield and Gaunt almost certainly had been killed at night—Bluefield on a Thursday, Gaunt late the night following.

What Bluefield and Gaunt had had to do with Lear perhaps remained to be seen. The shrouds of all three, so to call them, had been ticketed by the same hand. Somewhere a start had to be made, and there was valid reason to hold Ridinghood on a suspicion, at least, of complicity. Quite possibly, as a matter of argument, three men had committed the murders, not one; but if Ridinghood had killed Lear it stood to reason that he had knowledge of the other murders. And if Ridinghood had killed Lear he might conceivably have killed Bluefield and Gaunt.

Thus the police mind, functioning slowly, but with a certain muddled clarity. Miss Carvel, of course, had denied flatly ever having heard of Bluefield and Gaunt. So had Ridinghood.

The energetic Kelly and Sheets also had found a weapon that might have answered. It was among the stage properties at the theater, and no effort had been made to conceal it. Some sort of a carpenter's tool—long, slender, and with a stout wooden handle—a finely tempered boring instrument. Appealing to Rainfall, the police learned that such a weapon might very well have been the one used by the murderer. It was not large, therefore it could easily have been carried. Wiped on a piece of waste, and the waste destroyed, there would be no way, except in theory, to connect the thing with the murder.

There was no waste to be found answering the proper description, and such garments of Ridinghood's as could be unearthed at his hotel betrayed no signs of a bloody concealment. But, as Rainfall had pointed out, there would not of necessity have been any blood spilled.

"And, by George!" exclaimed the doctor, "*there* was a blind diagnosis that went right with a vengeance! I told you, Saxon, the police would grab Ridinghood sooner or later. But I thought I was just being clever when I said it."

They were dining together, which was a habit when the physician happened to be in the Loop.

Howard Saxon nodded. "I thought of that when I read about the arrest," he said. "I wonder what Mr. Ghost thinks of this latest development."

"Ghost?" echoed the physician. "Have you been in touch with him since he left the hospital? Do you know, I miss the beggar, although I suppose he's glad enough to be away from *me.* Is he back at his maps?"

"He's gone to stay with Professor Moment—the old geezer whose daughter is supposed to have seen the man who killed Bluefield. They're old friends, it seems. I wanted him to come and stay with me, but he refused. Maybe he's interested in the girl."

"I can't imagine it," said Rainfall. "Ghost isn't a marrying man. And the girl, I believe, is just a kid—but a good-looking one, if her photographs do her justice."

"Or if they don't," grinned Saxon.

"Well, I'm glad he's there. If that girl had seen just a scrap more than she did see I wouldn't give a nickel for her life. As it is, she may be in danger. More than likely *that's* why Ghost went there."

"I knew the professor at college," remarked Saxon. "I

wouldn't trust *him* to protect anybody, as far as I could see him. He's a rabbit!"

The doctor laughed. "Is he? Well, Ghost, I should say, is a horse—or rabbit—of another color. I have a lot of respect for that astonishing citizen."

"You may find *yourself* in danger before you get through, Rainfall," suggested the newspaper man. "You haven't been exactly idle in this case, you know."

Rainfall smiled wickedly. "I haven't done anything," he said; "but I wish somebody *would* try to 'get' *me!* I haven't had any real excitement since the war. The new generation looks at the old doctor pityingly, Howard—observing his thinning hair and his pathetic little limp. But there's life in the old dog yet! Alas, I am forty-two years of age," he added quizzically. "That seems pretty ancient to a spry youth like yourself, I suppose."

"I feel ninety-eight at seven o'clock every morning," responded Saxon. "But, joking aside, you *might* be, you know!"

"Forty-two? I am! Word of honor."

"In danger," said Saxon. "You are known to have been a friend of Lear's, and God knows what *that* might mean to the man who killed him. He doesn't know what Lear may have told you. Also, it was you who showed up the ways and means of murder, so to speak; and in the papers, to-day, you are quoted as identifying a certain weapon found in the theater."

"I didn't identify it. How could I? I said it *might* have been the one."

"It's the same thing."

"It's nothing of the sort," said Rainfall. "But," he added, flexing his strong surgeon's fingers, "I certainly hope somebody *will* have a try at *me*. Boy, I'd love it!"

"Get a tank of tear gas ready," advised the newspaper man. "You may need it."

"No such luck. Don't do any worrying about *me,* Howard—if you *are* worrying, which I doubt. I'm out of the picture."

That night, however, John Rainfall received a start.

As he entered the door of his apartment in East Division Street, a little square of paper looked up at him from the threshold, across which, beneath the door, it had been partially pushed. He picked it up, closed the door, and in the same movement snapped on the lights in the hallway. His hand dropped to his side pocket, where he carried a small automatic pistol, removed each evening from the side pocket of his automobile.

There was no sound in the old-fashioned flat save the loud ticking of the clock upon the wall.

He reached a hand around the corner of another door and flooded the sitting room with light. Carefully, his right hand still in his pocket, he progressed from room to room, and in each he snapped on a blaze of electricity. With infinite caution, he poked into every corner that might harbor a man or a machine.

The tour was a slow one and fraught with a certain tension. He trod softly, and at closet doors he removed the pistol from his pocket.

But the apartment was empty of peril.

Returning at length to the sitting room, at the front, he read again the words blocked upon the square of paper. The window shades were already down.

YOU ARE NEXT, DR. JOHN RAINFALL

And a little sketch, so badly done that Rainfall had some difficulty in making it out. It looked like an eagle sitting on the corner of a box.

At last it dawned upon him that it was a plume—a black plume—and that the box was intended to be the corner of a hearse.

CHAPTER FIFTEEN

PHILDRIPP'S CASE was a puzzle. He had been a sort of assistant cashier at Bluefield's. He had handled money and he had handled books. But he had done neither importantly. He was merely one of the necessary cogs. Nevertheless, he was an interesting cog, and Dawson, the clever reporter, and the police sleuths, Kelly and Sheets, paid him the dubious compliment of close attention.

First of all, Phildripp was unmarried. This was no crime—but was it not possibly significant that he was, of all the men employed in the shop, the only man who had failed to marry? Married men with wives and children to support—or even just wives—were supposed, on the face of things, to have enough to worry about without going around murdering people. Not that married men did not commit murder: they did—they murdered their wives and other men's wives. But superficially a case involving three dead men was more likely to be the work of a single gentleman, it was believed, than the work of a man charged with responsibilities remote from the very idea of murder.

Also, Phildripp, a callous individual, upon learning that his employer had been murdered, had calmly gone off to a musical comedy. That was the Friday evening after the memorable Friday morning on which Rufus Ker had opened the shop upon the tragedy. Phildripp merely explained that he had had tickets for some days and saw no reason to waste them. He lived at home with his mother, a respectable widow, and had a sweetheart.

After the show, Phildripp had taken his girl to her home, deposited her with her parents, or within sound of her parents, and had himself gone home alone. Presumably he had gone to bed. The plump detective assigned to Phildripp's trail had seen the lights in the house go out, and had himself, then, returned thankfully to his station. Phildripp, it was argued, could have left the house again, in the early morning hours, met Gaunt at some lonely tryst, lured him to the park, murdered him with neatness and precision, and even have managed to get the body of Gaunt onto the statue of General Burke.

The latter feat had not been difficult, it was thought. A rope around the body of the corpse, the other end of it around the body of the murderer, and the trick was half done. Now the murderer climbs the statue, slightly impeded by the shrouding canvas, and hauls up the body of the gambler. He unties the rope at either end, climbs down—and there he is! It had been, no doubt, an awkward job, but not necessarily a difficult one.

Two bright young reporters, indeed, had turned the trick themselves, to prove the relative ease with which it could have been performed. The reporter who played the part of the murderer was, of course, a husky youth; he had been at one time a football player. The reporter who played the part of the corpse—young Mr. Dawson—was a slight youth of no especial weight. Some admirable photographs of the feat had been taken and had entertained a great many readers of Mr. Dawson's paper.

Gaunt had been a slight man, and Phildripp was notably a burly fellow. He, too, had once been a football player. Bluefield had been pestered by Gaunt, there was reason to believe; conceivably, therefore, *he* might have murdered Gaunt. But as Gaunt's body had been found a day after Bluefield's, it was more likely that the murder had been the other way about, and that somebody then had murdered Gaunt. Why not Phildripp?

Just why Phildripp, if Gaunt had murdered Bluefield, should have taken it upon himself to avenge his employer was not apparent, perhaps; still, the whole argument was plausible enough in the absence of proven facts. It was also just possible that Phildripp, for reasons best known to himself, had murdered both Bluefield and Gaunt. Supposing that Gaunt had had something "on" the haberdasher, which seemed likely enough, it was not unlikely that he (Gaunt) would have an ally in the shop. Phildripp might have been that ally. Then supposing the allies to have quarreled, it was easy to imagine Phildripp as taking over both murders on his own.

If, then, Gaunt had murdered Bluefield and Phildripp had murdered Gaunt, or if Phildripp had murdered both Gaunt and Bluefield, might it not be possible, by perseverance, to link up Phildripp with the murder of Lear?

All of which would have been the idlest of speculation but for a trivial point disclosed by the Kellian and Sheetsian investigation. That point suggested remotely the link with Patrick Lear. Inquiring into the earlier states of their several suspects, it had developed that Phildripp's sweetheart, a certain Nancy Maxwell, had once been a member of a theatrical chorus.

"Aha!" said the police, in effect. "A chorus girl!"

Everybody knew what chorus girls were. Ergo, Miss Maxwell, who was probably no great bargain, had once been associated with Doris Carvel or with the actor Ridinghood. Why not? Even, conceivably, with Lear.

And if this were true it would be unnecessary, while adding Phildripp and Miss Maxwell to the list of suspects, to forget the suspicion attaching to Ridinghood and Miss Carvel. Was it not possible, indeed, that the entire group—Ridinghood, Phildripp, Miss Carvel, and Miss Maxwell—and just possibly Gaunt—had been responsible for *all* the murders, and that the actual performancc of tlie deeds had been divided?

It was a messy sort of theory, and usually at about this point the police department, and young Mr. Dawson, its confidant, threw up their several hands and said, "My God!"

Phildripp, at any rate, was unmolested. But he was carefully watched. So was Nancy Maxwell. The rest of the Bluefield working force—i. e., Regan, Jacobs, Thain, Humphries, *et al.*—were tentatively dismissed from calculation. *They* had nice wives, all of them, and some of them had children. *They* were not running around to musical comedies with erstwhile chorus girls.

Ghost, too, meanwhile, was thinking it all over—and getting nowhere in particular. It had become his habit to discuss the case with Professor Moment and the professor's daughter, after breakfast and at other appropriate hours.

The "something bright" that had attracted the eye of Holly Moment on the murderer's coat still bothered the amateur. At length, he had an inspiration.

"I wonder," he observed one evening, and quite irrelevantly, "if it could have been a pair of eyeglasses! They often hang at about that point—by a cord, I believe."

Miss Moment jumped. She knew at once what was in his mind. "Why, yes," she agreed. "Eyeglasses! Why not?"

"You are sure it was the *right* side?"

"It would have had to be, wouldn't it? He was facing me—and the glint was from the left, as I faced the window."

"I suppose so, unless he was curiously twisted. Let us see now—he would probably push the curtains aside with his right hand and put his right eye to the aperture. It was my right hand you saw during our experiment. Or *would* he? If he wore his eyeglasses on the right side, as you think—and supposing them to have been eyeglasses—he would have had to be left-handed."

"So he would," said Holly Moment. "Why, of course! And that reduces the number of the men who could have done it quite a bit, doesn't it?"

Ghost smiled. "Hardly enough to get excited about. The world is full of left-handed men—and of men who wear eyeglasses. Anyway, we don't know that the thing you saw—or think you saw—was a pair of eyeglasses. No, I'm afraid this isn't getting us very far."

Miss Moment was thoughtful. "Now, who, of the men already partly under suspicion, wears eyeglasses?" She looked at Ghost. "*If* he should prove also to be left-handed, that fact would help materially. The coincidence, at any rate—in the light of our conversation—would be unusual."

Suddenly she was greatly embarrassed. Her father was staring at her open-mouthed.

"Good gracious!" she exclaimed. "*Father* wears eyeglasses and is left-handed!"

Ghost laughed outright. "It was your father's eyeglasses that gave me the idea," he confessed. "Shall we agree that it couldn't have been your father?"

"Oh, don't, please!" begged Chandler W. Moment. "Can't you see me, Walter, standing there in that window—peeking out between the curtains at my own daughter? Such a likely coincidence, too, darling—that I should have looked out, after finishing off Bluefield, at the exact instant you and Stephen passed the shop! Really, I must congratulate you both. How on earth you deduced it, I can't imagine; but it is quite true. I am the murderer of Amos Bluefield! I also killed Hubert Gaunt and hung him across the bronze horse. *That* was rather difficult, but I managed it. I killed Bluefield because of his name: it's incongruous and silly. Who ever heard of a blue field? Gaunt I slew because he saw me murder Bluefield, and I had to protect myself."

"How about Lear?" asked Ghost, twinkling.

"Carried away by the success of my first two murders," said Chandler W. Moment, "I determined to end the careers of all whom I disliked. I disliked Lear's acting—it was abominable. That was the hardest job of all. You can't imagine the difficulty I had getting away without being seen. I used the fire escape, of course. It's just outside the dressing-room window. I may as well go the whole hog, while I'm at it, and confess that I am in love with Lear's wife." He paused for breath.

"I had not as yet decided upon my next victim. That is to say, I was wavering between the curator of the Field Museum—who was to have been killed and then stuffed for the Prehistoric Group—and Frank Birmingham."

"Why Frank Birmingham?"

"I don't like his books," said Chandler W. Moment.

Then the doorbell rang. They were getting used to the doorbell.

It was not the newspapers, this time, nor the police. The call was for Walter Ghost, and at the door, somewhat agitated, Ghost discovered the wiry slenderness and eager voice of Howard Saxon.

"I live out this way, you know," explained Saxon apologetically. "Forgive me for butting in, but—I wanted to talk with you."

"Of course," smiled Ghost. "Come in."

A moment later he was saying: "Mr. Saxon, sporting editor of the *Telegram*. But don't be alarmed—he is not here on business."

Then something else happened, so swiftly that only Saxon and Holly Moment were aware of it. They discovered that they had never laid eyes upon each other in the world before, yet had known each other for years and years. Centuries, perhaps!

This astonishing circumstance made it difficult for Saxon to proceed with his accustomed sprightliness. However, he talked for some time, on many subjects and not always coherently. Professor Moment wondered if the young man had been drinking.

After a time young Mr. Saxon remembered that he had some news.

"Rainfall will take my head off, I suppose, for blabbing it," he said. "He's tickled to death about it and wouldn't tell the police for worlds. But the fact is, he's received one of those notices!"

"No!" cried Ghost.

"Not 'Dead Man Inside,' of course—just a warning to mind his own business or he'll be the next. Something like that. He expects to bag the murderer, single-handed, when the fellow tries it."

"More than likely he'll be killed," said Ghost sharply. "The murderer has proved himself a very competent fellow, to date. Rainfall ought not to take any foolish chances. He's too valuable a man to invite that sort of attention."

Saxon shrugged his shoulders. "I know! I said something to the same effect, myself. All the good it did me! Of course, the other fellow's taking chances, too. Rainfall is no set-up."

"He's afraid, I suppose, of what Rainfall may know about Lear's affairs," continued Ghost.

"Which is pretty nearly nothing."

"True, but thc murderer doesn't know that. Well, it may be only another bluff—a warning intended to head off any secret plans the doctor may have. But tell him not to do anything silly, Saxon. I'll tell him myself! Couldn't we have him up here to dinner, some evening—to-morrow evening—Professor? Mr. Saxon, too, of course."

"Of course," agreed the professor.

"He'll snap my head *off* about this," grinned Saxon. "I know he will."

"I'll square you when I call him up," promised Ghost.

He accompanied the newspaper man to the door, and they stood together for a moment, looking out into the street. It was beginning to get late.

Saxon drew a long breath. "Say," he remarked. "I wonder if you are here because that girl's in danger, too. Are you?"

"Perhaps," smiled Ghost. "Partly for that reason—yes! I think the danger is slight, however. She has received a threatening letter, similar I suppose to the doctor's. That, also, is something that has not been reported to the police. Say nothing about it."

"Trust me," said Saxon.

Suddenly he repassed the amazed Ghost and stalked back into the living room. "Miss Moment," he barked, almost too dramatically, "if ever I can be of the slightest—*ah*—service to you—*er*—don't hesitate to call upon me—*ah*—at any hour of the day or night!"

Then he stalked back to the door, fell down the first three steps, finished the descent properly, and strode off with immense dignity in the wrong direction.

CHAPTER SIXTEEN

A NOTABLE repast was prepared in honor of the occasion by the Moments' Alabama negress. The professor did not afford a large staff of servants, but Heliotrope was a ménage in herself. She was mammoth. Her advent upon any scene had somewhat the appearance of the mountain bearing down upon Mahomet. Her noodle rings, however, were beyond comparison or rhetoric.

By the time the larded tenderloin had run its course, the conversation was established. Rainfall, it developed, was not inclined to become excited over the warning he had received.

"As a matter of fact," he observed, "it may be sheer tomfoolery—a practical joke. I can think of seven of my colleagues who would have done it if it had occurred to them."

"Sophomoric humor," commented Saxon. "Fellows like that ought to grow up."

The physician shrugged. "Nobody ever does grow up, you know—and I'm not sure that it's such a good thing." He laughed. "As a student, I once thought it amusing to put a set of human fingers in a bowl of oxtail soup. The resemblance to—" He interrupted himself. "I'm sorry! Do forgive me, Miss Moment."

"What a ghastly notion!" said the girl. "Whose soup was it, Dr. Rainfall?"

"Chapman's," grinned the doctor. "He was one of our lecturers. I'm afraid I didn't like him."

He was in excellent form. He rattled on for some time about his student days, and they gathered that life at medical school was a joyous sequence of rows with the professors.

"Well," said Ghost, after a pause, "I don't know that I exactly blame you. In similar circumstances, I'd take my own chances, too. I'm blessed if I know what could be done to protect you, anyway. You are bound to come and go between your home and the hospital."

"Exactly," said Rainfall. "And I don't want a collection of policemen hanging around either place. It isn't good business. Naturally, I'll be careful in the streets—but I can't call out the militia to guard every avenue I use."

He was secretly of the opinion that the threat was not a joke at all, but he saw no reason to advertise his belief. He still hoped, in point of fact, that the attack would be made. His plan of defense, in such event, was carefully considered, and he was satisfied with it. There was nothing timid about Rainfall.

"Of course," continued Ghost, "your warning may be in the same category as Miss Moment's. You are probably being warned not to meddle with what does not concern you."

"That may be it," agreed the physician. "But what have *I* done?" he complained. "I don't know what else I *could* contribute."

"A very sound idea, however, on general principles," observed Professor Moment complacently. "I have myself a magnificent passion for minding my own business. It keeps one out of a great deal of mischief."

Howard Saxon was still dubious. "What bothers me," he said, "is why the fellow took the trouble to warn you. He's been lavish enough with his murders, Heaven knows. And if Mr. Ghost's idea of a murder sequence has any merit, he isn't through yet. He may be planning something particularly devilish for *you,* Rainfall. Watch your step! Both you and Miss Moment, as a matter of fact, should be carefully guarded. I'll do it myself, if nobody else will."

"Oh, I'll be careful," promised Rainfall lightly. "Miss Moment, happily, is already well protected."

Nevertheless, it was his own idea, also, that the new development had been oddly handled. He too had wondered why he had been warned instead of being promptly murdered. In view of the definite terms of the notice, the warning was a gesture incongruous and unnecessary.

He had not told the others exactly what the square of paper had said.

"Of course," he added, after a moment, "if I am attacked—and the attack fails—we've got the murderer."

"How do you mean? Why have we?" The questions came from Howard Saxon.

"If he doesn't get me first," said Rainfall, smiling, "I shall certainly get *him.*"

For a little time the meal continued in silence. The physician's quietly positive assertion had shocked them all. For a chilling moment something sinister and immediate had seemed to threaten everyone at the board. A frown was gathering on Ghost's brow. With crisp irritation he broke the spell.

"The police," he observed, "have been very remiss. There is an explanation of this affair, if they would only quit running in circles and look for it."

Rainfall glanced up, surprised. "You mean that you can see some sort of pattern in it?" he asked.

"Not clearly—no! But there is a pattern, and there is an explanation. These murders aren't anything casual, a scheme hatched by some ingenious madman to attract attention to himself. I have already said that it all dates back to something in the lives of the men murdered. Somebody has nursed a long grudge. Now he's paying it off. He waited, I think, until he could get his victims together—in the same city—at the same time. Bluefield, of course, lived here; but what of Gaunt? Lear came only occasionally. Was it coincidence that brought them here together, in the space of a few days? Possibly it was, but it furnished the opportunity the murderer had been waiting for."

They were all looking at him with fascinated interest.

"That's all simple enough, isn't it? And why were the three murders so sensational? There was no effort to cover them up, if we except the faint suggestion of suicide in Bluefield's case—which nobody could take seriously for a moment. Publicity is the keynote. Bluefield and Gaunt and Lear were not quietly murdered and their bodies hidden, as we might have expected them to be. The actual murders may have been quiet enough; but in every case there was a blare of trumpets waiting, just around the corner. Bluefield's body was placed in his own window—Gaunt's on a statue about to be unveiled. Could anything more clearly indicate the murderer's wish to call attention to what he had done?"

"Hardly," agreed Rainfall.

"Lear's case is only slightly different. He was killed while an audience waited for his appearance on the stage. What I am trying to say is that, in every case, the murderer knew that discovery of his crime would follow hard on the heels of the crime itself. He wanted it that way. He invited discovery by the most ingenious advertising methods he could imagine. Not discovery of himself, of course, but discovery of his deeds."

"What do you argue from that?" asked the doctor.

"That his injury—the thing that made him do all this—his grievance, whatever it may have been—was quite possibly of a similar sort. That's not very clear, perhaps. I mean, his methods may very well reflect a sensational publicity attendant on the injury for which he seeks revenge."

"'An eye for an eye' quite literally, you mean?" asked Holly Moment. "That ought to make it easy to trace him, Mr. Ghost."

"One would think so—but there's no telling how far back it all goes. I thought at first that the original grievance might be something fairly recent. My feeling now is that it is not. If it were something within easy memory, the similarity of the cases would have been apparent to somebody; the newspapers of the entire country are featuring the case. But we have heard nothing. . . . Well, that's part of what I had in mind. I suggest also, as I have suggested before, that there may be other men marked for murder. I won't be dogmatic about it, but I think the death notices indicate the possibility. If I'm right, then other men already are aware of their danger. In effect, every 'Dead Man Inside' has been a warning to the next man on the list."

Rainfall demurred. "If that were so," he asked, "wouldn't the others, realizing their danger, hustle off to the police?"

"Possibly they can't," said Ghost. "For reasons of their own, they may not want to. As I say, I don't insist on any of this. I do say that it's possible—the suggestion is there—and nobody *has gone to* the police for protection, although that circumstance, as evidence, is pretty negative."

"It all sounds a bit melodramatic, don't you think?" Rainfall was faintly quizzical.

Ghost laughed. "It does," he admitted. "It *is!* It's a flight of the imagination, nothing else. I might *go* farther and suggest that the entire episode is a chapter of *criminal* history. That is, an episode in the lives of four warring crooks. What do we know, after all, about Bluefield and Gaunt? About Lear, for that matter? Nothing but what they have been willing that we should know—the surface facts of their lives. We don't even know the *surface* facts about Gaunt."

"I think it's gorgeous," said Saxon. "Follow through, Mr. Ghost! I mean, what's the rest of it?"

"Well," said Ghost, "it's a theory that fits the facts as we know them—that's all. I may be twisting facts to suit the theory. It's a habit of mine."

"But what possible grievance could such a man have?" asked Holly Moment eagerly. "Do you mean that—"

"That somebody once killed *him* and set him in a window?" finished Ghost, smiling. "Not exactly. But I think reasons may be imagined. For instance, suppose that, years ago, these citizens who are now being murdered, one after another, were part of a conspiracy by which the father or the brother of the man now committing the murders was done to death in similar fashion and his body posted in public for neighborhood inspection! Something like that. Suppose even a similar death notice to have been employed. That is fantastic, to be sure; but no more fantastic than the present series of murders."

Rainfall shook his head. "It won't do, Mr. Ghost," he said. "An affection for a parent, or a brother, even complicated by a scheme of vengeance, wouldn't carry over the number of years you appear to be suggesting. I mean, an affection for a *dead* parent or brother. Children grow up; they have their own lives to live, their own problems to solve, without worrying about the past. They might *threaten* vengeance—but I think the idea would fade after a few years."

"Possibly it would," agreed Ghost. "I'm not suggesting anything *too* youthful. There is a very significant circumstance, however, that has not been considered. It fits in at this point. Do you realize that the murdered men were all of about the same age? Now what does that suggest? Surely not a crank with a grudge against men of forty!"

"What *does* it suggest?"

"The associations of a man of middle age are business associations, or golf associations, or—well, something like that. The point is, the men they meet and get to know at all intimately, are men of all ages—young and old and in between. But when several men of the same age are apparently closely associated—so closely that some other man finds it expedient to wipe out the group—the suggestion is that the murdered men made one another's acquaintance at the time of life when men of the same age are thrown together. In other words, in youth. Not babyhood, of course, or even childhood. Adolescence!"

"Whew!" cried Rainfall, laughing.

"You don't agree?"

"I don't know! As you explain it, it's almost immorally plausible; but you *could* be wrong, you know. Men of forty do foregather, I suspect, even in middle age."

"No doubt they do," admitted Ghost. "My theory was intended to fit this case; and it is as likely to be right as it is to be wrong." He smiled. "Well, whatever occasioned the murders, and whenever they were planned, I think the motive was revenge."

"I should have preferred a solution involving a woman," said Rainfall. "That way, I agree, a man's vengeance might achieve a very respectable longevity. Give your murderer a sweetheart, Ghost—one who was in some way snatched away from him by these others. Even so, I should prefer your solution if the grievance were less ancient—if it went back only a few years."

Ghost spread his hands in good-humored disclaimer. "It isn't a solution, I know! It's a little journey in what you once called retrospective penetration. And there may very well be a woman in the case. There usually is, I believe. But I visualize the murderer as a man of about the same age as his victims; and I think there are a number of men still in the world who, if they would, could tell us who he is."

"On that we are agreed," said Rainfall. "Your entire argument, for that matter, is fascinating—and you may be right."

"Oh!" cried Holly Moment. "If only I had had a really good look at him!"

"You saw quite enough, in my opinion," said her father; and Saxon nodded emphatically.

"Thank your stars that you didn't," added Rainfall. "If you were known to be able to identify him, your life wouldn't be worth that!" He snapped his fingers. "We are in the same boat, Miss Moment!" He smiled at her. "But since neither of us knows any more than he has told, we are probably safe enough. If only Mr. Ghost, now, would appoint himself a committee of one to solve this mystery!"

Ghost laughed heartily. "As my physician, do you recommend it? I'm supposed to be convalescent, am I not?"

"Your mental agility would seem to be unimpaired."

"It must serve," said Ghost, "such as it is. The case fascinates me, I confess—and blush for the confession."

The coffee was coming in, backgrounded by the immense bulk of the negress Heliotrope. She set the tray down carefully upon the table and moved to the buffet. Miss Moment lifted the silver urn and poured the brown coffee into blue enamel cups.

Suddenly, Ghost, who had been looking idly into the adjoining front room, stiffened in his chair.

"Excuse me," he said quietly, and rose to his feet.

Then, while the others stared in amazement, he stepped swiftly and silently to the front windows, opening upon a wide veranda, and flinging up the center frame, looked out into the darkness. An instant later, he had stepped through the aperture onto the porch and vanished.

Three men got quickly to their feet and followed, the professor's chair crashing behind him. But even before Saxon, the most agile, could clamber through the window, Ghost was back.

"Gone!" he said laconically. "Don't everybody come out."

He climbed inside and again stood among them. "It was a man," he continued easily. "He was looking in at the window. I suppose he saw me as I stood up."

Saxon exploded into something resembling passion. "There!" he cried. "You see?" He looked at Ghost as if daring him to deny, ever again, that the life of Holly Moment was in hourly peril.

But Ghost only shrugged and smiled. "It's all right, old chap," he observed soothingly.

Rainfall was examining some faint spots on the window pane. "Here are his fingerprints, Ghost," he exclaimed. "By Jove, perhaps we've got him!"

"Yes," agreed Ghost, "I noticed them. We'll want to get those while the impressions are fresh."

"Did you *see* him, Mr. Ghost? Did you see his face?" asked Holly. She was standing with her father's arm around her.

"About as much of him as you did, I imagine," smiled Ghost.

"Supposing him to have been the same man! It doesn't follow that he was, of course. This fellow may have no connection whatever with—with the subject of our conversation."

Saxon disagreed warmly. "Excuse me, Mr. Ghost," he apologized, "but I think he has."

"So do I," said Ghost, "but we can't prove it; and certainly he chose an awkward evening, if it was murder he had in mind. He might easily have picked out a less formidable occasion. There are evenings when Miss Moment is less thoroughly surrounded."

It was puzzling. Had some new development, as yet unknown to them, he wondered, been responsible for this espionage? All things considered, the move was more likely to be directed against Rainfall than against Holly—but why, at the moment, against either?

"Hadn't we better notify the police at once?" asked the professor a bit nervously. "Maybe this fellow is still somewhere around."

Ghost hesitated. It was, of course, exactly the thing that should be done, as a matter of sensible routine.

"Look here," said Rainfall, "this is more likely to be my affair than Miss Moment's. Don't you think so, Ghost?"

"Yes, I do."

"Well, then, I'm getting out of here—now. I won't involve any of the rest of you in this."

"Nonsense!" said the professor. "You'll stay here, of course. There's plenty of room." His hospitality rose triumphant over his apprehension. "We'll heat up the coffee again and make a night of it!"

It sounded like an invitation to some sort of a debauch.

"To tell the truth," answered Rainfall, "I'm afraid that fellow may have been merely a spy for somebody already at work in my apartment. I must really get back there. There's nothing to fear; but if it will make you feel any better, I'll pick up a policeman en route."

Ghost nodded. "I think the doctor is right," he said. An idea had crossed his own mind, and he was eager to test it.

"Good," cried Rainfall. "I'll call a cab at once."

"I'll go with him," said Saxon, as the physician hurried off to the telephone.

Ghost shook his head. "Let him alone," he advised. "He knows what he's doing." He hesitated. "I may want you to stay here, Saxon, until *I* get back. But say nothing of that, please, to anybody."

They accompanied Rainfall to the curb, when the taxicab had arrived, and Ghost took careful note of the driver's number. It was unlikely that the call had been anticipated and a ringer substituted, but at the moment no chances could be taken. Saxon watched him with fascinated interest.

"Tell your man to drive fast, Rainfall," Ghost whispered to the doctor, "and keep to the lighted thoroughfares. You're armed, I suppose?"

"Hip and thigh," grinned the physician. "I'll telephone you from the flat as soon as I get there."

"All right—and be careful!"

The motor purred softly; there was a shifting of gears, and the cab was away.

Ghost put his lips to Saxon's ear as they walked back.

"Into the house with you, now," he said, "and close the door with a bang. I'll be after you in a minute."

Saxon stared at him, bewildered; then complied. The front door closed after him in memorable fashion.

Left alone upon the sidewalk Ghost pushed into the deep shadows of a great bush, close to the stairpost, and waited. It was his first definite move in the case, single-handed, and a little thrill of excitement added itself to the emotions thronging inside him. In a moment it passed, and he waited coolly for whatever might occur.

Would the fellow, if he were still around, return to the house? Or was the attack, as he was inclined to suspect, directed against the physician?

Another moment passed. Then, in the next street, a hundred feet beyond, a second motor sounded, roared for an instant, and took on the smoother accents of locomotion. A dark and powerful car spun quickly around the corner and passed the house with flying wheels.

Rainfall's conveyance was crossing the intersecting avenue, two blocks away. Forgetting that he was still convalescent, Ghost ran swiftly to the house. "Another cab, Howard!" he said. "Call it quickly, while I'm putting on my things; then stay here with the professor and Miss Moment until you hear from me again. Rainfall is being followed, and I'm going after him myself."

CHAPTER SEVENTEEN

RACING TOWARD the city, John Rainfall leaned forward in his seat and addressed his driver.

"Step on it, François," he ordered briskly. "Don't get yourself arrested, if you can help it—but, if you do, I think I can square it for you." He added: "There's another car coming up behind us that I want to lose."

The taxicab driver answered something that sounded like "Gotcha," and stepped on it. The cab shook itself and leaped forward. It shot down the long street as if it had been hurled from a catapult. Foot passengers turned to look after it, open mouthed.

It was an admirable hour for speeding. The dinner at the professor's had been a long one and had been dragged out by conversation. As a consequence the streets were now reasonably deserted. Theater traffic long had gone its way, and it was not yet time for it to begin to return. Children were safely off the streets and, it was to be hoped, in bed.

The green signals at important intersections were with them almost consistently, Rainfall noted with satisfaction. When they were not, the reckless chauffeur turned into cross streets and swung northward again with the change of lights. He was a cunning driver. His knowledge of little crescents and obscure diagonal thoroughfares was accurate and bewildering. Apparently he had done this sort of thing before. In time, they entered a long white boulevard whose lamps, in narrowing perspective, fused in the distance into a single blob of radiant white fire.

Rainfall contrived to light a cigar. Twisted in his seat, he looked backward from time to time for the pursuing car. It was well within view, and its headlong speed identified it beyond question. Another driver apparently was breaking the speed laws with impunity. It was a miracle that no motorcycle policeman had turned up in the path.

The doctor's story was ready, however: "Sorry, officer, but I am a physician hurrying to the beside of a patient. A matter of life and death. Here is my card."

Rainfall smiled happily. He had experienced no such tingling excitement since the war. Would the fellow try a shot? he wondered. But of course he would do nothing of the sort. Shots attracted attention, and attention was something the intending murderer of John Rainfall would not care for.

It would be possible, of course, in the event of an upspringing policeman, to indicate the pursuing vehicle and point out that it contained a dangerous criminal. But Rainfall put that idea out of his mind as quickly as it had entered. For one thing, it might be difficult to prove, in a hurry, and, for another, the man behind belonged not to the police but to him, John Rainfall. To hell with the police!

He patted the pocket of his overcoat, on the right-hand side, where an automatic pistol lay ready.

With reluctance he put aside also the alluring notion of drawing the pursuer into some darkened cul-de-sac, where they could shoot it out together. Ghost, he remembered, would be waiting for his call. Failing to receive it, the island seeker would turn out the entire police department, perhaps.

The pursuing car was still within view. It seemed, however, to be losing ground. Possibly the idea was not to catch up at all, but merely to hang on. Was there a second murderer waiting at the house?

Rainfall determined upon a small experiment. The moment was propitious. There were other cars now along the boulevard, and innumerable lights. He spoke again to his driver: "Slow up a minute, Alphonse. Let's see what this fellow will do."

Their speed began to fall off until, by comparison, they seemed to be only creeping. Behind them their pursuer still thundered on. But in a short time he had realized the situation, and his own speed fell off. Rainfall chuckled.

"All right," he said. "He doesn't want me just yet. Keep her at about thirty-five."

"Thirty-five," echoed the obedient driver; and at that rate they loafed across the city and approached the congested areas of the Chicago Loop.

At sober speed they entered the business district and threaded the crowded traffic lanes. Occasionally they halted, stopped by the tides of opposition, but there was no longer any fear that they would be overhauled. Whatever the intentions of the man in the pursuing car, he had been left behind in the jam of downtown traffic.

Crossing the bridge, they emerged in the northern section of the city, and rapidly clicked off the remaining blocks that lay between them and the Division Street apartment.

Rainfall's money, as they approached, was in his hand. The house, he saw at once, was dark; the street deserted. He paid his fare quickly through the window, added a generous gratuity, and hurried up the steps.

On the doorsill he halted. The taxi that had brought him across the city was backing and turning. No second car as yet had turned out of the lighted boulevard into the darkened cross street. Twice he drew back, his hand upon the doorknob; then, pistol in hand, as once before he had entered his apartment, Rainfall pushed into his own rooms and stood an instant in silence.

As before, there was no sound but the ticking of the old clock that had been his father's. He stooped in the darkness and felt cautiously for the line of slender thread that he had stretched across the hall before leaving the house that morning. His fingers encountered it. It was still intact. Still unbroken. No one had entered from the front, at least.

Treading softly, he worked rearward to the door at the back, and again felt cautiously for his second thread. It, too, was unbroken. Then, still in darkness, he walked from window to window and tried the locks.

Nothing had been disturbed. The apartment was just as he had left it. There had been threads across the windows, too, and they were, like the rest, unbroken, unmolested.

He returned to the sitting room and, lighting a fresh cigar, seated himself to think it over. Then he remembered the call he had promised to make. The telephone was in the hall.

How absurd, he thought, the entire episode would be, if, after all this excitement, the pursuing force did not arrive!

He plucked the receiver from its hook and started to give a number. Then carefully he replaced the instrument upon its standard and listened to the cautious footsteps mounting the outer flight. . . .

At the same instant, Walter Ghost leaped from a car immediately around the corner and approached the house on foot.

It had been a wearisome drive for a convalescent, and Ghost was conscious of a number of aches. His fears for Rainfall's safety, however, were high. The doctor, in an emergency, he was certain, would act with a maximum of courage and a minimum of caution.

How far behind he was himself he could not be sure. There had been some notable racing, but there had been also a number of irritating delays. If anything had happened to Rainfall, he decided, he would not easily forgive himself. Stubborn as the physician had been about going, it was possible that he might have been persuaded to stay the night with the Moments, if he, Ghost, had not added his authority to the situation.

A fearful fraud, this Walter Ghost, after all, he told himself. He had vowed, after the *Latakia* murders, forever to eschew the excitements of detection; yet here he was again—a sober student and booklover—in the thick, of murderous contemporaneous events! He would probably be fortunate, this time, if he escaped another operation.

There were no other vehicles in sight. But he had discharged his own driver out of sight and earshot, and no doubt the other man had done the same. Why the devil, he wondered, had not Rainfall lighted his front porch?

However, that must be the place. Saxon had described it well enough. Old-fashioned, four-storied, and gloomy as a penitentiary. . . . And quite suddenly Ghost observed that a man was turning in at the house in question and cautiously mounting the steps. So quiet had been the approach of both men that neither had observed the other.

For just an instant Ghost halted, shrinking against an iron fence. When the other had reached the darkened porch, again he stole forward. A sudden emotion had tightened all his nerves. . . .

What followed was like a troubled dream.

Over the head of the man upon the porch an electric globe blossomed whitely, flooding with light the figure beneath it. In the sudden glare, Ghost clearly saw the intruder's face, and saw the man's eyes blink shut before the blinding illumination. At the same instant the door was flung violently outward and Rainfall stood framed within the aperture. His right arm was already raised, and it seemed that the reports which followed, and the flashes of flame, emanated from the tips of his fingers.

The man on the porch dropped instantly in a huddled heap. His own weapon clattered upon the boards.

Ghost ran quickly to the scene. "Rainfall!" he called.

The physician coolly stooped across the body of the man he had shot, lifted his head.

"Hello, Ghost!" he answered, with mild surprise. "Is that you? Well, I got him! Help me to carry him into the house."

He bent again above the figure on the porch. "Dead?" asked Ghost in a low voice.

"Absolutely—and not a minute too soon, either! Another second and he'd have had *me*. That's his gun, there, beside your foot."

Ghost picked it up and dropped it in his pocket. "I followed you," he explained. "I saw him take off after you, so I was bound to come along. I'm afraid I can't do much lifting."

"Damn!" said Rainfall. "I forgot your wound. Sorry! I can handle him, myself."

"Quickly, then. We'll have the neighborhood around our ears in a minute. I'll hold the door."

Up and down the block doors and windows were opening upon the night, and curious citizens were thrusting forth their heads. Shots, in Chicago, are not a novelty, but for every disturbance there is always a prospective audience.

Between them they managed to get the limp body through the door. Rainfall carried it inside and placed it upon the floor. Then, for a little time, they stood above it and looked down into the face of the man who had been slain.

It was an intelligent enough face—almost a handsome face, although marked by signs of dissipation—and somehow, about the lips, it seemed to the imaginative Ghost there lingered the traces of a secret smile. The eyes, however, stared with a certain quaint surprise, an illusion perhaps heightened by the high sweep of the brows. To both men, for an instant, it was as if the dead man were about to speak—to utter some tremendous revelation.

They continued to look down upon him, silent and a little shaken. The man's clothing, they saw, was well tailored and of excellent material. The coat, however, was dabbled now with blood, and a slow stream still oozed from the wound in the breast. It streaked his shirt and vest.

Flinging off his coat, stained by contact with the corpse, Rainfall knelt and with careful fingers revealed the inner pocket of the man's jacket. He turned down the edge. With a slender flashlight from his own pocket he illumined the interior. Ghost bent forward, and together they read the name inked on the tailor's label: *Nicholas Aye.*

"Somewhere," observed Rainfall, rising to his feet, "I have heard that name before."

"It's an unusual one," said Ghost thoughtfully. He hesitated. "I suppose we really have no right to examine him, this way, before the arrival of the police."

Rainfall agreed. "I suppose not—but in the circumstances I think I have a few privileges. The fellow tried to murder me, after all. Poor devil!"

He whistled an eerie little tune. "Well, I've killed a man, Ghost! It's not quite in my line of business. I've often wondered if I could. It's an experience—for a man whose job is keeping people alive."

"Shaken up a bit?" asked Ghost.

"Yes, I am. So much so that I'm going to have a drink."

"Well," said Ghost, "it was probably your life or his."

He continued to stare thoughtfully at the dead man on the floor, whose blood was soaking into the physician's rug. There were papers in that inner pocket, he knew. He had seen them. If only he might have a look at them!

Nicholas Aye.

Was he the long-sought murderer of Bluefield and Gaunt and Lear? There was excellent reason to believe so. But why had he come armed with a pistol? The murderer of Bluefield, *et al.*, had been far more subtle.

Suddenly, in his turn, he knelt beside the body.

"It's quite unorthodox, Rainfall," he remarked, "but I'm going to have a look at this fellow's pockets." He drew out the sheaf of papers and laid them gingerly beside him on the floor. There was blood on all of them. "The police, I suppose, will be here at any minute."

"I suppose so," answered the doctor gloomily. "Some of my neighbors will have telephoned by this time and saved us the trouble."

Again there was a creepy silence. It was broken by the physician, now slightly restored by a stiff dash of whisky.

"What's that in his side pocket, Ghost?" he asked. "There, on the left."

"More papers," said Ghost. "Well, we ought to find *something*, with all this evidence to help us."

He drew out a square of white paper, and they exclaimed together.

It was more than twice as large as any that had been used before, and the letters, too, were bigger and more staring; but it had a familiar look.

DEAD MAN INSIDE!

"By George," observed the doctor, raising his eyebrows, "he *did* mean business, didn't he!"

For some moments they looked at the sinister document, realizing its intended purpose. Then outside, on the stairs, they heard the footsteps of the police.

CHAPTER EIGHTEEN

All things considered, it had been a busy evening for the police. Once more the story of the earlier murders, after a day or two of relative obscurity, was rehashed and restored to the front page.

The attack on Rainfall, it appeared, had not been the only development of the hours of darkness.

Far out on the west side of the city, near Garfield Park, another body had been discovered, seated lifelessly at the wheel of a closed car and ticketed with the now familiar placard. That is, the car was ticketed.

"Get along there, now," a patrolman had remarked, good-naturedly enough; and then, when the man did not reply, he had opened the door of the car and repeated his command.

Still the man at the wheel had not spoken. As previous to this one-sided conversation the patrolman had passed the parked car a number of times without comment, he felt justified in his annoyance.

Then he had shaken the man's shoulder, believing him to be asleep.

Discovery of the murder had been effected about midnight, according to the morning journals, but death, the police said, had visited its victim some hours before—approximately at nine o'clock, or about the time that Rainfall, more fortunate than the man in the car, had left the dinner at the Moments'.

There was no difficulty about identity. The man in the car had belonged to everything worth joining and carried membership cards in number. He was Ellis Greene, a young man of good reputation, and a bond salesman for a famous house. He had been murdered with admirable neatness, exactly as had been Bluefield, Gaunt, and Lear.

Save for the square of white paper pasted to the glass, which the patrolman had mistaken for an election poster, there was no clue to the murderer. None, at any rate, that could at once be made useful. A number of finger prints had been taken from the automobile, some of which were certainly Greene's own and some of which were those of a stranger. The car, however, had belonged to Greene, who was unmarried, a Republican, and a collector of postage stamps. His age had been about thirty years.

Detective Sergeants Brandt and Noble had been placed in charge of the investigation—Kelly and Sheets being still engaged with the theater mystery—and they were reported to be following up a clue.

The sensation in Rainfall's case was the identification of the man he had killed. Nicholas Aye was well known to the police, although he had no criminal record. He was, in point of fact, a bootlegger of repute—in his own district a sort of king or overlord.

In the light of Rainfall's testimony, and that of Ghost, it was manifestly impossible that Aye could have murdered Greene, then hurried to the south side of the city to spy upon Rainfall. On the chance, however, that the elapsed time between the moment of Greene's death and the discovery of his body had been underestimated by the coroner's department, the available finger prints were compared.

Those found on Professor Moment's window were definitely the finger prints of Nicholas Aye; those on the panels of Greene's car were not.

There was only one possible conclusion, if the cases were related—that the "Dead Man" murders were not, as had been supposed, the work of a single hand. Rather, they were the work of a number of hands, albeit the hands might have been directed by a single brain.

Who, then, was the brain? Query: was he Nicholas Aye?

But what could such a man have had to do with Amos Bluefield and Patrick Lear? Yet it was certain that Aye had visited Rainfall with murder in his heart and a placard in his pocket. And Rainfall had been Lear's friend and a prime mover in the Lear investigation.

For that matter, argued the police, if alcohol were the keyword to the puzzle, there could be no guessing how many citizens, reputable and widely diversified, the situation might ultimately touch.

Aye's pistol had seemed an incongruous weapon for a murderer committed to cold steel, but it was less incongruous the morning afterward than it had seemed the night of the assault. In the bootlegger's careful garments had been discovered a slender length of tempered steel, fitted with a wooden handle, which he had found no opportunity to use. Its point was guarded by a protector of stout leather, and it appeared to have been made to order for the murders.

Ghost was dismayed. The murder of Ellis Greene did not fit his theory at all. The bond salesman was too young to have been involved in the origins of the case, as he saw it. Nor was he pleased with the revelation of Aye's identity.

"A bootlegger!" exclaimed the amateur disgustedly. "To what base depths hath this our case descended? Chandler, do you mean to tell me that a bootlegger is the brain and center of this web? That Bluefield and Lear were murdered because they had knowledge of thc unlawful activities of a rum runner?"

Professor Moment looked reproachful. "My dear Walter," he retorted, "I have said nothing of the sort. I have thought nothing of the sort. Why pick on me?"

"Because I'm annoyed, I suppose. I am merely raving aloud."

"For that matter, though," argued the professor, "why shouldn't they have been? This is Chicago, after all. Rum running—bootlegging—is an established, indeed an accepted, fact. It is a profitable and recognized profession. It is perhaps our third industry. If somebody attempted to interfere with one of the systems, that somebody would be—I believe the phrase is—'bumped off.' Yes, sir, whether he were a haberdasher or an actor!"

"I'll tell you why it simply can't be," said Ghost. "Because the idea of it is comic. If Bluefield had been a policeman, and Lear a politician, then Gaunt—a gambler—would fit the scheme admirably, and we would have a typical Chicago crime which would fail to interest me in the slightest degree. Greene, too, would fit, perhaps. But the early history of this case is on too high a plane. Bluefield's murder—and Gaunt's—and Lear's were not low farce, but high fantasy. Each, or all, requires an explanation as satisfying as the murders."

"I am perhaps less sensitive to the nuances of murder," observed the professor aggravatingly. "To me, Walter, it seems reasonably obvious that this Aye—a sufficiently remarkable name, by the way, to satisfy your aesthetic sensibilities—is either the murderer or one of the murderer's tools."

"Granted," said Ghost, "for the sake of argument; but surely not in his capacity of bootlegger."

"What would you have him?"

"An auctioneer," said Ghost, "a country editor, a bishop of the Anglican church—a whirling dervish—a teacher of the mandolin! Anything but a bootlegger."

"You've been reading *Sherlock Holmes,"* accused the professor. "All right, Walter, I'll take that back! But it does seem a bit unreasonable to refuse an easy explanation because you are determined it ought to be a hard one."

Ghost shrugged. "Maybe you're right," he said. "Maybe I'm an ass. I've often suspected it. But I'm not demanding a difficult explanation. I ask only an explanation that fits the crime."

He was silent for a moment. Then, "I'll tell you what I'm going to do, Chandler," he continued. "I'm going to investigate this latest murder myself. The Greene affair. Last night, I thought I had a solution—vague, nebulous, a little crazy, but artistically satisfying none the less. To-day it's been shaken, and I'm beginning to doubt my intuitions—which is bad. I'm going to visit the morgue and have a look at young Mr. Greene, and then I'm going to talk with the detectives who are in charge of his case."

"All right," said the professor. *"Nihil obstat."*

"Thanks," said Ghost dryly, and went away to the telephone to call a taxicab.

At the county morgue, a singularly cheerless place, he found a bulky police sergeant in charge of the victim's garments, looking at them with listless eye while smoking a cigar.

"Yeh," nodded the sergeant, "I'm Noble! Ghost, eh? Your

name was in the papers, wasn't it? Sure, I remember. Friend of Dr. Rainfall."

Nevertheless, the sergeant looked suspicious.

"What can I do for you, Mr. Ghost? Wanta see the body?"

"Not particularly," responded Ghost. "I mean, I've seen bodies before, and there are pleasanter sights." He smiled disarmingly. "Yes, I suppose I do. I should like, also, if it isn't forbidden, to see the clothing and the contents of the man's pockets."

"Nothing interesting," said the sergeant. "Couple of letters of no importance—a patent cigarette lighter, worth about a dollar—some cigarettes—and his business card. A flock of membership tickets. He was quite a joiner."

"Nothing scandalous, eh? Too bad! Well, let me see them."

The detective officer indicated a large wallet—his own—on a table beside him. "It's all there," he nodded obligingly. "Help yourself. Sort of an amateur detective, ain't you?"

"If you don't mind," smiled Ghost.

"Oh, I don't mind! The woods are full of them. We've had sixty on this case, already."

"This case?"

"Not Greene—no, all these murders."

"I see! What do my colleagues seem to think?" Ghost contrived to make his tone deprecating, and the big detective grinned.

"My God! You should hear them!"

"I'm glad I don't have to," said Ghost. As he talked he was turning over the several articles mentioned.

He produced a newspaper clipping from the wallet. "Here's something you didn't mention."

"That! Oh, yes—it don't amount to much."

"Still, everything found on a man's body is interesting. Bootlegger out of circulation, eh?"

"What?" cried the sergeant. He looked over Ghost's shoulder. "You've got the wrong side of it, buddy." He obligingly turned it over. "Bond sales. That was his job."

Ghost read the other side. It was as the detective had said. Under a Wisconsin date line, report was made of an issue of bonds that was shortly to be placed on sale.

He returned to the obverse and read again a short account of the death, in a hospital, of a man who some time previously had been shot by federal agents. The man had been a minor rum runner, one Anthony Carr. What an extraordinary coincidence! thought Ghost—if it was a coincidence. For the man Greene was certainly a bond salesman by profession, according to police investigation. Nothing could be more natural than to find in his pocket a clipping having to do with a prospective sale of municipal bonds. Yet it was astonishing that the other side of the clipping should reveal the death of a rum runner. Both sides contained the notices complete.

Ghost was troubled. Again his more artistic and satisfying theory of what had occurred seemed to be going glimmering.

"These are his garments, I suppose?"

"Yep, all he had on."

"Good stuff, isn't it?"

"First rate," agreed Sergeant Noble.

Ghost turned the clothing over as idly as the sergeant had done. The shoes were singularly fresh and clean. They had just been half-soled. Suddenly his heart leaped and sank. Sank dismally.

In the right coat lapel of the man's jacket was a glittering button. Its significance to the police had been slight. It certified merely that Ellis Greene had been a member in good standing of the Chicago Lodge of the Royal Bison. But Ghost's mind carried back to the eerie scene in the Moment drawing room and Holly Moment's puzzled inquiry: "Are you wearing something on your coat, Mr. Ghost? On the right side?"

Something bright—that glittered for a moment in the poor light!

Great heaven, was it possible that the body of Bluefield's murderer lay there, only a few feet away?

Ellis Greene, bond salesman?

Many men, it was true, wore lodge buttons on their lapels; but Green was dead in circumstances that related him in some fashion to the other murders.

And if Greene had killed Bluefield, and somebody else had killed Greene, where did it all begin, and where would it all end? It was a circle—one murderer killing another murderer—the second murderer killed perhaps by a third murderer . . .

Gamblers, bootleggers, bond salesmen! Incredible!

And which side of the newspaper clipping had Ellis Greene been saving? To Ghost, it made all the difference in the world.

His æsthetic badly shaken, his theory in similar plight, the amateur thanked the detective sergeant for favors shown and drove thoughtfully homeward.

CHAPTER NINETEEN

Howard Saxon called the following evening upon Holly Moment, who appeared pleased at his coming. The evening before he had merely telephoned, having found it necessary to attend the wedding of a pugilist. At the pugilist's wedding there had been a barrel of liquor and a dozen attractive young women, but Saxon had been bored and unhappy from the beginning. His anxiety for the professor's daughter was still high, and the attack on Rainfall had been anything but reassuring.

It was his hope that he might be allowed to look in on Miss Moment whenever he happened to be in the neighborhood. After all, the household must be pretty lonesome! Thinking upon the little strolls taken, in sunlight, by Ghost and Holly, his blood turned cold. What madness! What reckless madness! His imagination ran riot at the thought. He conjured swift and terrible pictures in which always he saw himself standing between Holly Moment and some fantastic peril. Somehow, when he was himself upon the spot, the danger that appeared to threaten seemed less immediate.

He had arranged, in point of fact, a sort of tentative schedule of appearances for himself. On one evening, with or without invitation, he would visit Ghost—who as a friend would doubtless be glad to see him—and on another evening he would frankly call upon Miss Moment herself. Between whiles there was always the telephone, that remarkable instrument.

Miss Moment was happy to see him.

"How was the wedding?" she asked brightly. Saxon shook his head. "Blond and dismal."

"Oh, come," she laughed, "something of interest must have occurred. I suppose it came off? Why didn't you ask me to go with you?"

"Great Scott!" cried Saxon, amazed. "You don't mean to say—Why, if it had crossed my mind, I'd have asked you in a minute. No, I wouldn't, either! But wait until you can go places, and—say, I'll take you places that will make your hair curl! Well, maybe I will."

"You are curiously uncertain, aren't you?" asked Miss Moment. "Was the bride pretty?"

"Not a particle!" said Saxon. "Oh, I suppose Bat thought she was pretty. Blond and—*ah*—puzzled. You know? Why are blondes always puzzled, Miss Moment?"

"Are they? It hadn't occurred to me. And what of brunettes?"

"Decisive," answered Saxon. "Decisive and—overwhelming!"

"Dear me," smiled the professor's daughter, "I *am* learning things about my sex this evening."

What an ass he was, he told himself grimly. As a rule he was sane enough. Now he could think only of nonsense. God knew there were plenty of things he wanted to say to her. Her own ease was superb, he noted.

Nevertheless, she was slightly embarrassed.

"Speaking of brunettes," she contrived cleverly, "what do you think I discovered Heliotrope doing to-day?"

"What?" Saxon was relieved.

"Playing with a Ouija board!"

"Not really?" He had a swift vision of the mountainous negress bending over the little varnished board. "Something about our case?"

"I don't know. She blushed when I caught her at it, so I suppose it was a love affair. I *think* she blushed. It's hard to say when Heliotrope is blushing and when she isn't."

"So I should imagine."

"I thought it might be amusing to borrow the board and—"

"Try it ourselves? Why not!"

"Not that I have any faith in such things. Have you?"

"Not a faith," said Saxon.

"Then I'll get the board and we'll see what Little Chief Skookum has to say for himself."

"Is Little Chief Skookum her lover?"

"Her control, I think. Does one have controls when one uses a Ouija?"

"I must have forgotten," grinned Saxon. "I think Ouija herself is the control."

"I'll get the board, anyway," said Miss Moment. "Mr. Ghost will be down soon, I think, and then we'll have a—But we mustn't make puns about Mr. Ghost. He's too nice."

She departed for the kitchen in search of the negress.

"Now," she continued, reappearing after a time, "shall we hold it on our knees or put up a table?"

"Let's hold it on our knees," suggested Saxon. It was an idea that appealed to him.

A slow step sounded on the staircase, and in a moment Walter Ghost entered the room. He greeted Saxon warmly.

"Am I *de trop?*" he asked. "Hello, what are you youngsters

doing with that thing? I didn't know you went in for supernaturalism, Holly."

"I don't," she said. "It's Heliotrope's. Of course you're not *de trop*. Is he, Mr.

Saxon?"

"Certainly not," said Saxon. "You look tired, Mr. Ghost."

"I *am* a bit tired," confessed Ghost. "I've been thinking too much about this absurd murder business, I suppose. It *is* absurd, you know. Were you about to ask the spirits for assistance or advice?"

"What *were* we going to ask?" Miss Moment laughed. "I guess we hadn't got that far, Mr. Ghost." She looked at him with sudden doubt. "Surely *you* don't believe in such things!"

"Don't I?" Ghost was quizzical. "How do you know I don't? I believe in everything."

"You're joking, of course. Well, you may ask the first question." She seated herself and took the board upon her knees, which met Saxon's under the improvised table.

Her fingers rested delicately upon the smaller instrument that spelled the mystic words, and Saxon's moved to join them. Ghost whipped out a pencil and a notebook.

"I'll record the revelations as they come through, shall I?"

The dark head of Holly Moment was bent seriously above the board. "Concentrate!" she said; and suddenly she was a little timid in the face of this new experience. Almost a little afraid.

What if, after all, there were something in it?

Ghost's eyes were sparkling with interest. On his own tongue a dozen questions were waiting to find utterance.

Miss Moment's voice was slightly strained, but her diction was precise and accurate: "With whom am I about to speak?" After all, she thought, it was perhaps as well to know.

There were some instants of breathless indecision. The little instrument moved faintly under their fingers, then stopped. After a time it began again. It moved slowly toward a letter—wavered—backed away—returned to the attack. . . .

The motion was circular and crablike, and to Holly Moment it was curiously disturbing. She was not pushing the pointer a particle; of that she was certain. Was Saxon?

The guide moved forward—paused—hesitated above a letter—stopped still.

There was no further movement. "H," said Walter Ghost crisply.

"By Jove!" exclaimed Saxon. "It does work, doesn't it?"

"It's beginning again," cried Holly Moment. "Concentrate!"

The weaving, circular motion was reëstablished. The little guide moved more rapidly now, as if it had gained confidence in its powers. The pointer settled upon another letter.

"O," said Ghost.

"Absolutely spooky!" observed Saxon, with profound interest.

"Concentrate!" warned Holly Moment.

Under their fingers the three-legged guide was moving again. It was moving swiftly, like a skater with keen skates upon polished ice. It cut a wide swath across the board, running crazily toward the end of the alphabet.

A curious thrill passed through the skeptic soul of Holly Moment.

"W," said Ghost. He laughed suddenly. "This won't do at all. It's spelling out your name, Howard. Let me ask it a question." Addressing the painted board, he asked: "Do you mean Howard?"

The pointer moved affirmatively toward a corner of the board upon which was painted the word "Yes."

"Silly!" exclaimed Miss Moment chidingly. The board made no reply.

"Well," said Ghost, "I suppose there are several Howards in the world and out of it. We've got somebody, anyway. You've established a connection. Go ahead."

"You ask a question," suggested Saxon.

"Very well! Suppose we try a shot in the dark." Ghost bent above the board. In a low voice he asked: "Who killed Amos Bluefield?"

The silence that followed was eerie. Slowly the little stool began to move. . . . "L . . . E . . . A . . . R."

Miss Moment took her fingers abruptly from the board. "It's ghastly," she observed. "Also, it's complete foolishness! We ought to be ashamed of ourselves."

"Perhaps I ought not to have let you do it," admitted Ghost. "It isn't necessarily foolishness—I mean the board's answer isn't—but it does seem an unlikely reply. Lear was playing in Milwaukee until the end of the week in which Bluefield was killed. Still," he laughed, "it would have been even more unlikely if I had asked, 'Who killed Lear?' and the board had answered, 'Bluefield!'"

In their interest they had forgotten everything else. With a sense of shock they heard a key turn in the outer lock.

An instant later Professor Chandler W. Moment had entered the room. He stared, speechless, from one member of the group to another.

"What under the canopy—" he began.

"A little experiment, Professor," laughed Ghost. "We were upon the point of solving the mystery of Bluefield, Lear, *et al.* Won't you take a hand? Holly and Howard are about fed up with it."

"Not I," said Saxon. "I love it!"

"Really? Then you and I will try our hands at it. Let me have your chair, Holly, and you take the notebook."

"Quite lunatic, all of you," observed the professor from the doorway. Nevertheless, he hung up his hat and stick in haste and moved to join the investigators. "Ask it what happened to my second pair of spectacles," he said. "Where did you get that thing, Walter?"

"Hush!" said Ghost. "It's Heliotrope's. We've got a ha'nt named Howard on the celestial line, giving us information."

"And a Ghost named Ha'nt supplying the information," muttered the professor, drawing up a chair. "All right, I won't say another word."

In breathless silence the séance was resumed. The board was now supported by the knees of Ghost and Howard Saxon.

There was a moment of immobility, then a surprising thing happened. Without a question asked, the little guide began to move beneath their fingers. It moved rapidly, accurately, and without pause, from letter to letter until it had spelled out a sentence.

The professor's eyes were bulging.

"A . . . canary . . . used . . . to . . . hang . . . where . . . you . . . are . . . now . . . sitting."

"Good God!" exploded Chandler W. Moment. "My aunt Eliza!" He turned reproachful eyes on Ghost. "Walter, you rascal, you're pushing that thing around."

"Am I pushing it, Howard?"

"No more than I am, I guess," answered the amazed Saxon. "And I certainly never heard of your aunt Eliza or her canary, Professor. Did she have one?"

"She did," said the professor stiffly. "It hung there, from the chandelier, immediately above your head. Upon my word, I never heard of anything like it."

"It's odd," agreed Ghost. "Suppose you question her, Professor."

"I should feel like a fool," said Chandler W. Moment. "What under the sun would I ask her?"

Nevertheless, he moved forward, and bending wrathfully above the board he barked his question: "Are you the old woman they used to call 'Catty' Calthrop?"

At this insult there was a slight movement, as of protest, on the part of the board. But the reply was sweetly complacent.

"It . . . made . . . no . . . difference . . . to . . . me . . . what . . . I . . . was . . . called."

"Exactly what she would have answered!" gasped the professor. "Walter, what is the meaning of this?"

"I can't imagine what your aunt knows about these murders," replied Ghost coolly, "but if there is anything she wants to tell us, I think we should give her the opportunity."

The professor nodded wildly. "Go ahead," he gulped.

Ghost bent again above the varnished board. His voice was low and melodious. "There is something I want to know," he said. "Answer me, if you can. Somewhere there is a solution to our problem. It is a solution that dates back many years. Perhaps it is in an old street in an old city, and perhaps an old woman can give it to us. I do not ask for names—for names of people. What is the town I must seek to find my answer?"

For an instant the world appeared to stop turning. Totality seemed closing in upon them.

Then for the last time the pointer started upon its wayward course. Once more out of a child's alphabet there emerged slowly three meaningless syllables:

"Wal . . . sing . . . ham."

"Wal . . . sing . . . ham," repeated Ghost. "Walsingham!" He looked up. "Is that a city, Professor?"

Professor Moment was excited. "A college town, Walter! A little college town in Connecticut!"

"H'm," said Ghost.

He turned again to the board.

"Do you mean Walsingham in Connecticut?" They grew old waiting.

"Yes," said the board.

CHAPTER TWENTY

THERE IS a compound German word—*Ohrfeigengesicht*—which, loosely translated, means a face that invites a box on the ear. Something like that. Certainly there are such faces. They are the unenviable characteristic of at least one member of every community. Their magnetism is irresistible. The owner of such a face has only to put his head inside a door to make everybody within hurling distance yearn to heave a pot at it.

Adrian Bluefield had such a face. It had annoyed the reporters; it had annoyed the police. In time it was destined to annoy the undertaker and embalmer. At the moment, however, there existed in the minds of the reporters and the police only the vague memory of an irritation. After the funeral of Amos Bluefield, Adrian had been half forgotten. It was tacitly assumed that he was going about his brother's business, clearing the decks, settling the estate, arranging for a return to Portland, Maine. Not even the murder of Patrick Lear had any more than casually recalled the man.

In the excitement that followed the murder of Ellis Greene, the second Bluefield was suddenly remembered. A certain amount of stock-taking was imperative, and looking back over the long list of persons in any way touched by the several tragedies, the distracted police chief of Chicago observed to his chief of staff—not with inspiration, but almost listlessly—"Bluefield!"

He added: "By the way, whatever became of that fellow Adrian? Was that his name? Amos's brother."

The chief of staff replied that he was damned if *he* knew.

This brief exchange of words served to remind the chief of police that the credentials of Adrian Bluefield never had been questioned. There had been, indeed, as he recalled it, no credentials to question. The man had arrived in Chicago, given an interview, taken command of a situation, buried his brother, and dropped out of sight.

The chief of police thought it over. The merest routine demanded investigation. Also, it was conceivable that Adrian Bluefield, who had heard of Gaunt from his brother's letters, had heard, too, of Greene.

He asked a subordinate to call up Adrian's hotel, and at the same time scribbled a telegram to the head of the police department in Portland.

The subordinate returned. "Mr. Bluefield checked out the day of the funeral."

"The deuce he did!" observed the chief. "H'm! That's funny. Call up his brother's hotel. Maybe he went *there* to live."

In a few minutes the subordinate reported again. "Not there," he said. "They don't know anything about him. Everything has been moved out. They think the stuff went to storage, but they don't know."

"Well, well," said the police chief, or words to that effect. "Well, well, and well!" Then, suddenly, with that tardy inspiration that made him, after all, a better man for his job than nine out of ten others, he added: "Wilk, I'll bet that fellow's a crook!"

"No!" cried Wilk, scandalized.

"Yes, sir," said the chief of police, "I'll bet he's a crook."

"Tchk, tchk, tchk!" deprecated Wilk, humorously ironic. "Then he's the thirteenth known crook in this city. We'll be getting a reputation, first thing we know."

His superior frowned. "That will be about enough from you, Wilk," he remarked, and scribbled another telegram to the Portland police department.

In this fashion it was discovered that no Adrian Bluefield was known in Portland, Maine, and the dark suspicion grew that the man from the East had been guilty of falsehood. If he had lied about his place of residence it was inferred that he might also have lied about his name and business, about the letters from Amos Bluefield, about Gaunt, and about everything else.

It became apparent that the man calling himself Adrian Bluefield must be found at once and asked a number of questions.

The usual inquiries were begun. With customary shortsightedness, the department revealed its doubts to the press, thereby warning the man sought that he was again an object of interest. In this connection it was the police idea that Adrian, if he were on the square, would at once come forward.

But Adrian did not come forward. Instead, the friends of Amos Bluefield belatedly expressed an earlier surprise. Their first news of the relationship, they confessed, had come to them through the newspapers. Previous to the arrival of Adrian and the appearance of his interview in the journals, they had not known that Amos *had* a brother. He had never mentioned one. They had supposed his relations all to be dead.

"A pity they didn't mention it earlier," commented Ghost, when the doubts had found their way into print. "Typical citizens of the greatest nation under the sun! They saw it in the papers, so they believed it. It is in such fashion that opinions are formed, important conclusions reached; and it is the same in politics and religion and in everything else. The average man—or woman—depends upon a sort of magic to determine his course as citizen or factor. He arrives at complete conviction with the slightest possible information, and that usually false, mistaken, or intentionally colored by the newspapers."

He shrugged. "I suppose I should have questioned that relationship myself, since I am such a fount of wisdom; but who could have supposed the police would not investigate?"

The case of Ellis Greene still bothered him, and the appearance of yet another suspect in the field inclined him to irritation. There were points about the Greene episode that made it difficult to dismiss, greatly as he would have liked to dismiss it. He would have liked to believe that the case of Ellis Green had nothing to do with the earlier murders; that it was one of those predictable crimes called by criminologists "imitative." Murder as a result of suggestion. There were always several such after a murder that was really novel and different. They involved a peculiar psychological quirk in certain minds.

Once an old woman in a fairy tale had gone off to market after warning her children not to put beans up their noses. The idea had not occurred to the children, and would not have occurred to them; but as soon as her silly back was turned they stuffed their noses full of beans. Imitative murders were somewhat of that order of phenomenon, Ghost thought. Anything out of the usual stupid run of things was as certain to have as many begats as a paragraph of the Old Testament.

His experiments with a Ouija board were still a topic of conversation, and he had not confessed his duplicity in the matter, although it was suspected. He had not told the professor that it was Heliotrope herself, that admirable gossip, who had revealed the former existence of an Aunt Eliza and a canary. The incident had been, in point of fact, merely a dramatic gesture to lend point to his proposed departure for the East. It had struck him as a good idea to mention the town of Walsingham, for which collegiate township hc proposed to leave.

The earlier phases of the ghostly dialogue were, he was convinced, the sheerest nonsense. Yet it occurred to him to wonder whose subconscious—that of Saxon or that of Holly Moment—had dictated the name "Lear" in response to the question, "Who killed Amos Bluefield?" Saxon's given name might have been—in response to Holly's first nervous question—an emanation from either.

There was still another possibility in the case of Greene, it occurred to Ghost, reflecting upon all things that had passed. Perhaps an intending murderer, with a grudge against the bond man, had cleverly utilized the situation as a background for his wholly personal scheme of vengeance. Saxon, he recalled, had once suggested the idea in connection with the case of Lear—Saxon or somebody.

Confound Ellis Greene! Remotely, the newspaper excerpt found upon his body—if it were not indeed only a notice of a sale of bonds—seemed to link the man with Nicholas Aye. The button on his coat lapel suggested the man in Bluefield's window. Each item in itself was valueless—almost childish—but taken together, in connection with the manner of the fellow's death, they had an aspect of profound significance.

If, now, Greene also had been a member of that "forty" group, would the case of Bluefield, Gaunt, Lear, *et al.*, be helped or hindered?

It was similarly disturbing to realize that Adrian Bluefield might not now be Adrian Bluefield at all, but a new and sinister figure in the tale. And if he were not a Bluefield, who, in heaven's name, might he be? Who might he *not* be! He had appeared promptly enough after the death of Amos.

"Well," Holly Moment spoke soothingly when she had heard his several doubts on this score, "he isn't Greene, Mr. Ghost, and he isn't Nicholas Aye. That ought to be a comfort."

"It is," said Ghost, "it is, Holly! He is at least somebody to look for—somebody who has been seen by a number of persons—somebody who can be recognized, if sighted. Sooner or later he is bound to be discovered. When he is, he will have some explaining to do."

"And what a jolly mess it will be, Mr. Ghost, if he turns up dead and labeled, like the others! I suppose that's possible?"

"Jolly indeed," agreed Ghost, without enthusiasm. "Oh, it's quite possible. This whole affair is taking on a nightmarish quality in which *anything* is possible."

He was tempted to take her into his confidence on a number of matters. The ideas he had not discussed. The letter from Connecticut that had come in answer to his own. Little things! He had been turning them in his mind for a number of days. Significant things that might have no significance whatever. Insignificant things that might take on the utmost significance. Discrepancies—odds and ends of fact and fancy. They didn't fit, it was true—but who could say what the future might disclose?

But he decided against a confidant. He would play his own hand to the end, and if he were wrong, no one would be any the wiser. If he were right . . . ?

He smiled at the eager girl. "Well, Holly, if anything like a solution of all this muddle occurs to you, don't hesitate to mention it! I am really very much interested." He laughed his whimsical little laugh.

But the afternoon papers completed his annoyance.

Up north, in the Wilson Avenue district, a shopkeeper of no importance pushed beans into his nostrils—that is, he blew out his unimportant brains in the back room of his establishment, after placarding his window with a duplicate of the original Bluefield notice.

"I am dead," said the note dispassionately. "This store will not open to-day."

Suicide, of course. There was no doubt of it. Everything was present to prove it. The revolver, the powder burns, the position of the wound, all gave evidence of self-extermination. Nobody particularly cared. The man had been frankly a neurotic and a nuisance. He had been for some time near the end of his rope. Sick, broke, more or less insane, he had been following the "Dead Man" murders with profound attention, the neighbors deposed. He took in all the papers. He discussed the case with his customers. Now he was dead by his own hand. Even the police admitted it.

But it was irritating. It confused the issues anew. It raised again, and more strongly, all the old doubts. Was it conceivable that every murder after the first had been merely an echo of that fantastic performance—each unrelated to the other?

Ghost didn't believe it. The case of the Wilson Avenue shopkeeper was unrelated; but the rest—even possibly that of Greene, he was afraid—were definitely tied up one with another. There was a high significance in the warnings received by Holly Moment and John Rainfall. Holly's had grown out of the murder of Amos Bluefield; Rainfall's had been clearly connected with the murder of Lear. Aye had been a bootlegger, and there had been an odor, at least, of liquor in the case of Ellis Greene. All these things were related. They must be. All were full of meaning.

But liquor was not the keyword! The keyword had not been uttered, perhaps, but it was not liquor.

Out of nowhere an idea came to Ghost, new and attractive and entirely mad. "The old pirate!" That was what Chandler Moment had called the murdered Bluefield in a number of his household lectures.

What if "pirate" were the missing word? The word that would unlock the puzzle! Something hot and romantic that went back, in its origins, to the murderous rovers of the Caribbean! Bluefield and Blauvelt were the same name; there could be no doubt of that. A pirate hoard—a *map*—a group of men, now all of them about forty (bother Ellis Greene!), who went in search of it! And perhaps quarreled?

And, of course, even bootleg liquor—some of it—came from the sea-girt islands among which, years agone, the great Colon himself had ventured.

Ghost laughed quietly to himself. The notion pleased him, and he played with it for a time, finding relaxation in the exercise. But it was sheer madness, and he knew it. It didn't fit at all. The wish was father to the thought. He was a little tired of the city on the lake. The lure of islands was upon him. But it was a picturesque notion, and it had its points.

One thing was certain. The solution—barring a sudden and unlooked-for confession—lay in another quarter. It lay, indeed, in another decade. More and more he was convinced of it.

"I must go East to-morrow, Chandler," he told the professor that evening. "I shall be back again shortly, I hope; at any rate,

I shall be in touch with you. Yes, I am going to have a look at Walsingham."

The Twentieth Century Limited next morning sped him eastward on the new adventure. As the train was leaving the station he heard a newsboy shouting his wares beneath the train shed and thrust his head from the window.

But he was too late to learn what it was all about, and, quite probably, he reflected, it did not matter.

CHAPTER TWENTY-ONE

In other parts of the city other newsboys were similarly advertising their profession. Out of the jumble of sounds thus broadcast there emerged a name, upon hearing which interested persons purchased copies of the extra edition.

"Arrest of Adrian Bluefield" was the legend across the top half of one of them. It was followed by half a column of type chronicling the event.

Bluefield, it appeared, had been found in lodgings so close to a north side police station that he might have put his head out of a window and watched the squad-room patrolmen at their pinochle. A very jolly dodge indeed—to hide next door to a police station. The public laughed heartily.

Howard Saxon, who, as an employee of a newspaper, received the several editions of his own journal in advance of the man in the street, also was cynically amused.

"Another fairy story exploded," he commented to an assistant, when the extra edition had been dropped upon his desk. "It is a popular notion among writers of detective fiction that the safest place for a criminal to hide is under the police chief's bed—the last place anybody would think of looking for him, eh? Like the story of the Jew who wanted to be buried in a Catholic cemetery so the devil couldn't find him. Or was it the other way round?"

He continued to read the account of the capture.

There was little else of interest, however. Bluefield was not actually under arrest, in spite of the headlines. He was in custody—a distinction with a slight difference in law and no difference whatever to Adrian Bluefield. He was being held, unbooked and incommunicado, at the station near which he had established his headquarters.

His assertions were profane and added nothing to the solution of the mystery. He was himself, Adrian Bluefield, he insisted; he had done no wrong, and, what was more, the police had better have a care what they were doing.

He had been apprehended the night before. A detective, leaving the north side station on an assignment, had seen him entering the lodging house and had recognized him from photographs published in the newspapers the day of his arrival.

But had there been an arrival? It seemed to the police more likely that the man called Bluefield was a Chicago product who had been stricken with a great idea. Yet surely he had known a great deal about Amos Bluefield. Had he been an associate?

He might even, it was privately conceded, have been the murderer of the haberdasher.

Groups of experienced detectives passed through the room in which the suspect was being interrogated the morning after his capture. None of them ever had seen the man before. His photograph was not in the "gallery." He had all the known facts of Amos Bluefield's life at his finger tips. It was admitted that there was even a slight resemblance between the dead man and the living claimant.

"Still," as Rainfall observed to Saxon, when the latter had

called him on the telephone to report the latest news, "all fat men look alike. After a fashion, anyway. A sort of family resemblance. They have protuberances in common."

Rainfall had been puzzled by the case of Adrian Bluefield for some time. Anticipating Ghost and the police, he had privately doubted the identity of the stout man from the beginning. He had found no valid reason for assailing Bluefield in public, however, and as a consequence he had said nothing. The man's arrest interested him deeply, and he found himself wondering, a bit fantastically, if there could be any connection between Adrian Bluefield and the murdered Greene.

The doctor, in fact, agreed with Ghost, although they had not talked it over, that Greene was definitely out of the picture. The island seeker's "men of forty" theory had impressed Rainfall profoundly, in spite of the flaws he had indicated that it contained. The psychology of imitative murder was perfectly well known to him, and he, also, had been inclined to lay the death of Greene to this curious homicidal simianism.

With the sudden Bluefield notion in his head, and a pipe between his teeth, John Rainfall turned the entire situation over afresh.

He had heard from Saxon of Ghost's extraordinary performance with a Ouija board, and later of the amateur's departure for the East. For Walsingham in Connecticut! How under the sun had Ghost pitched upon Walsingham? But, of course, he had been simply looking into *Who's Who,* and the Connecticut township was the scene of Lear's early studies.

Time and again Ghost had insisted that the solution lay elsewhere and in another day. Now he had gone East to demonstrate it. That much was clear enough; but Ghost was not the man to act hastily or without excellent reason. Had he found a genuine clue, the doctor wondered, or was he merely in search of clues that might exist?

The board, it occurred to Rainfall, was merely a bit of Ghostian melodrama to explain the amateur's hurried departure. Or was the Connecticut journey, perhaps, just a fiction intended to conceal another activity?

Other questions came to the doctor as he smoked. What was Ghost's notion of the Greene affair? He had probably investigated it. And about Adrian Bluefield? Bluefield, to be sure, had been taken after Ghost's departure—or, rather, announcement of the capture had been made too late for Ghost to hear it. He would hear of it en route, however, in all probability. Certainly he would hear of it when he reached his destination, for the clever amateur would not fail to keep open his line of communication.

Rainfall refilled his pipe. Smoking was a privilege allowed him, in his own quarters, even at the Gatacre Memorial.

Bluefield's game, of course, if he were not a brother of the haberdasher, was obvious. He was a smooth crook endeavoring to get possession of a valuable estate. Was it conceivable that, for some purpose of his own, he had wished to complicate the earlier issues by a little murder on the side?

Unwittingly treading in the footsteps of Ghost, the doctor took some time from his duties to visit the morgue and have a look at Ellis Greene. It was a workmanlike job that Greene's murderer had done, he was forced to admit. The newspaper excerpt bothered him, too, as it had bothered Ghost. Was it possible that Greene and Aye had been in some manner associated? What in the world, he wondered, had liquor to do with Ellis Greene?

An idea struck him with some force. What if he, John Rainfall, in the absence of Ghost, were to be able to prove Bluefield the murderer of Greene! The trail seemed reasonably fresh, and the theory was attractive. And if Bluefield could be shown to have murdered Greene—what followed?

John Rainfall, Detective! He laughed a bit sardonically. What idiocy was he contemplating now?

Ridiculous! Greene was still definitely outside the picture, a victim of circumstance and suggestion. Bluefield was an oily scamp halted in an effort for a fortune. And John Rainfall was still a physician with duties to his fellow men.

At the hospital he learned that Saxon had called a second time. Developments? Perhaps there had been word from Ghost.

He called the *Evening Telegram* and in a moment was listening to the latest tidings from the scene of action.

"Bluefield has confessed," said the sporting editor, with the satisfaction of a man possessed of private information. "I thought you'd like to know."

"Confessed!" Rainfall was staggered. "Confessed to what? Do you mean to say that Bluefield murdered Ellis Greene?"

"To his identity," said Saxon. "He still denies that he murdered anybody, but from the looks of things he's in a bad hole. It wouldn't surprise me to hear that he'd murdered Amos—and Lear, too. Just possibly, his brother."

"His brother!"

"His name is Gaunt," explained the sporting editor of the *Telegram,* "and he's a brother of the man who was found on the statue—Hubert Gaunt. He knew about Bluefield from his brother, instead of the other way round—if you know what I mean. Just trying to make a little easy money, he says. He confessed when the police accused him of murdering Amos. I think, myself, that he murdered everybody, including Lincoln and Mary, Queen of Scots."

Rainfall was still incredulous, but his mind functioned quickly and clearly. "I think Ghost ought to hear of this, Saxon," he said. "It may help him. It may even change his plans."

"Right," agreed Saxon briskly. "I've already sent him a wire. If anything else happens, I'll give you a ring."

"If anything else happens," said Rainfall ironically, "give me ether."

CHAPTER TWENTY-TWO

Messrs. Kelly and Sheets, meanwhile, had not been idle. Between them they had settled upon a workmanlike plan of action. It had the merit of sanity and common sense, virtues abundantly possessed by both detectives.

It was by now reasonably certain, they agreed, that all the murders had been the work of a single directing mind, even—it seemed likely—of a single hand. The situation offered difficulties of reconciliation, to be sure, but to the hard, logical minds of Messrs. Kelly and Sheets difficulties were only temporary obstacles. Once a common factor had been established, they would become actual aids to investigation.

In short, to solve the murder of Ellis Greene it was necessary first to solve the murder of Amos Bluefield. Similarly, to solve the murders of Gaunt and Lear, it was imperative to return to beginnings. After a fashion, it was the method of Walter Ghost.

To date, the activities of the two police detectives had resulted only in the apprehension of Clay Ridinghood. It had been quite a coup, in its way. But it was beginning to worry them. Was Ridinghood, after all, the common factor in all the crimes? That he had murdered Lear was easy to believe, since there had been both motive and opportunity; but to connect Ridinghood with the deaths of Bluefield and Gaunt had been another matter. No motive was apparent, and as for opportunity, it was certain that the stage detective had been playing his part in Milwaukee, with his principal, at the time of the first two murders.

It had begun to look as if Ridinghood would have to be freed, unless stronger evidence against him could be found. Certain it was that he had not murdered Greene. The lockup keeper would not have let him out long enough to accomplish that.

"And I'll tell you something in confidence, Billy," observed Detective Sergeant John Kelly to his associate. "He didn't kill Lear, either!"

Sheets agreed—reluctantly. "Neither did the Carvel female," he returned sadly. "They both of them just *wanted* to."

"It ain't a crime," said Kelly, without emotion. "There's a flock of wrong birds I'd like to bump off myself—not all of them criminals. Lear had it coming to him, if the lady told the truth—and she probably did. But it's a wonder some shyster hasn't got Ridinghood out, by this time. We haven't a thing to hold him on. We certainly get away with crime, ourselves, in this business! If the Carvel person was better looking we'd probably have the town around our ears."

He shrugged. "Well, they're digging up Amos and Hubert this afternoon. Like to see 'em?"

"Hell, no!" said Sheets. "An exhumation gives me the willies. You find out too much about what happens to you after you're planted."

"I kinda like 'em," said Kelly, with a grin. "Keeps a guy's hat from getting too small for him. They won't find out anything we don't know, anyway. Bluefield and Gaunt were killed the same as Lear and Greene, don't make any mistake about that."

"Pity they couldn't find a stickpin, or something, on Bluefield Mex," observed Sheets. "He's the one person who *could* have killed them *all*—except all the people in the world we don't know anything about," he added dryly.

Detective Sergeant John Kelly spat accurately for a distance of twenty feet. "We'll get him," he said. "We'll get him! Whoever he is, we'll get him, and we'll get him plenty." He drained his glass.

"Suits me," said Sheets laconically. After a moment he continued: "And when we get him he'll have a dress suit in his wardrobe."

Kelly was startled. "He'll what? *Why* will he have a dress suit in his wardrobe?" He looked suspiciously at his companion. "You've been thinking again!"

"I know it ain't safe." Sheets was apologetic. "But I remembered last night that Bluefield wore a dress suit when they found him in the window."

"So did the dummy," said Kelly. "It always wore one."

"It wasn't Bluefield's," argued Sheets defensively. "The dummy wore his own suit on the hook, and Bluefield wore *his* own in the window. They didn't swap."

"What are you getting at?"

"The man who killed Bluefield had to catch him while he was wearing a dress suit—didn't he? So he could be planted in the window and look like the dummy!"

"Hmph!" said Kelly. "Where was Bluefield the night of the murder, eh?" He thought about it for a minute.

Sheets was impatient. "Where was he just *before* the murder? That's the question. Nobody ever found out."

"Well, where *was* he?" asked Kelly.

"How do I know? The worst of fellows like that is, they wear evening clothes after six o'clock every night, anyway." Sheets was disgusted with the whole tribe of them. "Maybe he was with a girl. Maybe he went to a show! That's what I was thinking."

"Say!" Again Kelly was startled. But he shook his head impatiently after a moment. "We keep forgetting that Lear's show wasn't in town the night Bluefield was killed."

"Who said it was? There were other shows in town. What I mean is this: We've got to prove that Bluefield and Gaunt were theatre hounds, or something of the sort, to connect them with the Lear case. It's a series of theatrical murders, Johnny, me boy, any way you look at it. Every one of the killings was stage-managed by a veteran. What's more, I believe *Greene* was at a theater the night he was killed."

"He was killed at nine o'clock," said Kelly. "Everybody knows that."

"*Maybe* he was! They didn't find him till midnight, though. These doctors don't know everything. There's that Maxwell girl, too. She used to be on the stage, and what is she now? Engaged to marry one of Bluefield's clerks!"

"Sands and Clarke are watching the Maxwell girl," said Kelly. "They say she's all right."

"Sands and Clarke!" sneered Detective Sergeant William Sheets. "Are we taking the word of Sands and Clarke for anything? A couple of Orangemen! Well, what about it?"

"I think you're crocked on the theater," admitted Kelly. "You're stage-struck! But you may be right, at that. You think we ought to go to all the theaters and ask about Bluefield?"

"Don't you?"

Kelly thought it over. "Maybe I do," he agreed. "We might do worse."

He looked about him. The jolly little barroom in which they sat, and in which the conversation had gone forward, was a pleasant spot. One did not leave it without reluctance. Detective Sergeant Kelly raised a thick forefinger, and a sleek Italian-looking individual rushed forward solicitously.

"Two more beers, Sebastian," ordered Detective Sergeant Kelly, "and make it snappy. We've got work to do, whether you have or not. Got any pretzels?"

"No pretzels!" The man called Sebastian smiled apologetically. "Got ham sandwich, got hot dog, got bin sup! What you like, keed?"

"No pretzels!" observed Detective Sergeant Kelly. "This is a hell of a speakeasy! Well, bring me some 'bin sup'! How about you, Billy?"

"'Bin sup,'" grinned Detective Sergeant William Sheets.

They inhaled their bean soup with great gusto and went forth again into the wicked world on the trail of the murderer of Amos Bluefield.

One theater, after all, they agreed, was as good as another, and the Alhambra was perhaps better than most. It had been the scene of the murder of Patrick Lear, for one thing, and its employees were all familiar suspects. For another thing, it was close at hand.

Their assurance as they entered the manager's office suggested that at least they had been born in the house.

Sam Sultan, the manager, was out, but a sleek assistant gave them cigars and apprehensive appraisal. Nobody else had been murdered, he confessed, in reply to Kelly's first sardonic question, and the show was doing very well. Very well indeed.

He regretted that he was unable to say whether Amos Bluefield had been in the theater on the evening of the first murder. He had not known Mr. Bluefield personally, although once he had purchased a tie in the Bluefield shop. It was unlikely, he thought, that anybody around the place would know. Just possibly, the box office clerk! Just possibly, the principal usher, who had a good memory for faces! But he doubted it.

He hardly cared to answer for Mr. Sultan, but he was certain the house manager and Bluefield had not been acquainted. Had they been, he felt sure, Mr. Sultan would have mentioned it at the time of the murder. Certainly he would have mentioned it at the Lear inquest.

"There wouldn't be any reason to mention it at the inquest over Lear," said Kelly morosely.

He shrugged. Everybody he wanted to talk to was out. None of them would appear until after dinner. He drew moodily on his cigar and cocked an eye at Sheets, who had just risen from his chair.

On the wall of the office, among many others, was a photograph of a pretty young woman, boldly and angularly inscribed across the lower righthand corner. It was this portrait that had caught the eye of William Sheets during a lackadaisical inspection of the gallery. It had occurred to him that the subject looked astonishingly like the young woman known as Nancy Maxwell.

With suppressed excitement he approached the photograph and read the inscription diagonally across its corner. His face fell.

"To Sam Sultan, with all good wishes," ran the legend, with no particular originality; and then there was a name: "Roberta Ballantyne."

"Roberta Ballantyne," repeated Sheets aloud. "Never heard of her!"

He looked appealingly at Kelly, who joined him, leisurely, in front of the photograph.

The substitute manager hastened to their aid. "You must

have heard of her," he chuckled, scoring one at the expense of the police. "She's in the show."

"Of course she is," said Kelly. "Ballantyne! She's the old housekeeper in the first act, isn't she? Good Lord, what a make-up! We saw her before she'd taken it off, Billy. This is the way she really looks, I suppose. Why, she's just a kid, and she takes the part of an old woman!"

The assistant laughed. "She ain't exactly a kid," he observed. "The photographer did that. But she ain't very old, either. About thirty, I guess."

"Well, well," said Detective Sergeant Kelly, and he contrived to jostle his associate with his elbow. "Thirty, eh? Quite a baby! Quite a baby! I'd kinda like to adopt her. Tell Sultan we'll see him after the show starts, to-night, will you? We can't wait here all afternoon."

In the street he seized his companion by the arm and registered delight.

Sheets, also, was beaming.

"You saw it, then?" he asked happily. "Saw what?"

"Who she looks like."

Kelly was puzzled. "You mean you thought she was someone else?"

"Holy cow!" observed Sheets profanely. "She's either Nancy Maxwell or her sister."

Kelly looked at his accomplice for a moment in complete surprise.

"Bunk!" he ejaculated, at last. "That's the bunk, Billy. What put that into your head?"

"It's what made me look at the picture," said Sheets. "Why the devil did you *think* I looked at it?"

"I thought you recognized the Ballantyne woman without

her make-up," groaned Kelly. "I was handing you a lot of credit for it. She doesn't look like the Maxwell person any more than I do. What I want to know is why she gave her picture to Sultan."

"Because he collects 'em, and she's a goodlooking girl. There's others on the wall."

"She's a minor character," asserted Kelly, "and she gave Sultan her picture because they're playing around together. Collects 'em? He collects women, that's what Sultan collects. It's a hunch, Billy, and take it from me, it's a good one. Why, you crazy bum, don't you see it yet?"

"See what?" Sheets was truculent. "I saw that she looked like Nancy Maxwell."

"To hell with Nancy Maxwell! All actresses look alike, anyway. This Ballantyne woman is the old housekeeper of the show. She came into Lear's dressing room the day he was killed—while the bunch was standing around looking at him. It was this Ballantyne woman that picked that square of paper off the floor—'Dead Man Inside!' And Sultan was in the room and took it away from her!"

Sheets agreed. "That's right. I forgot all about it."

"And now we find her picture on Sultan's wall, inscribed to Sultan. To hell with Bluefield! I'm going back on the Lear case."

CHAPTER TWENTY-THREE

Sultan!

What mugs they had been not to think of him before! Sultan, devotee of night clubs and manager of the Alhambra Theater. Sultan, collector of women and of women's photographs.

"Love to Sam!"

"Kindest regards!"

"With happy memories!"

The office had been filled with similar inscriptions. Miss Ballantyne's, Kelly admitted, had been less florid—somewhat more chaste—than a majority of them. Probably a nice girl till Sultan got hold of her. Were actresses ever nice girls?

It seemed clear enough, now, what had happened. The little drama in Lear's dressing room had been carefully arranged. Nobody had actually seen the woman pick up that square of paper; she had merely appeared to do so. It might have been in her pocket just before she entered the room. She had stooped down quickly—and when she came up the paper was in her hand.

"What's that?" Sultan had inquired, or words to that effect. And he had taken the paper from her. After that everybody had seen it. In the excitement of the moment nobody would doubt that it had been there all the time.

"Easy!" said Detective Sergeant Kelly. "So easy that everybody muffed it! That's the way things are, sometimes."

Sheets was still faintly dubious. "What about the marks on Lear's window sill?" he asked. "What about the fire escape and the car parked underneath?"

"There's always marks on window sills," said Kelly. "As for the car, maybe it was there and maybe it wasn't. I never did like that doorman. He remembered things too quick, once I'd put them into his head. But it don't mean anything, even if it was there. There's always cars in alleys. For that matter, maybe it was all a plant, to make it *look* like the murderer went down the escape."

"Well," said Sheets, "what's your idea now, Johnny?"

"Lear's a bum—*was* a bum—everybody knows that. His wife told us all about him. He was making faces at this Ballantyne girl, and she didn't like it; she liked Sultan. Well, maybe it was Sultan that didn't like it. Anyway, it got pretty bad, and one of them—Sultan or the girl—bumped him off. Then they framed this thing between them to make it look like the murder was part of the other two. How's that?"

"It *could* be," admitted Sheets cautiously. "That trick in the dressing room looks suspicious, all right. But I don't think the girl did it. She was on the stage."

"How do we know she was? We don't know when Lear was killed. That's what the Carvel woman said about herself."

"Oh, Lord!" prayed William Sheets piously. "We'll be back believing Ridinghood did it, again, first thing we know."

"No, we won't! Ridinghood's out. Maybe he suspects what happened, though. You never can tell. Maybe the Carvel dame suspects. I'll tell you what it is, Billy: we went wrong when we began to believe all these cases had to be hooked up. That was a mistake. Maybe they are; but they don't *have* to be—see? This hunch looks pretty good to me. What we've got to do is stick to the Lear case. It's all we've got, really. The rest is all buried somewhere. Let's get the man that killed Lear. If he turns out to be the man that killed the other fellows, too—which he won't—it'll be swell. But, anyway, we'll have *somebody.*"

They proceeded forthwith to the Alhambra, the hour being shortly after nine in the evening, and requested audience with Sultan, the manager, who was anything but pleased to see them. He had heard, with a certain dismay, of their earlier visit. Their interest in the portrait of Roberta Ballantyne had bothered him more than he cared to show.

"Anything I can do for you, gentlemen," he said suavely, in response to their greeting. "Anything at all!"

There was an admirable directness about Kelly at times. He jerked a brutal thumb at the portrait of Roberta Ballantyne and asked: "Who's this Ballantyne woman?"

"An actress," answered Sultan, smiling. "You know who she is, Kelly. She's in the show."

"What's she to you?"

"Nothing," said the house manager promptly, "nothing at all. She's a friend, of course. Everybody in the company is a friend of mine."

"Why'd she give you her picture?"

"Because I asked her for it. I collect photographs of the people who come to this theater."

"Ever had her out?"

Sultan's red face became redder. He frowned. "Honestly, Kelly," he said mildly enough, "I don't think it's any of your business—but I'll tell you. Yes, I have! She's had dinner with me—supper, that is, after the show—a couple of times."

"What's she know about this Lear case?"

"Not a thing," snapped Sultan. He added more courteously: "On my honor, not a thing!"

"Did she tell you so?"

"Well, yes, she did. Naturally, after it happened, we talked it over. I asked her if she had any suspicions, and she said she hadn't."

"Not a suspish, eh?" Kelly grinned sardonically. "Were you out together the night before Lear was killed?"

The manager hesitated. It was a shocking situation, after a fashion. Kelly perhaps knew all about it, and if he lied he might be inviting disaster. On the other hand, the detective might be merely bluffing. He decided to tell the truth.

"Yes!"

"Talk about Lear?"

"Somewhat. A bit, perhaps."

"She didn't like him?"

"Yes, she did! She liked him a lot. She said so."

Kelly was puzzled. The answer had come like a shot. It had all the ringing quality of truth.

"Oh, she did, did she? Had no complaints to make about his conduct, or anything like that?"

"Certainly not. Mr. Lear's conduct was always exemplary."

"Whatever that is," grinned Kelly. "Well, come clean, Sultan!" He lied easily. "We know you were out together the night before it happened. We know more than you think. Exactly what *did* you talk about? Had you been out together before that?"

Sultan shrugged and was suddenly cynical. "I can't answer more than one question at a time," he sneered. "I'll tell you what I know, and you can think what you damn please about it. I don't know what tree you're barking up, Kelly, but whatever it is you think you know, you're wrong. Yes, we had been out together—but not on this engagement. I've known Miss Ballantyne for more than a year. We used to pal around a bit when she was here in another show, a year ago. That's why we went out together this time. We were already friends."

"Get down to Lear," suggested the detective. "You talked about him."

"She said she had been to Mr. Lear to make a complaint." The words came reluctantly from the manager's lips.

"What kind of a complaint?" Kelly was excited underneath his brusque exterior, but he was careful to maintain his front.

"There was a man in the company who had been bothering her, and she didn't like it. She'd told him so, and he continued to bother her. So she complained to Mr. Lear."

"Why to Mr. Lear? Why not to the manager of the company?"

"Mr. Lear was a sort of father to the members of the company—if you know what I mean."

Kelly's sneer was beautifully apparent. "I can guess!"

"I doubt it," answered Sultan. "You're one of those fellows who believe that all stage people—But what's the use!"

"Who was the actor that was bothering her?"

Sultan was silent for a moment. Then he spoke slowly. "You're dragging all this out of me—and you're going to get a wrong notion about things after I've told you. Well, I can't help it!"

"Who was he?"

"His name is—Moore."

"What!" Kelly almost bounced in his chair. "You mean the stage manager? The fellow who testified at the inquest?"

"Yes."

"Good grief!" said the detective, and tried hastily to readjust his thoughts to fit this surprising piece of information. "Why, he's—he's an old man! Isn't he?"

"Oh, no—and what if he were? He's about forty or so, I guess."

"Hm-m!" Detective Sergeant Kelly shot a swift glance at his associate, the silent Sheets, who spread his hands helplessly.

"Hm-m!" said Detective Sergeant Kelly.

His mind raced. It *could* be! It could be so! And, of course, if it were Moore, then nothing that Moore had said at the inquest was to be depended on. What had Moore said at the inquest? Kelly couldn't remember—rather, he could remember only a long series of negatives and denials. That little runt! There had been a row, of course, when Lear had called him down—probably a grand one.

Again he had a picture of the scene in Lear's dressing room as it had been described to him on his arrival. He saw the entrance of Miss Roberta Ballantyne—saw her stoop and rise again—with a paper in her hand—saw Sultan snatch the paper.

Saxon had told the story, and it had been very vivid. Was Sultan trying now to fool him?

"Why haven't you said anything about this before?" he asked.

"Because I'm satisfied that Moore had nothing to do with the murder of Mr. Lear. I know Moore, and he wouldn't hurt a fly."

"He was bothering Miss Ballantyne, you said."

"He wasn't hurting her. He wouldn't have hurt her. I hope I haven't given you the wrong idea, there. But his attentions displeased her, and when he persisted in them she complained."

"She preferred yours," said Kelly brutally, and the house manager writhed in impotent anger.

He mastered himself. "Yes," he retorted coolly, "she preferred mine. What I'm telling you is that Moore didn't kill Lear. It's what I was afraid you'd believe. I was protecting Moore from you two infernal blockheads. Do you want to pinch me for it?"

But Kelly was as cool as Sultan. "Maybe," he said, without emotion. "I'll take care of that later." He hesitated. "About that square of paper, Sultan. You didn't happen to write it yourself?"

"Good God, no! Why should *I* have written it?"

"I can think of a reason. Miss Ballantyne didn't write it?"

"Do you think we're both crazy?"

"I'm hanged if I know exactly what I do think of you," confessed Kelly. "I'll tell you when I've made up my mind. Meanwhile, keep your mouth shut. Understand? Not a word to Moore about any of this, or you'll be in trouble yourself."

"I won't say a word," growled Sultan, "but I'm sorry I ever heard of you two birds."

"That's all right," said Kelly, with a smile. "Hate me and Sheets all you like. We can stand it."

"Thanks," said Sultan dryly. "Thanks a lot. I certainly appreciate all you've done for me."

Kelly returned the sneer with enthusiasm. "Don't mention it," he begged, turning to the door; and from the door sill he added significantly, "to anybody!"

For several moments, Sam Sultan stood looking at the closed door. Then he made a sudden gesture, and his laugh was harsh as an iron hinge.

"Oh, no," he observed aloud, "I won't say a word! Not a word!"

By which he meant that he would say many words, and that quickly, to Stanley Moore; for he was as certain in his heart that Moore had killed Lear as he was that he had not done so himself.

What was more, he was very glad of it.

CHAPTER TWENTY-FOUR

"'My name is Horace Gaunt. I am the only surviving son, now that Hubert is dead, of Harvey Gaunt, who died in 1903. I am a lawyer. My home is in Providence, Rhode Island. I did not come to Chicago from Portland, Maine, as I asserted when I was claiming to be Adrian Bluefield. Most of the things I said at that time were untrue, I am sorry to say. I came from Providence. I claimed to be Adrian Bluefield knowing that Adrian Bluefield was dead, but that no one except his brother Amos was aware of it. No one, that is, who knew Adrian. My brother Hubert found it out, and the plan by which I was to impersonate Amos's dead brother was hatched between us.

"'There were seven boys in our family, and my father gave us all names beginning with the letter H. The eldest was Henry, who has been dead for many years. The second and third sons, Harold and Howard, died in infancy. The others, in order, were Herbert, Horace (myself), Hubert, and Harvey Junior. My youngest brother, Harvey, was killed in the war. My brother Herbert died about a year ago. My brother Hubert, as I suppose the world knows by this time, was murdered and his body placed on the statue of General Burke in Lincoln Park.

"'I cannot say who killed Hubert, but I would ask the police to consider the possibility that he was killed by Amos Bluefield.'"

Professor Chandler W. Moment put down his paper, pulled his glasses downward upon his nose, and looked at his daughter over the tops of his panes. "What do you think of that, my dear?" he asked.

"Ridiculous," answered his daughter, "I could invent a better story myself. Mr. Bluefield was murdered the day before this Hubert Gaunt. Everybody knows that."

"No," said her father, "he was *found* the day before this Hubert Gaunt. There's a difference." He sipped his coffee reflectively. "This man's idea is really very engaging."

"He's saving his own neck," insisted Holly Moment. "He killed Mr. Bluefield himself, and probably he killed his brother too. If this Hubert Gaunt *was* his brother."

"Oh, I imagine there's no doubt of that," said Chandler W. Moment. "Of course he's saving his own neck. But he's got to tell the truth to do it. He knows very well that the police will saddle him with the entire chapter of murders if he doesn't. I think he is being very frank. Well, there's more of it. I wish Walter were here to read it."

He continued with his reading.

"'I realize that to all appearances Amos Bluefield was killed first, and the natural supposition is that he was killed by my brother. I will be honest and admit that I thought so, at first, myself. But although Hubert was a bit of a ne'er-do-well and was frankly a gambler, it is difficult to believe that he would commit a murder.'"

"Rather good, that, don't you think?—calling his brother a bit of a ne'er-do-well—after what *he's* just confessed!" The professor chuckled.

"'It will be asked why, when I admit that we had planned together to capture the estate of Amos Bluefield, I do not believe that Hubert had murder in mind. I can only reply that all of my dealings with my brother were by mail, and that at no time was murder even hinted at. Hubert was in the confidence of Amos Bluefield. He wrote me that Amos did not expect to live long, and I took it that he was ill. There was no date set for my appearance. Hubert was to let me know about that.'"

"And Hubert *did* let him know, and he came as planned," interrupted Miss Moment. "How, then, can he possibly assert that Mr. Bluefield murdered his brother, if Mr. Bluefield died first?"

"Wait a minute! You asked that before. He's answering that very question now. . . .

"'But I did not hear from my brother, and one day I picked up a newspaper and saw that Amos Bluefield was dead—murdered in Chicago! I was inexpressibly shocked. My first thought was that Hubert had killed him. My second was that it had been a fortuitous accident. With considerable doubt in my head, I took the train for Chicago, and on the way I made up my mind to act my part as planned. I had wired Hubert of my coming, but I know now that he never received my wire.

"'Almost as soon as I had reached Chicago I was seized by the reporters. I had to speak quickly and firmly. I told my story and asserted that I was Adrian Bluefield. Then I was told about Hubert.

"'The tidings were terrible. For a little time I reeled under them. What, I wondered, could have happened? Had Hubert killed Bluefield in a quarrel and then taken his own life? Had some third person killed them both in connection with a grievance of which I knew nothing? I was immensely agitated. My mind works quickly, and I even wondered in that moment if it were not possible that Bluefield had killed Hubert, then committed suicide in such fashion as to make it appear that he had himself been murdered by my brother.

"'I have since thought over the entire case, and I have read everything I could find about it. There had been bad blood between Bluefield and my brother, and perhaps it had continued to exist. Hubert owed Amos Blucfield money—I do not know how much—and possibly it had arisen out of that circumstance. When the nature of the wounds by which both men met death was made apparent it became evident to me that if Bluefield had murdered my brother, he had himself been murdered by a third person, since suicide seemed to be an impossibility.

"'Then I began to think again about my earlier idea—that a third person had murdered them both. It seemed the likeliest notion of all, in view of the similarity of the murders, but the curious fortuitousness of it repelled me. I could not imagine that any third person was party to Hubert's plans. But if Bluefield had killed my brother it was certainly not he who placed Hubert's body on the statue. The body was not there on the evening before the day it was found, and Bluefield's body *was* in the window.

"'I could not make head or tail of it, and I do not now assert that Amos Bluefield murdered my brother. I merely suggest that the police bear in mind that possibility, in view of the apparently strained relations between them. In view, also, of the fact that Amos Bluefield was not at all the unblemished citizen that he was popularly supposed to be. One thing only is certain: that a third person exists who is cognizant of both murders, whatever part he may have played in them. For myself, I can show, if need be, that I was in Providence when Amos Bluefield was killed, and that my brother was dead when I reached Chicago. About the murders since that of my brother, I have no knowledge, but I do not believe they are related to the first two cases. I do not see how they can be.'"

The professor shook his head. "His argument grows weak toward the end," he admitted. "Ghost would shred it in a minute. No, I agree with you, my dear, that he is slightly—*ah*—cuckoo when he asserts that Bluefield may have murdered his brother. The difficulty there—as he seems to sense, himself—is Hubert's body on the statue of General Burke. And the man who murdered Gaunt is the man who put his body on the statue. Who else would do it?"

Miss Moment agreed. "Whoever murdered Bluefield murdered Gaunt, too, and neither one murdered the other. And whoever murdered Bluefield and Gaunt murdered Lear and Ellis Greene."

"Quite possibly," said her father. "Quite possibly. Greene's case is, perhaps, less striking in its dramatic effects than any of the others; but the first three are, I venture to think, masterpieces. And as in all masterpieces, whether in art, fiction, or crime, there is a family resemblance that betrays the master hand—in this case, we believe, the same hand."

He leaned back complacently in his chair. It was a subject that pleased him, and he discoursed most ably on subjects upon which he was least competently informed.

"It is to be remembered, however, that emotion is at the root of it. Great art, for instance, however various and unlike, evokes the same emotional response, which in turn creates, perhaps, the possibly fallacious idea that—"

"Is that all of the Bluefield statement?" asked his daughter innocently.

"Not quite, I believe. Not quite!" He picked up his newspaper. "The rest appears to be family history, and rather ancient. How he does love to talk about his family! It's rather a pity there wasn't an eighth son. He might have been called Homer and have turned out better. Shall I read on?"

"Please do," begged Miss Moment earnestly.

"This would interest Walter. Bless my soul! I wonder if it isn't, perhaps, the very thing he is looking for. Listen to this, Golly!"

He began to read again.

"'I have been asked about the relations between my brother Hubert and Amos Bluefield. I do not know them in intimate detail. They were about the same age, however, and had been at school together—a preparatory school at Walsingham, Connecticut.'"

"Walsingham!" cried Holly Moment.

"You see?" said her father. The rebuke in his tone implied that he had been trying to din the word into her for hours.

"'A number of the youngsters ultimately got themselves into trouble, as I understand it, and several of them were expelled. I was in Europe, at the time, and did not learn all the details, but the difficulty grew out of a hazing administered to another boy. My brother was one of the group expelled, and he never returned to school. He drifted to the West, fell in with evil companions, was with a circus for a short time, I believe, and finally took to living by his wits. He used to write to me for money whenever he was in need, and I always sent it to him. In his latest letters to me, he frankly admitted that he was no better than a common gambler.

"'To the best of my knowledge, Hubert was never involved in the liquor racket. As for the man, Nicholas Aye, who appears to have been concerned in the case of the actor Lear, I have never heard of him, or, rather, I had never heard of him until I saw the announcement of his death in the newspapers.

"'With reference to Adrian Bluefield: he was the only brother of Amos. My brother never knew him, nor did I. Hubert knew he had existed, however, a fact he had learned from Amos. Adrian Bluefield went to Africa, a great many years ago, and vanished completely. A matter had arisen that in some manner compromised his integrity, and I suppose he felt that it was necessary to leave the country. For years no one knew what had become of him; then, in a roundabout way, Amos heard of his death. There were few left who knew him, and I anticipated no difficulty in carrying out my intended impersonation. I had been supplied with all necessary information by my brother, who, as I say, had learned it all from Amos. I should like to add that I am very glad the criminal enterprise was not carried through. It is my wish to return to my home without disgrace attaching to my name.

"'Such restitution as I have been able to make, I have made. Mr. Bluefield's papers, of which I took possession, are in the hands of the police, and I have yielded the receipts to all goods sent to storage. I should like the public to know that, sooner or later, I should have taken the action which has been, in a way, forced upon me. All the time I was in hiding, indeed, my thoughts ran in that direction. I should have fled earlier, but that I realized the danger of my position. It had come home to me, tardily, that my entire enterprise, if discovered, might point to me as the murderer of Amos Bluefield and my own brother. This fear, which I freely confess, and certain moral scruples which I was happy to find had not entirely died within me, had all but determined me to give myself up. I should have done so, I believe, within twenty-four hours, had I not been apprehended.'"

Professor Chandler W. Moment rose to his feet and moved toward the door.

There was something of determination in his stride.

"Where are you going, Father?" asked his daughter curiously.

"I'm going to send a wire to Walter," answered her father. "He ought to know about this as soon as possible. It may give him a hint."

"It isn't neccssary, really, you know," said his daughter. "Wire if you want to, but I imagine Howard already has done so."

"There is something fine and reckless about sending a telegram that appeals to me," said Professor Chandler W. Moment. "It is years since I have had an opportunity. So you call him Howard, do you?"

Miss Moment was surprised. "That's his name, isn't it?"

"I don't like names beginning with the letter H," said her parent severely. "Oh, well, I'll call him up and ask him if he wired to Walter."

He resumed his journey toward the front of the house just as the alarm of the doorbell rang through the place. At the door he received a yellow envelope from a uniformed messenger boy.

"What is it, Father?" asked his daughter, hurrying after him.

"It's from Walter," said Professor Chandler W. Moment. "It looks like code to me."

"It's Shakespeare," she laughed, leaning over his arm. "But what do you suppose he means? Mr. Ghost, I mean."

"Anyway," said the professor, "he's coming home to-morrow."

CHAPTER TWENTY-FIVE

Ghost's homecoming was characteristically unobtrusive. Although possessed, he believed, of the solution to the mysteries, he made no attempt to communicate with the police. Had he done so, it is possible that they would not have recognized his name.

At no time had he been a figure of importance in the investigation, as far as the public knew. His name had appeared in the newspapers a number of times, but few persons associated him with the problem. Save for the half dozen who knew him intimately, he was remembered, if at all, as a nebulous nonentity who had been present, almost fortuitously, at the violent passing of the bootlegger Aye.

From the beginning, he had played a lone hand. It was his habit—the way he preferred to play all games, including the larger game of life, in which, after all, his detective interludes, so to call them, were only deprecating gestures.

He liked applause well enough, but he had no obtrusive vanity. He quested truth because he believed in truth; but his notion of truth was not always that of other men. Right and wrong were terms that he seldom employed in serious conversation. He preferred to think in terms of wisdom and unwisdom. His admiration of the police, at times sincere enough, was always qualified.

He descended from his train without ostentation and was driven at once to the home of Professor Chandler W. Moment.

The Chicago morning papers had been delivered quite early aboard the train. One had been propped against his sugar bowl during breakfast in the diner. He was thus in possession of all facts concerning recent developments and found them not without interest. Again the headlines were large and black. The "Dead Man" murders, at one length or another, had clung to the front page now for many days.

Obviously somewhat of an impasse had developed. Two men were now virtually under arrest, charged with the same crime—Stanley Moore and Clay Ridinghood. It was still, apparently, a police idea that solution of the Lear murder was solution also of the others—or that the others were unrelated and, by comparison, unimportant. The police idea, in point of fact, was not very clear. Nevertheless, two men were being held.

Ghost remembered Moore very well; that is, he remembered his testimony at the inquest, as reported by the press. It had been very frank, he thought; very honest even in its implications. Now the fellow appeared to be in serious difficulty. He had confessed to having quarreled slightly with Lear the day before the murder. There had been words exchanged about another member of the company. A woman.

In the case of Ridinghood, too, there was new and rather sensational evidence. The Ballantyne woman—"H'm," muttered Ghost, "I had almost forgotten her!"—had also made a confession. She had confessed to withholding information at the inquest rather than seem to implicate the stage detective. It appeared, on reconsideration, that she had actually overheard the man Ridinghood in murderous conversation with Miss Carvel—i. e., with Mrs. Lear.

"By heaven!" Ridinghood had cried, "he ought to be killed!" And then: "By heaven, I'll kill the adjective noun, myself, if he ever—!"

Ever what? He had apparently been silenced by Miss Carvel before he finished. This had been some days before the actual murder—while the company was still playing in Milwaukee. Milwaukee had been the "dog," upon which the sensational comedy *Green Terror* had first been tried.

Well, it was a strong threat, if Miss Roberta Ballantyne really had heard it uttered; yet it meant nothing in particular, thought Ghost with a little smile. Stage people were that way—excitable, given to wild statements based only on a sudden choler. Few of them ever really indulged in massacre.

But why had Miss Ballantyne withheld so important a bit of evidence? From the police point of view, it was important in a high degree.

The answer seemed fairly obvious. None of the stage folk had been eager to implicate an associate, and Miss Ballantyne had spared Ridinghood and Miss Carvel almost as a matter of course or of professional courtesy. No doubt she had heard many similar outbursts in her time. But the arrest of Moore had opened her lips. She had remembered the Milwaukee threat at a timely moment, and had made it known. Ergo, she was more interested in sparing Moore than she was in sparing Ridinghood.

"Heigho!" said Walter Ghost. "'What a tangled web we weave,' indeed!" Which was, perhaps, the first time in months that he had failed to find an apposite quotation from his favorite book.

There was also in the morning papers a résumé of the earlier statement by Adrian Bluefield, or, as he was now known, Horace Gaunt. This latter, Ghost read with profound attention. It was surprising, he reflected, how closely the rascal approximated the truth in some of his conjectures. Was it possible that he *knew* the truth?

No, he was telling what he believed to be true—but with certain reservations dictated by caution. That Horace Gaunt had not known that his brother contemplated the murder of Amos Bluefield was beyond belief; and Ghost did not think it for a minute. On the whole, he reflected, it was probably a lucky break for Horace Gaunt that his precious brother had been anticipated.

Yet the beggar had actually mentioned Walsingham. Casually, to be sure. Would the police now take the hint and follow up that staring clue? Or would they, as before, continue to ignore one of the most significant circumstances of the entire episode?

It was Ghost's private thought that they would continue to ignore it. And he had no objections. It was not his business to instruct the police.

At the home of the Moments he was welcomed as might have been a voyager returned from the antipodes.

"Yes," he admitted, "I think I know the truth, at last. I think I have known it for some time. However, there is always the chance that I am a fool. I've demonstrated it often enough, heaven knows."

Professor Moment was not to be put off. "What I want to know, Walter, is who killed Bluefield—and Lear. I don't care who killed Gaunt and Greene. But I suppose it was the same man in each case?"

"No, I think not. I don't think Greene's case is related to the other three. It has never fitted into the pattern."

"And the others do?"

"The others *are* the pattern by which subsequent murders must be judged."

"Ah! And who killed Bluefield and Patrick Lear?"

Ghost laughed. "There is an appalling directness about your questions, Chandler. Until I can prove it, I'm not prepared to say. You may be sure I'll tell you as soon as I may."

Holly Moment looked at him with deep suspicion. "You hinted, Mr. Ghost," she said accusingly. "You hinted at it in that telegram! I'm sure you did. Now, didn't you?"

"Well, perhaps I did. I felt a trifle elated when I sent it off, and I may have been reckless enough to risk a long-distance suggestion." He smiled. "Did you identify it?"

"'Sit still, and hear the last of our sea-sorrow,'" she quoted. "Of course! It's from Shakespeare's *Tempest.* Father thought it was code. Prospero is talking to Miranda on the island. I thought you were just telling us to wait and we would soon know the answer to everything."

"Well, I had that in mind."

"But why 'sea-sorrow'?"

"Why not?" laughed Ghost.

He became more serious. "Look here: it's a long story. It goes back a long time, as I have said before. I haven't been to the police with it. I may never take it to the police. I don't know what I shall do. I'm not a policeman. My connection with the case isn't official. It isn't even known, officially, that I have any connection with it. I'm in this on my own, because—well, first I was in it because I believed Holly to be in danger, and later, I suppose, because the thing fascinated me. Anyway, I can do as I please. What I want is a little honest advice."

"Advice," said the professor, "given gratis and copiously."

"I know! Well, I thought I'd tell only four persons what I've discovered—you and Holly, of course, and Rainfall and Saxon. We've all mulled the thing over before, and none of us will tell, if we decide not to take it to thc police. We all have sense—I hope—and probably we can reach as fair a decision as any haphazard jury. What do you think?"

Miss Moment was delighted.

"When?" asked the professor. "To-night?"

"If you like, and if the others can come. Yes, the sooner the better, I suppose."

"I'll call up Howard at once," said Holly. "I've already told him about your telegram. He couldn't make anything of it, either."

Ghost gave her a curious little smile. "Couldn't he?" he said.

"But what about Greene?" asked the professor. "If he doesn't fit, what happened to him?"

"Oh, he was murdered, all right! I have an idea about that. I worked it out on the train, going down. I think somebody followed him to the shoemaker's."

"To the shoemaker's!"

"Yes. I reached that conclusion as a result of thinking about Greene's shoes."

"His shoes!" cried the professor weakly.

"He wore black Oxfords, and they had just been half-soled. You know, I saw him at the morgue. Yes, they had just been half-soled. *Just!* Not within a day or two, but within an hour or two. Probably less. The soles were bright and clean. They had hardly been walked on. The nails were fresh and new. The rubber heels were new. The polish on the shoes simply shone."

"Stepped into his car at the door of his house," observed the professor. "Possibly, but more than likely he went to a garage for it. To do that, he'd have to walk a little bit. The shoes were just from the cobbler's bench, I tell you."

"I still don't see—"

"The cobbler's awl, Chandler! The perfect instrument for such a murder. Somebody was with him or followed him. That somebody went into the cobbler's place with him. It may have been somebody who knew where Greene was going. Anyway, he stole the cobbler's awl, and—"

"Eureka!" cried the professor excitedly. "The cobbler himself!"

"Well, I thought of that," confessed Ghost, "but I couldn't imagine a motive."

"Owed him money, probably," said the professor.

Ghost smiled. "You solve these things with consummate ease, Chandler, once you get started. I wish I could do it in twice the time! Well, it's only an idea, as I say. But if I were a clever detective, working on the Greene case, I'd look all over the west side of town for a cobbler who had lost an awl."

Miss Moment came back, breathless. "They're coming," she said. "Howard and Dr. Rainfall were having dinner together, anyway, so Howard will bring the doctor here afterward."

She pouted. "Couldn't you give us just another little hint, Mr. Ghost?"

"'Sit still, and hear the last of our sea-sorrow,'" he answered smiling.

CHAPTER TWENTY-SIX

In the Moment living room a singing silence had succeeded the words of greeting and the early small talk of arrival. All eyes were fixed on Walter Ghost.

Rainfall, a long cigar between his teeth, was still relatively calm. Saxon, nervous and awkward, crossed and recrossed his bony knees. Miss Moment, bolt upright in her chair, was tensely impatient. The professor was almost bouncing with excitement.

For a number of intolerable seconds the amateur continued to draw placidly upon his cigarette while he arranged his thoughts. His own eyes were on a picture halfway up the wall. Then, with a gesture unconsciously dramatic, he dropped his stub into a receiver and turned his gaze upon his audience.

"A very curious case, Chandler," he observed almost casually, and although he addressed the professor his friendly smile seemed to embrace them all. "For anything like a *scientific* explanation, we shall probably have to ask Rainfall. The motivation is not entirely clear to me. It goes back, all of it, as probably you are tired of hearing me say, a great many years. I ventured to think about twenty years, and I missed by a single year. Oddly enough, the origins of the case were even more fantastic and extraordinary than the murders which grew out of them."

"You predicted that, also, I think," said the doctor with a smile.

"I have always felt that that *should* be the case, anyway. Well, it all began with a hailstorm in the state of Connecticut in the year 1911."

"A hailstorm!" cried the professor.

"You have heard legendary stories about the size of hailstones. Stories have come down to us of stones as large as paving blocks. I don't quite believe that. Anyway, these stones that I am talking about must have been large. It was an unusual storm.

"But I am already ahead of my story. I should have said, perhaps, that it all began with the hazing of a young man in the town of Walsingham. The hailstorm came later, although, if it had not been for the hailstorm, as I read it, there would have been no murders twenty years afterward. There is a preparatory school at Walsingham, a small one, where then, as now, secret societies were, and are, forbidden. The result of such a rule can be predicted. Unauthorized fraternities sprang up among the bolder spirits, and one of these seems to have been a singularly fantastic one. It was called by its members, with youthful bravado, the 'Terrible Ten.' It boasted only ten members, all, apparently, daredevils."

Ghost smiled. "I don't suppose they were really so terrible, but no doubt they thought they were. Certainly some of them turned out badly, though. The ringleaders of this group were Nicholas Allenwood, Amos Blauvelt, Patrick Stacey, and Hubert Gaunt. You may recognize the names, as I did, when I had been over the books of that period. Allenwood is obviously Nicholas Aye; when he changed his name he simply took the first letter of Allenwood and spelled it out. This is the purest speculation on my part, I must admit, but I am confident I am right.

"Amos Blauvelt is unquestionably Amos Bluefield; the latter name is a translation of the former—from the Dutch into English. Stacey we know to have been Lear's family name; and Gaunt, apparently, saw no reason for making any change and so stuck to his own. Make no mistake about these changes. In my opinion they had nothing to do with the crimes that followed years afterward. They were convenient changes, that is all. Stacey became Lear for stage purposes, Blauvelt became Bluefield probably because he sensed a Jewish flavor about Blauvelt and didn't like it; I really don't know. Allenwood became a bootlegger and perhaps decided to spare his family. Let us hope so. Save for Gaunt's brother, Horace, whom we have still in our midst, the families would all appear to be dead, which is just as well.

"Well," continued the narrator more briskly, "there came to the school a freshman named Tempest—Gregory Tempest. The others—Allenwood, Blauvelt, *et al.*—were sophomores and juniors, except for one who was a senior. It was a mixed company, you see. This fellow Tempest was what is called, I believe, a 'regular guy,' and as there was soon to be a vacancy in the 'Terrible Ten,' he was invited to join. He agreed, nothing loath, and in time plans were drawn for his initiation—always a weird and ridiculous piece of ritual and ceremony. The other members of the group, perhaps I should say, were named Frankhouse, Dawson, Delancey, Morgan, Moore, and Ker."

Saxon cried out in amazement. "Ker!" he said.

"Yes, it's almost beyond belief, isn't it? I doubt if any more remarkable coincidence ever occurred. In the group, besides those readily identifiable as the dead men, there were three other names that had figured, more or less, in the murder case. You noted the others, of course: Dawson and Moore."

"Dawson?" asked the professor.

"He's the young reporter who, as I understand it, sensed the body of Gaunt under the shroud of Burke's statue. He has since been prominent in the investigation. Of course, Dawson and Moore are quite common names, but Ker is not. I was immensely puzzled. If there had been a Greene in that list I think I should have thrown up the job! But, of course, Dawson, *in propria persona,* was out of the picture. He was too young to have been one of the Ten. Rufus Ker, on the other hand, was too old. But I was bound to wonder whether a son of Ker's or an uncle of Dawson's, or something of the sort, was not involved.

"Well, it was a frightful muddle. I put it out of my mind for a bit and concentrated on what had happened. You see, I was quite definitely looking for something out of the ordinary involving three men—Bluefield, Gaunt, and Lear. It was these names that turned my attention at once to the Ten. Happening across Allenwood was a bit of luck. Not that I did not have him in mind—he was so obviously a part of the murder conspiracy, in one rôle or another—but I had erred in believing him to be a minor figure. I now believe him to have been a very outstanding figure. Certainly, I have learned, he was the headliner in all the antics of the Ten.

"So much for the *dramatis personæ.* You must keep them all in mind." He lighted a cigarette, puffed twice at it, and threw it away.

"Walsingham is an interesting town," he continued. "In earlier years—earlier even than the time I am talking about—it was, after a fashion, a racing town. Just outside the limits a few miles, and nearer to Walsingham than the next village, was an abandoned race track—a one-mile track—which once had been a flourishing resort." He laughed suddenly. "Again, I'm getting ahead of my story. But the race track is part of it.

"To resume: Allenwood and his band of nuisances determined to give young Tempest an initiation calculated to chill his blood. They had never gone quite so far before. In preparation for the event a considerable quantity of liquor had been consumed by everybody concerned—which, also, I need not add, was against the rules of the school. Thus fortified, they all proceeded to an empty house, just on the edge of town, which was reputed to be haunted.

"What went forward in the haunted house is not certain—probably a lot of absurd rites and a lot of gibberish. I imagine that more liquor was consumed, then and there. At any rate, late that night, Allenwood, who had left the group, returned from town driving a hearse. Yes, a hearse. Empty, of course! He had rented or borrowed it from a local undertaker. They proposed to place young Mr. Tempest in the hearse and drive him around the town, as the concluding number of their program. You see the amusing sort of fellows they were!" commented Ghost dryly.

"Good gracious!" said Holly Moment, shrinking a little nearer to Saxon.

"I don't suppose Tempest cared," continued Ghost. "He was probably too drunk to be affected much. Anyway, he was placed in the hearse, or he climbed in, and the unholy procession started around the town. Nobody had noticed, or nobody cared, that a storm was brewing. All this was in the early spring, with winter still loitering in the neighborhood. It was still cold, and Tempest, in the hearse, was probably the most comfortable of the band. However, they had bound him, hand and foot, as part of the scheme of things, and they had put a huge placard on the side of the hearse. You can imagine what the thing said!"

"'Dead Man Inside!'" said Holly Moment and Rainfall, at the same instant. "Exactly. You begin to see, now, what happened; how, like a pantoum, the story begins to round on itself and make a pattern. 'Dead Man Inside!' And Tempest, drunk, was as good as dead. On the driver's box were Allenwood and Gaunt, and the rest of the precious company followed on foot, singing and carrying on. The town turned out to see them, but nobody thought of interfering. The doors at the back of the hearse were left open, and one of the boys—I fancy it was Bluefield—sat just inside, with his legs dangling. All this detail comes from an old file which I dug out of a country newspaper office in Walsingham. Perhaps the man who sat inside was Lear. It's a detail that wasn't reported.

"And then—to make the story short—the storm broke. It broke over them on the other side of town, as the procession headed out toward the open country. 'The rains descended and the floods came.' And the rain came down in large cold drops that became in a little time hailstones. The old newspaper says the stones were as large as walnuts, which is quite probable. They pelted down upon the hearse, and upon the horses that drew it, and upon the procession that followed. At a loud and sudden clap of thunder the horses took fright, and in a minute there was such a runaway as probably never had occurred before in the history of the world.

"The procession disbanded at once. Those on foot hurried back to town without stopping to worry about the group that still clung to the hearse. And the horses girded up their loins and ran furiously out into the open country, assaulted at every step by the great hailstones and more and more frightened by every fresh thunderclap that burst over them. Allenwood, who had plenty of nerve, stood upright on the swaying seat, trying to get the animals under control. He had to give it up. There was only one thing to do: to keep the horses in the road—full of ruts as it was—for if they left the highway and ran into the prairie alongside there would be a spill, he knew, that would endanger the lives of everybody in or on the vehicle.

"And inside—you can imagine! Tempest, bound hand and foot, rolled and thumped from side to side, now crashing against one wall and now against the other, until his face and body were bruised and lacerated and all his drunkenness had left him. I imagine, by that time, the drunkenness had passed for all of them. "Then the runaway reached the abandoned race track, and in the mind of Allenwood was born a tremendous idea. In its way it was almost epic. Since the horses *must* run until they fell exhausted, he determined to swing them through the gate and onto the track, where they might at least run on a smooth surface."

Ghost shook his head. "What a picture!" he said. "Can't you see it? By a miracle he negotiated the gate safely and got the hearse onto the track; and then those horses, under the scourging lash of the hail, circled that mile track three times—the cumbersome hearse swinging and swaying at their heels! Allenwood's face was cut by the icy rain and stones as if it had been lashed by knotted strings. And the horses ran and ran, mad with terror, until they were nearly dropping with exhaustion. An incredible picture! There is all the quality of a nightmare in that flying hearse, with its waving black plumes and plunging horses, circling a deserted race track under a sky torn by lightning and made hideous by thunder. The episode is almost monstrous, and I suspect it is without precedent.

"However, I am getting rhetorical. What happened was this: Completely out of hand, at length, the horses left the track and plunged toward an iron fence that bounded the course. A shocking accident impended, and Allenwood and Gaunt, on the box, abandoned the hearse. They both jumped, rolled over a few times, and came up, miraculously, with only minor bruises. The man who had ridden inside with Tempest had long since jumped for safety and was far behind upon the road, with a twisted ankle, limping back toward town. Then there were a grinding crash and showers of flying glass, a sickening moment for the man inside, and in the end—for Tempest—complete blackness."

"Dead?" asked the professor after a long moment of silence.

"They thought so," answered Ghost. "Allenwood and Gaunt had a look at him, and they believed him to be dead. So they left him there, left the horses there, still kicking at the traces, and fled back to town as hard as their legs could take them. On the road they met the man who had jumped first, I suppose, and later they met all the other members of the Ten. I assume this, and I assume they all took an oath of silence, for when the performance was investigated—as of course it was—nobody knew a thing about it.

"But the townspeople had seen some of the band, and so it was brought home to the Ten. Allenwood, Blauvelt, Gaunt, Stacey, and a couple of others were expelled."

"And Tempest?" asked the doctor.

"Was picked up, next morning, half dead. He had a broken leg, and many less serious injuries. Exposure, too, had all but murdered him, and for some time he lay at the point of death. In the end he recovered and left the school—naturally enough, perhaps."

There was another silence, broken this time by Saxon.

"And you believe that this Tempest had held a grudge all these years and that it was he who killed Bluefield and the others?"

Ghost nodded. "I throw out that suggestion," he answered. "Is it plausible?"

"It's plausible enough, I suppose," growled the professor. "As you tell that amazing story, Walter, it's very plausible, too; and assuredly, since you say so, it *did* happen. The thing to do, then, is to run down Tempest and accuse him?"

"Possibly—and if you think we have the right. After all, he had considerable provocation."

"But *did* he?" asked Holly Moment. "It was all frantic, of course; insane, for that matter; but, of course, no actual harm had been intended."

"Well," said Ghost, smiling, "I said I wanted advice in the matter."

Rainfall removed his long cigar from his lips. "You suggested that I might find a scientific explanation of the case," he observed tentatively. "You mean, of course, that some explanation is necessary to make plausible and understandable so long and well nursed a grudge. I suppose it is. I should imagine that only this man Tempest could justify it, and then only by his later experiences. The question is bound to arise: What was the effect, later on in life, of all that Tempest went through?"

"So I think," agreed Ghost. "I don't mean that I think it drove him insane—although long brooding, I believe, often has that effect. There would perhaps be other consequences."

"But have you a line on this Tempest?"

"I think so. I've been over the whole case a number of times, and I believe my conclusions to be sound. I believe Tempest committed the murders, and I believe Tempest can be found. The question, as I see it, is: Do we *want* to find him?"

Saxon sat up quickly in his chair. "Listen!" he said. "There's an extra edition. Do you hear?"

For a moment they all listened to the powerful accents of a newsboy some distance up the street.

"Bluefield!" said Saxon. "It's our case. He certainly said 'Bluefield.' Didn't he, Mr. Ghost? There wouldn't be an extra edition unless it were important. Wait a minute and I'll get a paper."

He dashed out of the house and went in search of the shouting boy, who was slowly approaching on the other side of the street. In a few minutes he was back, his eyes sparkling, his tongue thick with excitement—bursting with information. "Done!" he cried. "We're all of us sold, Mr. Ghost! Can you beat it? A crazy old shoemaker named Johnson has confessed to all the murders!"

CHAPTER TWENTY-SEVEN

THE NEW development dropped, bomb-like, into the lives of investigators great and small. The small army of detectives employed upon the many angles of the several murders stopped dead in its tracks and whistled softly to itself.

A crazy old cobbler named Johnson!

And the innumerable sleuths, in and out of uniform, private and professional, had been tracking minor actors and actresses from breakfast to evening prayers. They had been trailing innocent salesmen and stenographers of the Bluefield establishment from early grapefruit to late motion pictures.

Well, Dawson was having his inning at last.

"Dawson!" observed Detective Sergeant Kelly to his traveling companion.

"*Wouldn't* it be Dawson who'd spill this, just about now!"

They sat morosely in the office of the Detective Bureau and cursed the energetic reporter who had found a crazy old cobbler named Johnson. For where, now, was their careful case against Stanley Moore, stage manager for the late lamented Lear?

"It isn't possible," said Sheets savagely. "Even if he killed Gaunt and Ellis Greene, why the hell should he want to kill Bluefield and Lear?"

"And how?" asked Kelly. "Never mind the 'why!' There's always reasons."

"With his awl!" said Sheets bitterly.

They turned again to the extra edition, still damp from the press.

Young Mr. Dawson had been very clever, there was no doubt of that. He had observed a pair of shoes belonging to Greene, during his visit to the morgue, and had observed the exceeding newness of their soles. It had occurred to him that they had just been repaired. But why had they not been walked upon? he had wondered.

Obviously, Green had changed in the cobbler's shop, climbed back into his car, and driven away.

Where, then, was the second pair of shoes—the shoes that Greene had worn in going after the others? Had he left them with the cobbler? Or were the missing shoes, perhaps, a clue to what had happened to Greene? Had the cobbler—wild idea!—followed Ellis Greene for a purpose of his own?

It had also occurred to young Mr. Dawson that a cobbler's awl would be an almost perfect weapon for the kind of murder visited upon the several victims. His story was engagingly and modestly told, in the third person, as of a reporter for the *Evening Cry*, but his full name was at its head: *Ernest Crackanthorpe Dawson*. He signed up three abreast, as boldly as Ella Wheeler Wilcox, upon whose literary laurel wreath he had designs.

He had gone questing for the missing shoes and had found them where the murderer had thrown them—in a clump of bushes in the park, just across the road from where the victim's car had stood. The shoes had been curiously gashed. To find the cobbler had been only a little more difficult. His shop was in West Madison Street, hardly a block from the scene of the murder. He had willingly identified the shoes and as willingly had confessed the murder. He had no grudge against Greene, he said. But he had, somehow, felt impelled to kill him. The death notice he had prepared some days before and carried in his pocket.

He had asked Greene to drive him to the park, and Greene—with whom he had often done business before—had good-naturedly assented. At the edge of the park Greene had stopped his car and, sitting at the wheel, bent over to change into the newer shoes. In that particular only had young Mr. Dawson been at fault. The shoes had been changed in the car, not in the shop.

The opportunity was made to order. Johnson, in the rear seat, had leaned over and driven the awl into the bond salesman's brain as he bent forward over his shoes. The blow had been delivered with the cobbler's left hand, and Greene was dead before he knew that he was in danger.

Thereafter, the murderer had cleansed his weapon by driving it several times through the leather of the older pair of shoes, and later he had dropped the shoes in the clump of bushes in which they had been found.

Asked by Dawson if he had been moved to the murder by the earlier and similar crimes, Johnson had electrified the reporter by saying calmly: "I killed those other men myself!" He had autographed a confession to that effect, which was now in the possession of the *Evening Cry* (reproduction on page 3), and he was willing to give himself up to the police whenever they chose to claim him.

Details of the murders of Bluefield, Gaunt, and Lear were not supplied, but it was indicated that this omission might be remedied in later editions of the newspaper.

Detective Sergeant Kelly plucked up some hope.

"Hmph!" he observed. "If it wasn't for those damned shoes—and the gashes in them—I'd say this Johnson didn't kill any of them. Well, he'll be here before long, Billy—if he hasn't skipped before Tarzan lands on him!"

"Tarzan" was the irreverent name bestowed by certain of his friends upon Captain Michael Frogg, head of the Detective Bureau, who had gone in person to effect the capture of the cobbler.

"He's crazy as a bug," said Sheets. "I don't believe he even killed Greene. He's been reading about these murders, and when Dawson bounced in on him with a pair of shoes he saw a chance to get his name in the papers. It's always happening. You know that as well as I do."

"Well, the shoes *were* gashed," demurred Kelly cautiously. "It can be shown whether or not they're Greene's."

"Maybe Dawson gashed 'em himself," suggested Sheets. "I wouldn't put it past him."

Nevertheless, the shoes were Greene's. Upon comparing them with the pair that Greene was wearing when his body was found—now part of the Detective Bureau's museum—the fact was undeniable. In this particular, at any rate, Dawson had scored a triumph.

The reason he had not written the details of the cobbler's murder of Bluefield, Gaunt, *et al.*, was known, at the moment, only to Dawson and the editors of the *Evening Cry*. It was that he had not heard these details himself. After receiving the murderer's scrawl of confession it had occurred to Dawson—with the watery blue eye of Axel Johnson staring into his—that the cobbler was meditating another murder. He had left the shop and the vicinity in haste.

He was present, however, at the examination that went forward in the office of Captain Frogg shortly before midnight. Johnson had been taken without a struggle and now sat calmly at his ease in a chair that creaked and swung under a blaze of lights. For the first time in his life, perhaps, the cobbler was a center of interest. For the first time in his life, important persons hung upon his words and urged him to give his message to the world.

The weapon that had gored the bond salesman to death gleamed dully on the captain's desk, under the captain's hand—a slender steel instrument ground down until it was barely stouter than a heavy needle.

"Why did you kill Amos Bluefield?" asked the captain harshly.

"Because I did not like him," said the cobbler. "Once I stopped to look at the man in his window, and a policeman ordered me away."

"You mean the dummy?"

"I mean the dead man in his window."

"And a policeman told you to move on?" Frogg was puzzled. "And that's why you killed the proprietor of the shop?"

"I did not forget that insult," answered the cobbler serenely, and his watery eyes gleamed for a moment with placid triumph.

The man was obviously as crazy as a loon. Looking at the whiskered, fanatic face, Kelly, planted at the cobbler's elbow, wondered for a moment if the story might not be true. Certainly, if he always looked as unkempt as upon this occasion, he was the sort of citizen who would be told to move along.

"How did you get into the shop to kill him? How did you know he was inside?"

"I telephoned him to meet me there. We met at midnight and went in together. I asked him to apologize for the insult he had caused me, and he refused. So I killed him and put his body in the window. The other dead man I took out and put in a closet."

"What did you tell him on the phone? What made him come down to meet you?" Frogg's voice was as skeptical as his thought.

"I told him I was the man he had insulted and I demanded an apology."

Mad as it sounded, it was remotely plausible. At least the man's explanation was not fantastic and impossible.

"How did you know how to kill him?" asked the police captain, more curiously than severely. "Who taught you that trick with the awl?"

The cobbler smiled cunningly. He had anticipated that question.

"In my own country," he said calmly, "I knew a doctor who once told me it was a clever way to kill a man." He nodded sagaciously. "He had himself killed many men that way, he said."

"Whew!" whistled the captain under his breath. After a moment he continued: "Well, what about Gaunt—the man on the statue? Why did you kill him?"

The answer came plausibly and at once. "We had left the door of the shop open. The other man came in—I do not know why. He saw me kill this Bluefield. It was unfortunate, but I had to kill him also—this Gaunt."

"The same night!" Again Frogg's doubts rose triumphant over his worry. "Good God, man, what did you do with the body until the *next* night?"

Apparently it was a question for which the cobbler was unprepared. He hesitated. "I took it away with me," he replied at length. "I hid it until the next day."

"Where did you hide it?"

"In the park," said Axel Johnson.

Frogg's eyes traveled swiftly over the antique specimen that was confessing to four murders. He continued with some irony:

"Then the next night you dug it out of a bush, threw it over your shoulder, and climbed the statue with it—to put it on the horse! Is that right?"

It was an explanation that satisfied the cobbler. "Yes," he answered with relief, "that is what I did."

Frogg smiled genially. His voice became brisk and cheery. He was almost jovial. "And now about Lear," he said. "The actor, you know! Why did you kill Mr. Lear, Johnson?" He added: "And how?"

The eyes of Axel Johnson became dreamy and introspective.

"That was the hardest of them all," he said. "I went to the theater, that day, to kill a man named Davis. He was not there, and I walked around in the theater looking for him. After a while I saw a door, and I went inside. Mr. Lear, the actor, was sitting in front of his looking glass. He did not see me. Very suddenly I saw that he was the policeman who had insulted me that day I looked in Amos Bluefield's window, and I knew that he must die. I killed him before he could turn around. It was very strange meeting him there, like that."

For a moment they all sat in silence, looking back at Axel Johnson. Then Frogg rose heavily to his feet. He looked significantly at Detective Sergeants Sheets and Kelly and at Ernest Crackanthorpe Dawson.

"Very strange indeed, Johnson," he remarked, not unkindly. "But, of course, we can't have you going around killing policemen like that, you know. By the way, why did you want to kill the man called Davis?"

The cobbler's eyes flashed with a sudden and terrible anger. His mustache bristled. He seemed like a great cat about to spring.

"Because he has my head!" he screamed. "He cut off my head and would not give it back!"

"Ah!" said the captain, without emotion. "So that was it!"

To Sheets and Kelly he said: "Take him away, boys, and keep him by himself. Yes, downstairs, for the time being."

Then, as the detectives lingered for an instant at the door, the cobbler heard for the last time on earth the voice of Captain Michael Frogg, low-pitched for the benefit of Ernest Crackanthorpe Dawson. Neither of the two words spoken found any familiar echo in Axel Johnson's brain.

"Psychopathic laboratory."

CHAPTER TWENTY-EIGHT

IN THE Moment living room the tidings fell with a similar sense of impact.

Rainfall's long cigar jerked sidewise in his mouth, the ash cascading down his vest to spread, fan-like, upon the rug. He took the thing from his lips. "Are you joking, Howard? But of course you're not!"

The professor had jumped like a stricken stag. "Jehosophat!" he cried. "I've solved the mystery myself! It's what I said to Walter this very afternoon." He appealed to Ghost. "Didn't I, Walter?"

Walter Ghost smiled faintly. "You suggested that a cobbler had killed Greene, at any rate," he admitted. He had recovered from his own surprise in an instant, realizing what had actually occurred. "The man's insane, of course."

Saxon, still clutching the newspaper, began to read the account aloud. He read in a high, monotonous singsong.

"Dawson!" he said, in conclusion. "Clever beggar! I remember him as a cub."

"So that," mused Rainfall with curious emphasis, "is how Greene went."

Ghost nodded. "It's the way the others went, too," he said, "but the cobbler didn't kill them."

"I know! But I've often wondered about Greene. He never figured in the case. It had to be something like this, I suppose. The cobbler, as you say, is insane. He's been reading about the other murders. I suppose it occurred to him that his awl would make an ideal instrument of death. Your man Tempest, Ghost, would seem to have a lot to answer for."

"Ye-es," said Ghost, a bit absently. "You are right, of course, about the awl. That, and the newspapers, put the notion into his head. How many times do you suppose the madman looked at it and considered a possible victim? And all day long, no doubt, they came and went in his shop—men and women, boys and girls—while he pegged away at his last, exchanging insane pleasantries and waiting for the perfect opportunity. We shall never know, perhaps, why Greene was selected."

Saxon was a little put out. "Then you don't believe his confession?"

"I think he killed Greene," said Ghost. "I suggested as much, earlier in the day. Or was it you who suggested it, Chandler?" He smiled. "At any rate, Dawson has run down the murderer of Ellis Greene, which is feather enough in Mr. Dawson's cap. Possibly there had been a slight altercation between Greene and the cobbler. One way or another, the thrust followed—a lucky one, I fancy, to have been so accurate!—and later, to cover himself with glory, Johnson confessed to *all* the murders. The phenomenon is not uncommon in the history of crime and insanity."

"Do you agree with Mr. Ghost, Rainfall?"

"Quite," said the doctor. He was immensely emphatic. "All down the line, I agree with Mr. Ghost. From the beginning he has been the only person who has grasped any part of the situation."

Miss Moment had been thinking, also. Now she spoke quickly. "But is it certain," she asked, "that this old shoemaker killed Greene? If he lied about the others, he may have lied about Greene, too."

Rainfall laughed shortly. "He may even believe, by this time, that he really killed them all. That, also, is not uncommon."

"He killed Greene," said Ghost. "The shoes will prove it, if necessary." He hesitated. "Well, Saxon, your interruption was sensational and dramatically timed, but we are still exactly where we paused to listen. We are still, in effect, a jury sitting upon the case of Gregory Tempest."

Rainfall relighted his cigar, which had gone out. "Yes," he agreed, "what are we to say about Tempest?"

He puffed calmly at his tobacco for a few moments, then continued: "A physician learns a lot of queer things in his profession. Without excusing Tempest, I think I understand him. Accepting Mr. Ghost's assertion that Tempest is the guilty man and that he is prepared to prove it, let me undertake a defense of the luckless fellow. Miss Moment is no doubt correct when she suggests that the horrors visited upon him, and his subsequent maiming, were unintentional. Nevertheless, they were *facts*—memorable ones—and they were bound to leave their mark on him. The shock to his nervous system might be, in itself, enough to scar him for life. Supposing him to have been sensitively constituted, the effect of the entire episode might very well have been ruinous. Conceivably it might have made an abject coward of him to the end of life. And I venture to think that never again would he be able to look at a hearse without a shudder.

"However, I am thinking principally of the possible later effect of the accident on Tempest's social obligations. I suggested a moment ago that he had been maimed. Mr. Ghost did not say so, but, considering all that happened to Tempest, it is a likely enough supposition, and it would account, I think, for his well nourished scheme of revenge. Suppose him, in some fashion, to have been permanently injured, and in such fashion that the injury was apparent. The result would be a mounting self-consciousness, a self-consciousness that would increase rather than diminish with the years."

"I see," said Holly Moment, as he paused. "I think I do. You mean, if he had lost an eye, or something like that?"

"Precisely! To the end of his life that sightless eye would be a torture to him. Privately, that is—for, no doubt, in public he would pretend not to mind. Yet he would be constantly conscious of it, and self-conscious *about* it. He would see pity in the glances of others—perhaps even repugnance—when, quite possibly, no such emotion was being displayed. Conceivably the deformity would keep him from marrying. At the least, it would, in a greater or a lesser degree—depending upon the man—set him apart from other and more normal human beings."

"And all the time he would be planning his revenge?" The question came from the professor.

"Perhaps not *all* the time. But there would be moments when the idea of revenge would fill him—horrible moments when the consciousness of his deformity was sharply contrasted with the perfection of others—possibly with the smug perfection of the very men responsible for his condition. The cumulative effect of many such moments would be, I think, a cold hatred for the men who had injured him—even a constantly increasing cynicism toward a majority of mankind.

"Well, that might be one aspect of Tempest's case. On the

other hand, I am bound to admit, the accident might have made of him something kindly, charitable, and forgiving. Misfortune often operates that way, but as a rule only where the victim's case is complicated by a strong religious belief. Finally, it is possible, I think, that the moods of contrition and hatred might alternate. Personally, I rather like a hearty hater, and where sufficient justification can be shown, I confess, I feel no particular horror toward a murderer. Nor any sentimental regrets about a murderer's victim."

He cocked an eye at Ghost and smiled a bit sardonically. "What do you think of all that, Dr. Ghost?"

"We are not *too* far apart," admitted the amateur, "although your notions are perhaps a trifle advanced for popular consumption. Certainly not every prospective murderer can be allowed to be his own judge and his own jury, in advance of the crime. Or after it, for that matter! It is only the exceptional murderer who can be trusted to dispense an accurate justice, don't you think?" He laughed. "Our argument, you realize, is thoroughly immoral, or unmoral, if you prefer. Should we put such ideas into the tender minds of Howard and the professor? You suggest, in effect, that unless a private justice is visited upon certain persons, justice will not be obtained. Well, I agree that there are many scoundrels deserving of death whom the law will never touch. I have never, myself, felt it my duty to murder any of them—possibly because I have never been in the position of Gregory Tempest."

"But in his position you might?" asked Holly Moment incredulously.

"No," laughed Ghost, "since you pin me down with a question, I am bound to admit that it is most unlikely. That is, if I know myself at all. Probably it is dangerous nonsense that we are talking, Holly. Still, I do not pretend to judge the case of Tempest. Dr. Rainfall has suggested a state of mind that might well be productive of a murder, or of several murders. If he should happen to be right, the murderer's motive is at least understandable. We may sympathize with his grievance without committing ourselves to approval of his performance."

Saxon shrugged. "For my part," he said, "the number of murders in Chicago is beginning to annoy me. Whether as a sport or a profession, I think the practice should either be legalized or discouraged."

It was at this instant that Professor Chandler W. Moment came unexpectedly to the aid of the mysterious Tempest. He had been fidgeting in his chair for some time.

"For *my* part," he contributed with extraordinary bitterness, "I think that Tempest acted quite within his rights, if not within the law. I have, myself, been through a number of hazings—as a boy—and I still remember some of them with anger. There was the time I was tied to a pony and galloped through the streets of Weewaukee until I was nearly dead. I could cheerfully have killed the boys who did it, immediately after the event, and upon my honor I could cheerfully kill them to-day. That's the sort of a hater I am! Another time I was tossed into the lake by a group of students who knew that I couldn't swim a stroke. I nearly drowned before a policeman got me out. After throwing me in, the young devils who were responsible calmly walked off and left me. Do you mean to say that those unholy rascals do not still deserve to be murdered and stuck up in a shop window? I've watched their subsequent careers. Not one of them has amounted to a damn!"

"Father!" breathed his daughter.

"What's more," continued the truculent professor, "I have

frequently had students brought before me charged with the most fiendish tortures. One precious bunch had strung up another boy by his heels over a slow fire, just out of reach of the flames. They almost smoked him to death. It was my pleasure to recommend the expulsion of those particular scoundrels, but I give you my word I should have liked to crack their backs over my knee! The ringleader of that group is to-day a cheap political boss, and as cowardly a rascal as the day he smirked and sniveled in my office.

"No, gentlemen," concluded Chandler W. Moment—"and Miss Moment," he added with a florid gesture—"there are some fine boys in the colleges; perhaps a majority of them are fine boys—although I often wonder!—but there are also some singularly abominable young dogs, in whose ranks a little judicious murder would work wonders for the future of the world. I rejoice that one man—Gregory Tempest—had the lasting courage of his convictions. If Dr. Rainfall's reading of our riddle is correct, four eminent rapscallions are no longer a stench in the nostrils of the community."

It was a magnificent outburst, and it came from the heart.

"And that," added the professor, with shamefaced realization of his anticlimax, "is my strictly private opinion of hazing and hazers. It is not, of course, for publication." And he looked at Howard Saxon with mingled supplication and menace.

"Certainly not," agreed Saxon politely.

Ghost laughed a little shortly. "And our discussion has ended where most such discussions do end," he commented. "In rhetoric and indecision. It was really admirable, Chandler, but is it evidence? At any rate, I understand that you cast your vote in favor of Tempest and against any proceeding against him."

"I do!"

"And you, Howard?"

"I don't know. Dr. Rainfall's analysis of the case was, after all, the merest guesswork, wasn't it? He may have misread Tempest's case entirely. If the dead men were actually scoundrels, and Tempest was—and is—actually an admirable citizen who never again will commit murder, then I am for Tempest. But I don't see how we can put ourselves on record."

"What do *you* think, Holly?" asked Ghost kindly.

"I think I am a little sorry for Mr. Tempest—but he shouldn't have done it."

"One *for,* two against," said Rainfall. "If I also vote in his favor, do you cast the deciding vote, Mr. Ghost? And what, I wonder, will it be?"

"I shall not vote," answered Ghost quietly.

His strange, kindly eyes burned upon them all for a moment, then returned to the doctor. "No, I shall not vote. I have a feeling of respect and admiration for Tempest, based on information that has come to me quite outside of this criminal investigation. Whatever may have been his provocation, I believe him to have been in his own mind justified; and I think that any decision in the matter must come from the man himself. He is acquainted with my knowledge of his deeds. I did not tell you that before, but it is true. I have no notion what he will do or whether he will do anything. I shall myself do nothing. If I were to vote, I should vote in his favor; but there is no necessity. I am through with the case."

"You plan to take no action at all?" In varying forms the question came from all within the room.

"No action at all," said Ghost. "Heaven help us! Who are *we* to point the finger of accusation?"

CHAPTER TWENTY-NINE

"Dear Walter," began the long letter in Ghost's morning mail, and the amateur's hand trembled a little as he held the paper to the light.

So Tempest already had reached a decision. The letter was his message to the man who had given him a choice.

What had been the decision?

"I hope—" muttered Ghost—"I sincerely hope . . . ! Damn it, what do I hope? I'm afraid to look!"

"Dear Walter—I have not called you that before. There have been few whom I have ever cared to address familiarly. You are different. You understand—and I am grateful. Thank you! And again, from my heart, thank you! My decision is taken, and you will learn in time what it is. And now as to Gregory Tempest.

"I realized, of course, why the conference was called. I knew, even before your return from Walsingham, that you *knew*. Saxon heard of your cryptic telegram to the Moments, from Holly, and naturally he told me of it. Perhaps you had counted on that? Perhaps even then you were telling me that you knew, and giving me a chance to escape? For, of course, I understood your message. *Any* line from *The Tempest* would have answered, but the one you selected was clever. In other words—to Holly—'Be patient. The end is in sight.' To *me*—'Tempest, you are known!'

"You know, of course, that I would not have harmed *her.* There is a type of murderer who, once his program is accomplished, is forever finished. He will never kill again. Thereafter, if he is not hanged for his crimes, he will be a safe and law-abiding citizen. But I had to bluff, at first. I had only a newspaper version of what she had told the police. God knew what they were concealing! God knew what she had really seen of me—that night in the window! I tried to stop her mouth with a threat; but it was only a threat. She was safe from me, whatever happened. After Allenwood, *everybody* was safe. He was the last. I thought I had fooled you, that night when I shot Allenwood. But were you really fooled, I wonder? Possibly from that night dated your suspicion of me.

"There were only the four from the beginning —Allenwood, Bluefield, Gaunt and Lear. The others of the group that tortured me were nonentities—colorless cowards—abject followers of their ringleaders. I forgave them and forgot them. Bluefield, Gaunt, and Lear I killed in order—and without compunction, I confess. They were *rats,* Walter. You must believe me, when I say this. I cherish your good opinion of me—a murderer. Allenwood was to come last. What a turn you gave me, that day in the hospital, when you asserted, quite calmly, that the 'Dead Man' tickets might be, in effect, a progressive threat to other victims as yet unmurdered! It was the exact truth, although only Allenwood was left. I *wanted* him to realize what was happening—if he had wit enough—and to squirm in anticipation.

"Well, he understood. And, naturally, he came seeking me *first.* He was in no position to denounce me—a reputable physician, and he a bootlegger. Nobody would have believed his story. So to save his own life, he decided to kill *me* before I killed *him*. It was clever of him, and nervy of him, to warn me beforehand. It was also clever of him to bring a ticket in his pocket. Had he been successful it would have confused the issues completely, and possibly the mystery of none of the murders would ever have been solved. I don't know, though. You might even have seen through that! Good God, Walter, what a fellow you are! You do nothing at all, apparently, but sit in a chair —you take no steps of active investigation (well, very few!)—but in your mind is born a complete picture of all that has taken place and is to come. You're right, old man—you're no detective. That isn't detection—it's genius.

"There was no difficulty about any of the murders except Lear's. I had been watching all the scoundrels, off and on, for years. They were no good to themselves or the communities they infested. You must take my word for this, too. I *know!* Bluefield was a seducer who preached morality in public—an oily, horrible devil. I've had some of his—his victims—at the hospital. Can you imagine him sending them to me? Oh, yes, he knew who I was. I attended to that a long time ago. Possibly he thought because I had changed my name he had some hold on me. I don't know. He was always suave and patronizing. Well, I risked my professional reputation for Bluefield more than once—but I always knew his day was coming. Why did I do it? I was sorry for the girls, I think.

"He was glad enough to meet me in his shop—at midnight—when I telephoned him. I told him it was about one of his victims. I killed him with actual pleasure, I think. Am I insane, Walter? If so, what is insanity?

"The notice I posted on the door before I left. The dummy

was partly an afterthought, although I had often wondered what I could do to make the murders as public a performance as possible. The dummy set the key for all that followed. Poetic justice, eh? They had ticketed *me*—and displayed me in a *hearse.* Talk about show windows! You were right about the hearse, too. You've been right about a lot of things.

"Just before I stepped out of the window I parted the curtains and peered into the street. I was going to leave the shop soon, and wasn't anxious to run into a policeman. A young man and a young woman were passing, and I drew back in a hurry. The young woman, of course, was Holly Moment, although I didn't know, then, *who* she was. It was a fateful instant, Walter, but I didn't realize it at the time! It was that piece of caution—not an unusual action, surely—that dictated my warning note to Holly, and that brought *you* into the case. But I had no thought of anything like that, that night, as I let myself out into the street and hurried away from the staring eyes of Amos Bluefield.

"Gaunt I dug out of a cheap lodging house. Bluefield had told me he was in town and how to reach him. He was registered under another name. I think Gaunt had something 'on' Bluefield. I know Bluefield gave him money. Well, I bought Gaunt a few drinks, took him over into the park about midnight, and that was the end of Hubert Gaunt. It was the night after I had killed Bluefield. I put a rope around his waist, climbed the statue with the other end of it—under the canvas, which was a bit difficult—then dragged up the body, removed the rope, and climbed down myself. Just before climbing down I affixed my notice to the canvas, which was so thick I had to use a safety pin. There's a clue you overlooked, Walter! Those particular pins are hospital safeties; but maybe they look just like other safety pins. The whole thing was over in twenty minutes or less—a record!

Gaunt was only curious once. He wondered what I wanted the rope for!

"'*Two!*' I said—you remember old Monte Cristo?—and went home, satisfied.

Lear and Allenwood were the only ones left.

"I had heard that Lear was coming to town soon. It was an opportunity. I wanted them all in thc city together, at the same time, so that each one who followed Bluefield would have a chance to do some thinking. Allenwood, I knew, would be a hard fellow to get at. He was surrounded by gunmen and other vermin. I almost *had* to bring him to *me,* and I actually considered the possibility of his coming, although I should have managed it, somehow, even if he had stayed away. His warning notice I conveniently lost—which is why you didn't see it. It contained a picture of a hearse! That was too near to being a clue for me to advertise it.

"I was telling you about Lear, though. I heard he was coming to town, and I made ready for him. I had seen him before, and I had corresponded with him, casually, for some years. He sent me tickets, as usual. I met him the day before the murder, and told him I wanted tickets for the matinée. Howard was with me the day before, and I contrived to have tickets sent to him, also. You see, I needed Howard as a witness—a witness to the fact that I sat in my seat beside him throughout the beginning of the performance.

"It is curious, but the police had the facts of the Lear murder in their minds at the outset. With everybody else who saw the body, I was questioned, and it was obvious that they thought I *could* have committed the murder, although they never really believed it. But the thing they had in their minds was what actually occurred. I drove to the theater in my own car—foolishly, perhaps—parked it under Lear's window in the alley, climbed onto the fire escape when the watchman was inside (and you can't imagine how much the rain helped all through the whole chapter of murders!), and came upon John Patrick Stacey in his dressing room.

"He was surprised, naturally, to see me enter through the window. But I told him a cock-and-bull story and pretended to be a little drunk. He was annoyed but not too suspicious, being a drinking man himself. I told him the doorman had refused me entrance, and that I had determined to see him about his heart. It *was* weak. He had told me so the day before. After a time he went back to his looking glass, and it wasn't many minutes before he was as dead as Bluefield and Gaunt. I escaped the way I had entered, unseen, and drove away. I drove all the way back to the hospital, parked my car outside, took a taxi halfway back to town, then changed into another.

"That wasn't as good as it might have been, but it turned out all right. The second taxi was held up at the bridge, and as a result I got to the theater late. I was cutting it pretty fine all the way through. A big policeman at the bridge, whom I knew, helped considerably. I deliberately called his attention to me, in case I needed his testimony later on—and, by George, I *did!* However, I wasn't under suspicion for very long at any time. Nobody seriously believed I had killed Lear. There were too many other and better suspects. Even Howard had to give an account of himself, though. Poor old Howard! He's going to be shocked by all this. He's an excellent fellow, Walter. You and he are the only friends I've had in years.

"The weapon is gone, no matter where. It was a surgical instrument that I prepared myself, grinding it carefully to the proper dimensions. Did it occur to you, quite early, that all the murders had been rather *surgically* accomplished? From the beginning I realized that therein lay my principal danger. Had I committed only the Lear murder, I fancy I should have been apprehended. But the two earlier crimes made me an unlikely suspect. My association with Bluefield, such as it was, was not known—naturally enough. Certainly neither of us was talking about it!

"Greene's case puzzled me for a time. It was, in a way, favorable to me, in case of suspicion; but I wondered who had done it. I once considered saddling all the crimes on Greene's murderer, if he could be found—for it seemed likely enough that he was some insane follower of my example. But that clipping was a curious twist. The bootleg feature was sheer coincidence, apparently. Then I wondered for a time if this damned 'Adrian Bluefield'—Gaunt's brother—hadn't killed Greene. It seemed possible, but I couldn't figure out his game. By that time you were off for Walsingham, and I knew that revelations probably impended. I thought quickly and considered a bit of brilliant detective work intended to saddle all the crimes on Gaunt—who certainly wouldn't be missed if he were hanged!

"Well—it wouldn't work. Not that I'm sentimental, particularly. But I'm not a coward, either. From the beginning I had vaguely realized that probably the last 'Dead Man' would be Greg Tempest. He would be killed by John Rainfall. Or vice versa! Perhaps it would be John Rainfall who would be killed by Greg Tempest? Anyway, I wasn't making anybody else shoulder my crimes. Yes, you may put it down that from the beginning I had planned to kill five men. It will make you feel better, Walter, if you are thinking—about this time—that you are responsible for *my* death. You're not! It was sporting of you to give me a chance to escape. For a time I considered it.

But not for long. My decision had been made long before you offered me a choice.

"I hope you understood my story as told, left-handedly, in the Moment living room, a few hours ago. All its implications! Did you? I am sure you did. Your own story of the hearse was, for the most part, very accurate, except that the experience was infinitely more hideous and more revolting than you could have imagined. It left me with one leg shorter than the other and one deaf ear. You may have noted that I kept my left ear studiously away from all conversation—or perhaps you didn't. Few people have realized that I am hard of hearing; I've seen to that. But I couldn't conceal the limp.

"Well, what's a limp? I hear you say. What's one deaf ear? To you, perhaps, neither would count for much—but, then, you are Walter Ghost. If I'd known you earlier, Walter, I'd have become less cynical of life and the thing called man. But I was sensitive, self-conscious, filled with noble ideals, and all that sort of rot. As a youngster, I mean. I got over it. I wanted to be—conceive it, if you can!—I wanted to be an actor! Yes, I did! A *great* actor! Not a Patrick Lear. Do you know what I've heard Lear called? 'God's gift to women!' *Faugh!* Rather sickening, don't you think?

"But I was talking about Greg Tempest—once a rather decent youngster. You know what Lear was without my telling. His wife told the world about it, and I knew it even before she did. You ought to read some of the letters he wrote me. Filled with brag and bounce and selfishness and cruelty and—Well, well! I *was* talking of Greg Tempest, wasn't I? To hell with Lear—with Stacey! That's where he is, too—if there's a hell. With Bluefield, and Gaunt, and Allenwood. Maybe with Greg Tempest, in a little while!

"I became a very cynical young man, in time, Walter—after a horrible period of self-consciousness and general inferiority. A girl figured in that a bit. Need I go into it? I suggested, I think, that possibly Tempest had wished to marry. Well, he did! Wished to, that is. He didn't marry. The girl was sorry—awfully sorry. It hadn't occurred to her that his feelings were of that kind. You know? Not her fault, of course. I'm not blaming her—I don't know that I blamed her, then—not much. But it helped to push me down. I thought it was the limp—the deaf ear. As a matter of fact, I still think they had something to do with it. But I'm not blaming the girl. Anyway, I didn't marry. That's enough about that.

"I developed a philosophy, after a while. You've often heard it, I imagine. 'Nothing matters!' And nothing much *did* matter except getting even with Allenwood, Bluefield, *et al.* Wrong? Sure! Who said that the finest revenge was to forget? I'm not built that way, Walter. It seems a bit wishy-washy to me. I've always been wrong, maybe. I rather like being wrong. There are so damned many frauds in the world who are 'right.' Still, as I say, if I'd known you earlier, I think I might have realized that *everything* mattered. It's funny! To you, even little islands matter—the date of an old book—the origin of an old legend. Little things! And you're happy, aren't you? I wonder if you would answer that 'yes' or 'no'? Your eyes, old man, are about as sad as any I've ever seen. What have *you* been through? And how have you managed to weather it?

"Again I ask: am I insane? I suppose I am. But it's not the insanity represented in the asylums. Or am I one of perhaps a dozen sane men left on earth? If so, I'll bet you're another—and you've never killed anybody. You've never even wanted to! Howard isn't sane—he's in love. Not to be too frantic about it, what I'm trying to say is what everybody with sense *(What is sense?)* knows to be a fact. We're none of us sane—we're none of us insane. For what is sanity and what is insanity? Words! Susceptible of many definitions—like all words. *Integrity*—there's a grand word! I heard it used a little while ago, as I drove home. It floated to me out of another taxi. Well, what's integrity? A purely subjective term with no legal definition and no precise meaning. It means whatever the prevailing fashion in morals happens to make it mean.

"Forgive me! A lot of this is gratuitous, I know. I've rambled like an old vine, Walter. But have I given you any inkling of the boy who was Greg Tempest or the man who was John Rainfall?

"I'll finish quickly now. I entered a medical school, as you know, and became, in time, John Rainfall, doctor of medicine—the name was suggested, obviously, by my own. I liked the gloomy sound of it. I was well named from the beginning, I guess. And I took my job seriously, Walter, if anybody should happen to ask you. I was a good doctor—a good physician and a good surgeon. But not too sympathetic. Perhaps that's why I was good. A doctor's life isn't productive of rosecolored philosophies, unless he's an old woman, and then he isn't a good doctor. He sees life in terms of births, accidents, sickness, mutilations, deaths; and it all seems a bit futile. Unless he watches himself, he becomes a little callous—or a lot callous. The trundle of a stretcher through a hospital corridor doesn't bring tears to his eyes. It's just another job for *him,* and usually a damned ugly one.

"Then the war came, and it looked like Opportunity to me—Opportunity with a big O. If I could 'go out,' fighting—eh? I might even forget about the rest of it.

But, no!—my limp and my bum ear were against me. They

wouldn't have me at any price. I couldn't even fight for my country, it seemed. At that, I didn't care so much about the country, but the scrap would have been enjoyable. Not a chance! But they were glad to accept my professional services, and in a little while I was in charge of a base hospital—and there I stayed. Right there, behind the lines—a long distance behind. Couldn't get near the front. There I was, day in and day out, pouring iodine into torn bellies, even when I knew that the best service I could render some of the poor devils would be a permanent sleeping draught. Afterward, a lot of people called me 'Captain' and attributed my limp to a wound received in action. I let them. One didn't have to be self-conscious about a battle wound.

"Well, old man, I'm not getting any place, of course, with all this. One never does. I'll make an end of it in a minute now, and close as I began—with thanks to you, my dear Walter, for a little glimpse of what perhaps I might once have been. Your books, and your islands, and all your other interests almost converted me to a new order of thought. But I was too old to learn. I could only regret. You shook me, though! I might have come to care for everything, as you do, and yet be remote *from all that did not* please me. That splendid remoteness, that isolation in the midst of one's fellows! I had it, too—but with what a difference! I'll admit, if you like, that your way is better than mine.

"Thanks again, and my respects to Holly and her amusing parent. And—good-bye, old man!"

The name that Tempest had decided to use at the end was "John Rainfall." Reading it, Ghost's eyes were sadder than ever John Rainfall had seen them.

CHAPTER THIRTY

Saxon had come hurriedly in response to Ghost's telephone message. He read the long letter in silence. When he had finished he continued to stare vaguely away over the tops of the sheets.

"You had no suspicion of him?" asked Ghost, at last.

The newspaper man shook his head. "None," he answered. "I was too close to it all, I suppose. I had no perspective and no detachment. It's awful, isn't it! I don't know what to say. I still can't believe it. You knew, of course. You knew yesterday, when you were telling your story. He knew that you knew when he was telling *his*."

"Yes," said Ghost, "I've known for a long time."

"How long?"

"Subconsciously, I think, since the day you and he entered my room at the hospital and told me you had just come from the inquest. I had been reading about the other cases, and they had an appearance of surgical competence that I was bound to note. A surgeon was indicated, and one was, at least, near at hand. You were both friends of the murdered Lear and had been present in the theater when he—when he died. There was nothing conclusive about my thought, obviously; nothing even definitely accusative. I merely knew, in passing, that it was a situation calling for explanation. Naturally, I didn't at once believe Rainfall to be the murderer—not consciously, at any rate. I think my first *certainty* came on the night he killed Allenwood."

"Is it possible?" asked the professor. "If ever I had doubted Rainfall, his killing of Allenwood would have banished my doubts forever."

"In a sense, it was intended to," admitted Ghost. "He knew the killing would be called self defense, and he would be absolved. Rainfall was outwardly cool, that night, but inwardly he was immensely excited. I saw him at the instant of the murder, and I saw him afterward. Rainfall was no drinker, but it took a stiff dash of whisky to restore him. There had been no witnesses to his earlier crimes. In the case of Allenwood, he knew I had seen the shooting. It was a curiously puzzling affair, although I raised no question at the time."

"Puzzling?"

"He gave Allenwood no chance for his life. He flooded him with light and flung the door open so violently that the man had to give back a step to avoid being struck. Rainfall's pistol was raised as he opened the door, and Allenwood—who undoubtedly had a weapon of his own—was dead on the porch before he realized quite what had happened. It was all right, of course. Allenwood had come there to kill *him*—but how could Rainfall be sure that it was Allenwood who stood on his veranda? He had been followed, to be sure, but why might it not have been a patient, or a friend, just about to ring the doorbell? It struck me as odd—Rainfall's promptness—and there seemed to me to be only one answer to it. He had *recognized* the man in that instant when the light blazed over him. Not only that, but he had suspected from the beginning who the man was and was prepared to recognize and shoot him on sight. I have no objections, as I say; but if Rainfall *knew* the man who had sent him the note of warning, you see the suggestiveness of the situation. In other words, the warning was not that of an unknown criminal, directed against a stranger who might be interesting himself too closely in the murderer's affairs. Rainfall was definitely known to the murderer, and the murderer was known to Rainfall. And if that was the case, what followed?"

"What?" asked Saxon.

"Rainfall, obviously, had from the beginning concealed important information. If he were, himself, one of a group marked for death, then he was, or had been, quite probably, an associate of Bluefield and Gaunt and Lear, in whatever wrongs the murderer was avenging. Why, then, had he been warned in advance? As far as we knew, the others had received no warnings. They had simply been killed. As I say, it was a puzzling problem. Quite suddenly, inspiration visited me. It occurred to me that Allenwood, not Rainfall, might have been the prospective fourth victim, endeavoring to anticipate his own murder by abolishing his intending murderer. That would make Rainfall the murderer, supposing Allenwood to be correct in his assumptions—and, of course, supposing my own thinking to be accurate.

"There was no proof, of course, and I didn't at once accept my clever idea as the whole truth. Nevertheless, it was a valid idea, and, I thought, worth bearing in mind. It made of Allenwood, also, a very smart man, which, no doubt, he was. For if Allenwood were successful in killing Rainfall, and Rainfall were the actual murderer of Bluefield, Lear, *et al.*, the whole issue would be so completely fuddled that no police solution would be possible. There was the 'Dead Man' ticket in Allenwood's pocket, of course, which seemed to point to Allenwood as the original murderer; but I saw that it might very well have been a part of Allenwood's plan to turn suspicion from himself. No doubt, if apprehended, he could prove an airtight alibi in the cases of Bluefield, Gaunt, and Lear, whom he had *not* killed, and thereby escape any serious suspicion in the case of Rainfall. Where the plan went wrong was in Allenwood's allowing Rainfall to kill him before he killed Rainfall. I suppose that possibility hadn't crossed his mind.

"Well, as I was saying, Rainfall was excited that night. Not only had I seen the shooting, which he must have known looked a trifle fishy, but, afterward, we examined the body together—found the card in Allenwood's pocket—and *might* have found, as Rainfall well knew, something bearing more intimately upon himself as a member of the group."

"But you didn't," objected Saxon, still feebly defending his friend.

"No, we didn't; but there *was* something else. Not a paper. For some time I had wondered what it was that Holly saw glittering on the murderer's coat, that night outside of Bluefield's window. In Rainfall's apartment, after the killing of Allenwood, I thought I knew what it was. Again, it wasn't a certainty, but, in view of everything I was then thinking about Rainfall, it was something better than an insignificant coincidence. Rainfall had flung off his coat—apparently a habit of his when he had things to do. As we bent over Allenwood's body, he took from his vest pocket—on the *righthand side*—a thin, pencil-length flashlight, and used it to illumine the name on the tag in Allenwood's pocket. It was a natural action; he thought nothing about it. He knew nothing of what I had learned from Holly. The instrument itself is not unusual. Many men carry them. To the everlasting discredit of my thinking, I carry one myself! Why it hadn't occurred to me before, as a possibility, I don't know. Anyway, as he rose to his feet and replaced the thing in his pocket, I realized that it *could* have been such an instrument—the tip of it—that had caught Holly's eye."

"Still lighted!" cried Saxon incredulously.

"Possibly," said Ghost calmly, "but not necessarily. It *may* have been still lighted. There is a button catch on the thing. Or it may have been that the light of the street lamp, across the boulevard, caught it for an instant as he parted the curtains—caught the shining metal at the point where it protruded above his pocket. I don't know. It is quite conceivable, though, that he forgot to release the catch, however unlikely it may seem to us now. I think there is no doubt that he used the flashlight—there in the window. He had a difficult job to perform. Too difficult to carry out in darkness. But I don't insist that the light remained on when he parted the curtains."

"He had his coat off?"

"So I read it. He was handling a freshly murdered corpse, after all; and, later, he was to be seen in the streets. No doubt he was reasonably certain there would be no further bleeding—in the case of Lear, he testified to a single drop of blood—but in the case of Bluefield he was lifting and carrying the body. Yes, I think he had his coat off."

There was a silence. "What then?" asked the professor at length.

"I have already mentioned the warning Rainfall received. Holly had also received one. Both struck me as being a little out of key—when I came to think them over. I took the liberty of doubting their essential importance. In the beginning, I had not believed either Rainfall or Holly to be part of the murderer's original scheme of vengeance. They were, on the surface, innocent individuals who had blundered into the case, and who had to be warned to keep their mouths shut. But, in Rainfall's case, *had* he simply blundered in? It occurred to me that he had almost *barged* in; and what had he done, after all, to merit a warning? Really, very little. He had insisted on a more thorough autopsy on Lear than had been performed in the cases of Bluefield and Gaunt, and he was supposed to be a sort of police expert. But whatever he was, he had assumed the rôle himself. As for the autopsy, it would have been quite complete, in any case. Rainfall knew it and anticipated it by asking for it. That was clever. For a time I even wondered if he had sent the warning to himself; but that was before the night of Allenwood's death."

Ghost paused. "I never saw that note of warning received by Rainfall," he continued after a moment. "He never volunteered it. In his letter he refers to it as having been conveniently 'lost.' The letter makes it clear *why* it was lost. But the very fact that he did not show it seemed significant."

"He didn't show it to me, either," admitted Saxon. "Just told me he had received one."

"I suppose the rest is clear to you?" asked Ghost. "My vague suspicions crystallized into serious doubts, until I *had* to make sure I was either right or wrong. I preferred to be wrong. My idea that the origins of the case went back for many years had never been shaken. I consulted a very ordinary volume in the professor's library—a current edition of *Who's Who*—and learned that Lear had been educated at Walsingham. I wrote to Walsingham and had a letter from the college there, containing a list of Lear's classmates. It was a highly suggestive roster, as you know. Then I went to Walsingham, having first contrived that Rainfall should hear of my purpose through Saxon."

"No!" cried Saxon, thunderstruck.

"That was the purpose of the nonsense with the Ouija board," said Ghost. "You were almost certain to mention it to Rainfall. I wondered if, afterward, he would come to me. I even wondered if he would attack me. There, at any rate, I did him an injustice. Nothing happened, however—and I went to Walsingham. The rest you know."

Again there was a silence. "Hm," commented the professor, after a time. "It sounds simple enough, Walter, as you tell it. Very sound! Very logical!"

"Neither one nor the other," demurred Ghost promptly. "And it was all complicated by the Greene case and a dozen other false leads. Disentangling the possible truth from the possible falsehood was exceedingly difficult, and my thinking was at all times very confused. Rainfall's own attitude was consummately clever. He told no actual falsehoods; he merely suggested them. He was willing that everybody should go wrong as long as he cared to. It was not his part to turn suspicion upon himself. Yet if, at any time, I had gone to him frankly and asked him for the truth, I think he would have told me."

He added: "Rainfall speaks of the curious coincidence in the matter of Greene's reversible clipping; but the most extraordinary coincidence of the case seems not to have struck him. I mean the odd circumstances that Rainfall killed Bluefield just as Gaunt was getting ready to perform the same office! Had Gaunt anticipated Rainfall, he would have fled, I suppose, and thus escaped his own fate. In which case, I wonder whether Rainfall would have gone ahead? However, such speculations, after the fact, are always futile."

Something was still bothering the sporting editor of the *Evening Telegram*.

"That death notice, Mr. Ghost—that 'Dead Man' ticket—on the floor of Lear's dressing room?"

"Was dropped there by Rainfall after, or just *as,* you entered the room," agreed Ghost. "You came very close to the truth yourself, that day, Howard. You knew it was not there when you entered."

"Rainfall went in first," asserted Saxon. "I remember *that.*"

"Then he dropped back, an instant later, when the notice brought upon you both by your entrance was again centered upon Lear. It is the one point he forgot to mention in his letter, but there can be no doubt of what happened."

Saxon put his head into his hands. "It's awful!" he said. "It's simply awful, Mr. Ghost! There aren't words to touch it."

"I hope," said Ghost kindly, "there will be compensations."

At the words Holly Moment caught her breath for an instant, then blushed scarlet. Was he hinting at . . . ?

"There *have* been," she responded in haste, and with great presence of mind. "We have all known *you* better, Mr. Ghost, because of this horrible affair. That much has been gained, at any rate. But it is rather appalling to think that I began it all!"

"It should never cross your mind," said Ghost. "There is no saying where *anything* begins."

But Chandler W. Moment nodded his agreement with his daughter—a sufficiently remarkable circumstance.

"In every department of life," he observed, with irritating complacence, "I find my philosophy justified. I have a genuine passion for minding my own business. What a pity it is not contagious!"

CHAPTER THIRTY-ONE

A GREAT black headline lay across the tops of the latest editions of the city's journals as Ghost and Saxon proceeded through the Loop. Once more Detective Sergeants Sheets and Kelly were atoms in the public eye. At important intersections, fresh bundles of papers, damp from the press, were being dropped by mud-splashed motor vehicles driven by belligerent satraps. Newsboys were beginning to shout their tidings.

Saxon descended from the taxi and purchased a paper. He returned, dismayed and apprehensive.

"I knew it," he groaned. "I knew I ought to have telephoned the paper! They've arrested Moore, at last. Lord, what a mess!"

Ghost glanced at the screaming headlines and shrugged his shoulders. He read the opening paragraphs without emotion.

"There's no harm done," he said. "They can't hold him. They'll know the truth soon enough, I fancy. You can't telephone till you're sure of Rainfall. The whole unhappy boiling of them will be free shortly—Moore, Ridinghood, Miss Carvel, and whoever else they may have tucked away in their cells. How they all must have hated Lear, Howard! And how they all stuck together and protected one another! How they protected Lear! A curious animal is man."

They drove onward, crossing the bridge over the river's mouth, where Rainfall once had stopped to bestow a cigar upon a traffic policeman, and entered the opening block of the glistening boulevard. Following the stream of motors northward they proceeded upon their gruesome mission. Neither was happy about his errand. In the rolling cab, beside them, rode the familiar personality of John Rainfall, an emanation that lay heavily upon them both.

The taxicab waited for them at the curb as they ascended the steps in Division Street and paused for an instant outside the well remembered door.

With his hand upon the knob Ghost hesitated and drew back. The handle had turned under his grasp. With a little shock he realized that the door was unlocked and ready for their visit.

"I've a key," said Saxon. His voice trembled on the words.

"Unnecessary," muttered Ghost; and still he hesitated. "I have an odd notion, Howard," he added suddenly. "Suppose—just suppose—we find nobody here!" He smiled a little faintly. "Nobody and no *body!*"

His companion stared. "What do you mean?"

"It would be rather pleasant to go away without knowing," said Ghost. "*Never* to know! To wonder, sometimes, if in the end he had not decided to escape, to start again some other place. To try again for that happier life he would have liked. Eh?"

"Good heavens, Mr. Ghost!" cried the startled Saxon. "We'd *have* to know—some time! There are the papers to tell us."

"I know! But—if it were only a *book,* let us say, that could be ended here—without this ultimate revelation! Wouldn't it be happier for us all?"

He shrugged again and clapped the younger man on the shoulder.

"I'm a fool," he confessed. "And there's Moore to be considered. And my thought does Rainfall an injustice. After all, he preferred it this way. Pay no attention to me. The fact is, though, I thought I couldn't bear to see that note again."

The taxi driver was watching them curiously.

"Note?" echoed Saxon. For a moment he stared; then suddenly he understood. "You mean, you think that he . . . ?"

"I'm sure of it," said Ghost.

He pushed open the door with sudden decision and passed into the narrow corridor.

Then for a number of dreadful seconds they stood silent, looking at the square of white paper on the inner door.

THE END

DISCUSSION QUESTIONS

- What kind of detective is Walter Ghost?
- Were there any historical details in the novel that surprised you, given your knowledge of the era?
- Were you able to predict any part of the solution to the case?
- Aside from the solution, did anything about the book surprise you? If so, what?
- Did any aspects of the plot date the story? If so, which ones?
- Would the story be different if it were set in the present day? If so, how?
- What role did the setting play in the narrative?
- If you were one of the main characters, would you have acted differently at any point in the story?
- Did you identify with any of the characters? If so, who?
- Did this novel remind you of anything else you've read? If so, what?

MORE

VINCENT STARRETT

AVAILABLE FROM

AMERICAN MYSTERY CLASSICS

THE GREAT HOTEL MURDER
Introduced by Lyndsay Faye

MURDER ON "B" DECK
Introduced by Ray Betzner

OTTO PENZLER PRESENTS

AMERICAN MYSTERY CLASSICS

All Titles Introduced by Otto Penzler
Unless Otherwise Noted

Charlotte Armstrong, *The Chocolate Cobweb*
Introduced by A. J. Finn
Charlotte Armstrong, *The Unsuspected*

Anthony Boucher, *The Case of the Baker Street Irregulars*
Anthony Boucher, *Rocket to the Morgue*
Introduced by F. Paul Wilson

Fredric Brown, *The Fabulous Clipjoint*
Introduced by Lawrence Block

John Dickson Carr, *The Crooked Hinge*
Introduced by Charles Todd
John Dickson Carr, *The Mad Hatter Mystery*
John Dickson Carr, *The Plague Court Murders*
Introduced by Michael Dirda
John Dickson Carr, *The Red Widow Murders*
Introduced by Tom Mead

Todd Downing, *Vultures in the Sky*
Introduced by James Sallis

Mignon G. Eberhart, *Murder by an Aristocrat*
Introduced by Nancy Pickard

Erle Stanley Gardner, *The Case of the Baited Hook*
Erle Stanley Gardner, *The Case of the Careless Kitten*
Erle Stanley Gardner, *The Case of the Borrowed Brunette*
Erle Stanley Gardner, *The Case of the Shoplifter's Shoe*
Erle Stanley Gardner, *The Bigger They Come*

Frances Noyes Hart, *The Bellamy Trial*
Introduced by Hank Phillippi Ryan

H.F. Heard, *A Taste for Honey*

Dolores Hitchens, *The Cat Saw Murder*
Introduced by Joyce Carol Oates

Dorothy B. Hughes, *Dread Journey*
Introduced by Sarah Weinman
Dorothy B. Hughes, *Ride the Pink Horse*
Introduced by Sara Paretsky
Dorothy B. Hughes, *The So Blue Marble*

W. Bolingbroke Johnson, *The Widening Stain*
Introduced by Nicholas A. Basbanes

Baynard Kendrick, *The Odor of Violets*

Frances and Richard Lockridge, *Death on the Aisle*

John P. Marquand, *Your Turn, Mr. Moto*
Introduced by Lawrence Block

Stuart Palmer, *The Pengiun Pool Murder*
Stuart Palmer, *The Puzzle of the Happy Hooligan*

Otto Penzler, ed., *Golden Age Detective Stories*
Otto Penzler, ed., *Golden Age Locked Room Mysteries*

Ellery Queen, *The American Gun Mystery*
Ellery Queen, *The Chinese Orange Mystery*
Ellery Queen, *The Dutch Shoe Mystery*
Ellery Queen, *The Egyptian Cross Mystery*
Ellery Queen, *The Siamese Twin Mystery*

Patrick Quentin, *A Puzzle for Fools*
Clayton Rawson, *Death from a Top Hat*

Craig Rice, *Eight Faces at Three*
Introduced by Lisa Lutz
Craig Rice, *Home Sweet Homicide*

Mary Roberts Rinehart, *The Album*
Mary Roberts Rinehart, *The Haunted Lady*
Mary Roberts Rinehart, *Miss Pinkerton*
Introduced by Carolyn Hart
Mary Roberts Rinehart, *The Red Lamp*
Mary Roberts Rinehart, *The Wall*

Joel Townsley Rogers, *The Red Right Hand*
Introduced by Joe R. Lansdale

Vincent Starrett, *The Great Hotel Murder*
Introduced by Lyndsay Faye
Vincent Starrett, *Murder on "B" Deck*
Introduced by Ray Betzner

Cornell Woolrich, *The Bride Wore Black*
Introduced by Eddie Muller
Cornell Woolrich, *Deadline at Dawn*
Introduced by David Gordon
Cornell Woolrich, *Waltz into Darkness*
Introduced by Wallace Stroby